CONTENTS

CONTENTS

Number 7
Philibert Place

I

There are many dreary and dingy rows of ugly houses in certain parts of London, but there certainly could not be any more ugly than Philibert Place. It was shabby and cheerless on the brightest days, and on foggy or rainy days it was the most forlorn place in London.

At least that was what the boy thought as he stood near the iron railings watching the passersby.

It was the morning after he had been brought by his father to live as a lodger in the back sitting room of house Number 7.

He was a boy about twelve years old, and his name was Marco Loristan. He was the kind of boy people look at a second time when they have looked at him once. His face was not an English face. It was very dark in coloring. His features were strong, and his black hair grew on his head like a mat. His eyes were large and deep set. He was as un-English a boy as one could imagine, and an observing person would have been struck at once by a sort of silent look expressed by his whole face.

This look was especially noticeable on this morning as he stood before the iron railings. He was thinking of the long, hurried journey from Russia that he and his father and their old soldier servant, Lazarus, had made during the last few days. Cramped in a close third-class railway car, they had dashed across the continent as if something terrible was driving them.

And now here they were, settled in London as if they were going to live forever at Number 7 Philibert Place. He knew, however, that it was just as probable that in the middle of some night, his father or Lazarus might waken him from his sleep and say, "Get up. Dress yourself quickly. We must go at once." A few days later he might be in St. Petersburg, Vienna, or Budapest, huddled away in some poor little house as shabby and comfortless as Number 7 Philibert Place.

His strange life and his close association with his father had made him much older than his years, but he was only a boy, after all. The mystery of things sometimes weighed heavily upon him and set him to deep wondering.

In not one of the many countries he knew had he ever met a boy whose life was in the least like his own. Other boys had homes in which they lived year after year. They went to school regularly and played with other boys. They talked openly of the things that happened to them and the journeys they made.

When he remained in a place long enough to make a few friends, he knew he must never forget that his whole existence was a sort of secret whose safety depended upon his own silence and discretion. This was because of the promises he had made to his father, and those promises were the first thing he remembered. Not that he had ever regretted anything connected with his father.

None of the other boys had such a father, not one of them. When his father walked down a street, people turned to look at him even oftener than they turned to look at Marco. The boy felt as if it was not merely because he was a big man with a handsome, dark face, but because he looked as if he had been born to command armies—as if no one would think of disobeying him. Yet Marco had never seen him command anyone, and they had always been poor, and shabbily dressed, and often enough ill fed. The few people they saw no matter where they were treated him with a sort of deference, and nearly always stood when they were in his presence, unless he bade them sit down.

"It is because they know he is a patriot, and patriots are respected," the boy had told himself.

He himself wished to be a patriot, though he had never seen his own country of Samavia. He knew it well enough, however. His father had talked to him about it ever since that day when he had made the promises. He had studied curiously detailed maps of Samavia—maps of its cities, maps of its mountains, maps of its roads.

His father had told him stories of the wrongs done to its people, of their sufferings and struggles for liberty, and, above all, of their unconquerable courage.

When they talked together of its history, he always knew by the look in his father's eyes that his blood burned. His countrymen had been killed, they had been robbed, they had died by thousands of cruelties and starvation, but their souls had never been conquered. Through all the years during which more powerful nations enslaved them, they never ceased to struggle to free themselves and stand unfettered as Samavians had stood centuries before.

"Why do we not live there?" Marco had cried on the day the promises were made. "Why do we not go back and fight? When I am a man, I will be a soldier and die for Samavia."

"We are of those who must live for Samavia—working day and night," his father had answered. "We must deny ourselves, train our bodies and souls, use our brains, and learn the things that are best to be done for our people and our country. Even exiles may be Samavian soldiers. I am one; you must be one."

"Are we exiles?" asked Marco.

"Yes," was the answer. "But even if we never set foot on Samavian soil, we must give our lives to it. I have given mine since I was sixteen. I shall give it until I die."

"Have you never lived there?" asked Marco.

A strange look shot across his father's face. "No," he answered, and said no more.

Marco, watching him, knew he must not ask the question again.

The next words his father said were about the promises. Marco was quite a little fellow at the time, but he understood the solemnity of them and felt that he was being honored as if he were a man.

"When you are a man, you shall know all you wish to know," Loristan said. "Now you are a child, and your mind must not be burdened, but you must do your part. A child sometimes forgets that words may be dangerous. You must promise never to forget this. Wherever you are, if you have playmates, you must remember to be silent about many things. You must not speak of what I do, or of the people who come to see me. You must keep in your mind that a secret exists which a chance foolish word might betray. You are a Samavian, and there have been Samavians who have died a thousand deaths rather than betray a secret. You must learn to obey without question, as if you were a soldier. Now you must take your oath of allegiance."

Loristan rose from his seat and went to a corner of the room. He knelt down, turned back the carpet, lifted a plank, and took something from beneath it. It was a sword, and as he came back to Marco, he drew it out from its sheath. The child's strong, young body stiffened and drew itself up. His large, deep eyes flashed. He was to take his oath of allegiance upon a sword as if he were a man. He did not know that his small hand opened and shut with a fierce understanding grip because those of his blood had for long centuries past carried swords and fought with them.

Loristan gave him the big bared weapon and stood erect before him.

"Repeat these words after me sentence by sentence!" he commanded.

And as he spoke them, Marco echoed each one loudly and clearly.

"The sword in my hand—for Samavia! The heart in my breast—for Samavia! The swiftness of my sight, the thought of my brain, the life of my life—for Samavia. Here grows a man for Samavia."

Then Loristan put his hand on the child's shoulder and said, "God be thanked!" His dark face looked almost fiercely proud.

"From this hour," he said, "you and I are comrades at arms."

And from that day to the one on which he stood beside the broken iron railings of Number 7 Philibert Place, Marco had not forgotten for one hour.

A Young Citizen
of the World

—————— 2 ——————

He had been in London more than once before,
but he knew when he was brought a second or third time
to a city that the house he was taken to would be in a
quarter new to him. He would not see the people he had
seen before.

His father had never forbidden him to make chance
acquaintances. He had, in fact, told him that he had
reasons for not wishing him to hold himself aloof from
other boys. "You must not seem a foreigner in any
country," he had said to him. "It is necessary that you
should not. When you are in England, you must not
know anything but English."

The only barrier that must exist between them must
be the barrier of silence concerning his wanderings from

country to country. When he was in Russia, he must speak only of Russian places and Russian people and customs. When he was in France, Germany, Austria, or England, he must do the same thing. He had seemed to grow up in the midst of changing tongues that all seemed familiar to him. He did remember, however, that his father had always been unswerving in his attention to his pronunciation and method of speaking the language of any country they chanced to be living in.

Once, when he was seven or eight years old, a boy had asked him what his father's work was.

Marco brought the story to Loristan. "His own father is a carpenter, and he asked me if my father was one. I said you were not. Then he asked if you were a shoemaker, and another one said you might be a tailor. I didn't know what to tell them." He put a grubby little hand on his father's arm and almost fiercely shook it. "I wanted to say that you were not like their fathers. You are not a tailor or a shoemaker, but a patriot. You could not be *only a tailor*!" He said it grandly and with a queer indignation, his black head held up and his eyes angry.

His father laid his hand against Marco's mouth.

"Hush. Hush," he said. "Is it an insult to a man to think he may be a carpenter or make a good suit of clothes? If I could make our clothes, we should go better dressed. If I were a shoemaker, your toes would not be making their way into the world as they are now." He was smiling, but Marco saw that he held his head high, and his eyes were glowing as he touched his shoulder. "I know you did not tell them I was a patriot," he ended. "What was it you said to them?"

"I remembered that you were nearly always writing and drawing maps, so I said you were a writer, but I did not know what you wrote . . . and that you said it was a poor trade. Was that a right thing to tell them?"

"Yes. You may always say that if you are asked. There are poor fellows who write different things that bring them little money. There is nothing strange in my being a writer."

In the first days of a new place Marco often walked a great deal. He was strong and untiring, and it amused him to wander through unknown streets and look at shops and houses and people. He liked to branch off into the side streets and odd, deserted-looking squares. He often stopped to watch workmen and talk to them if they were friendly. He made stray acquaintances in his strollings and learned a good many things. He had a fondness for wandering musicians, and from an old Italian, he had learned to sing songs in his strong, musical voice. He knew many of the songs of the people in several countries.

This first morning was very dull at Philibert Place, and he wished that he had something to do or someone to speak to. To do nothing whatever is a depressing thing at all times, but perhaps it is more especially so when one is a healthy twelve-year-old boy.

Suddenly he turned away from the gate and went into the house to speak to Lazarus. He found him in his dingy room on the fourth floor at the back of the house.

"I am going for a walk," he announced to him. "Please tell my father if he asks for me. I must not disturb him."

Lazarus was patching an old coat when Marco spoke, and he stood up at once. He was very particular about certain forms of manner. Nothing would have obliged him to remain seated when Loristan or Marco was near him. Marco thought it was because he had been so strictly trained as a soldier.

Though he no longer saluted them in public, he omitted no other form of reverence and ceremony, and the boy had become accustomed to being treated as if he were anything but the shabby lad whose very coat was patched by the old soldier who stood at attention before him.

"Yes, sir," Lazarus answered. "Where was it your wish to go?"

Marco knitted his black brows a little in trying to recall distinct memories of the last time he had been in London.

"I have been to so many places and have seen so many things since I was here before, that I must begin to learn again about the streets and buildings I do not quite remember."

"Yes, sir," said Lazarus. "I also forget. You were but eight years old when you were last here."

"I think I will go and find the royal palace, and then I will walk about and learn the names of the streets," Marco said.

"Yes, sir," answered Lazarus, and this time he made his military salute.

Marco lifted his right hand in recognition, as if he had been a young officer. Most boys might have looked awkward in making the gesture, but he made it with natural ease.

Marco had seen officers returning the salutes of their men when they encountered each other by chance in the streets. He had seen many royal persons and many royal pageants, but always as an ill-clad boy standing on the edge of the crowd of common people.

"It is well to observe everything and to train one's self to remember faces and circumstances," his father had said. "If you were a young prince or a young man training for a diplomatic career, you would be taught to notice and remember people and things just as you would be taught to speak your own language with elegance. Such observation would be your most practical accomplishment and greatest power. It is as practical for a poor lad in a patched coat as for one whose place is to be in courts. As you cannot be educated in the ordinary way, you must learn from travel and the world. You must lose nothing—forget nothing."

It was his father who had taught him everything, and Marco had learned a great deal. Loristan had the power of making all things interesting. To Marco it seemed that he knew everything in the world. They were not rich enough to buy many books, but Loristan knew the treasures of all great cities and the resources of the smallest towns. Together he and Marco walked through the endless galleries filled with the wonders of the world. Because his father made the pictures seem the burning work of still living men whom the centuries could not turn to dust, because he could tell stories of what they felt and suffered and were, the boy became as familiar with the old masters as he was with most of the countries they had lived in. They were not merely old masters to him, but men who were great, men who seemed to him to have wielded beautiful swords and held high, splendid lights.

His father could not go often with him, but he always took him for the first time to the galleries, museums, libraries, and historical places that were richest in treasures of art, beauty, or story. Then having seen them once through his eyes, Marco went again and again alone, and so grew intimate with the wonders of the world. He knew that he was gratifying a wish of his father's when he tried to train himself to observe all things and forget nothing. These palaces of marvels were his schoolrooms, and his strange but rich education was the most interesting part of his life.

In time he knew exactly the places where the great Rembrandts, Rubens, or Raphaels hung. He knew whether this masterpiece or that was in Vienna, in Paris, or in Rome. He knew stories of splendid crown jewels, of old armor, and of Roman relics dug up from beneath the foundations of old German cities. Any boy wandering to amuse himself through museums and palaces could see what he saw, but boys living fuller and less lonely lives would have been less likely to concentrate on what they looked at or to store away facts with the same determination.

Having no playmates and nothing to play with, he began when he was a very little fellow to make a sort of game out of his rambles through picture galleries. There were always the blessed free days when he could climb any marble steps and enter any great portal without paying an entrance fee. Once inside, there were plenty of poorly dressed people to be seen, but there were not often boys as young as himself who were not attended by older companions. The game he had created for himself was as simple as it was absorbing—try to remember and clearly describe to his father at night of what he had seen.

These night talks filled his happiest hours. He never felt lonely then, and when his father sat and watched him with a certain curious and deep attention in his dark, reflective eyes, the boy was utterly comforted and content. Sometimes he brought back rough and crude sketches of objects he wished to ask questions about, and Loristan could always relate to him the full, rich story of the thing he wanted to know. They were stories made so splendid and full of color in the telling that Marco could not forget them.

The Legend of
the Lost Prince

3

As he walked through the streets, he was thinking of
one of these stories. It was one he had heard first when
he was very young, and it had so seized upon his imagination that he had asked often for it. It was, indeed,
a part of the long past history of Samavia, and he had
loved it for that reason. Lazarus had often told it to
him, but he had always liked his father's version best.
It seemed a thrilling and living thing. Loristan always
found some such way of making hard and comfortless
hours easier to live through.

"Fine, big lad—for a foreigner," Marco heard a man
say as he passed them this morning.

It was this remark that had led his thoughts back to
the story of the Lost Prince. He knew that most of the

people who looked at him and called him a foreigner had not even heard of Samavia. Those who chanced to recall its existence knew of it only as a small fierce country, so placed upon the map that the larger countries which were its neighbors felt they must control and keep it in order, and fought its people and each other for possession. But it had not been always so.

Hundreds of years ago Samavia had been as celebrated for its peaceful happiness and wealth as for its beauty. Legend held that Samavia had been the site of the Garden of Eden, and that its people had been of such great stature, physical beauty, and strength, that they had been like a race of noble giants. Among the shepherds there were poets who sang their own songs when they piped among their sheep upon the mountainsides and in the flower-thick valleys. Their songs had been about patriotism and bravery. The simple courtesy of the poorest peasant was as stately as the manner of a noble.

Five hundred years ago there had succeeded to the throne a king who was bad and weak. His father had lived to be ninety years old, and this his son had grown tired of waiting in Samavia for the crown, so he had gone out into the world and visited other countries and their courts. When he returned and became king, he lived as no Samavian king had lived before. He was an extravagant, vicious man of furious temper and bitter jealousies. He was jealous of the larger countries he had seen and tried to introduce their customs and their ambitions, but he ended up introducing instead their worst faults and vices.

There arose political quarrels and savage new factions. Money was squandered until poverty began to stare the country in the face. The big Samavians, after their first astonishment, broke forth into furious rage. There were mobs and riots, then bloody battles. Since it was the king who had worked this wrong, they would have none of him. They would depose him and make his son king in his place.

The young prince was totally unlike his father. He was a true royal Samavian. He was bigger and stronger for his age than any man in the country, and he was as handsome as a young Viking. More than this, he had a lion's heart. Before he was sixteen, the shepherds had already begun to make songs about his young valor, his kingly courtesy, and generous kindness. Not only did the shepherds sing them, but also the people in the streets. The king, his father, had always been jealous of him, even when he was only a beautiful, stately child whom the people roared with joy to see as he rode through the streets. When the king returned from his journeyings and found his son a splendid youth, he detested him.

The people began to clamor and demand that the king should abdicate. He became insane with rage and committed such cruelties that the people ran mad themselves. One day they stormed the palace and burst in upon the king as he shuddered, green with terror and fury in his private room. He was king no more and must leave the country, they vowed, as they closed round him with bared weapons.

Where was the prince? They must see him and tell him their ultimatum. It was he whom they wanted for a king. They trusted him, and they would obey him. They began to shout aloud his name, calling him in a sort of chant in unison, "Prince Ivor—Prince Ivor—Prince Ivor!" But no answer came. The people of the palace had hidden themselves, and the place was utterly silent.

The king, despite his terror, could not help but sneer. "Call him again," he said. "He is afraid to come out of his hole. He is afraid!"

A savage fellow from the mountain struck him on the mouth. "If he does not come because thou hast killed him, then thou art a dead man!"

This set them aflame with hotter burning. They broke away, leaving three on guard. They ran about the empty palace rooms shouting the prince's name, but there was no answer. They sought him in a frenzy, bursting open doors and flinging down every obstacle in their way. A page, found hidden in a closet, owned that he had seen His Royal Highness pass through a corridor early in the morning. He had been softly singing to himself one of the shepherd's songs.

In every nook and cranny they sought for him, believing that the king himself had made him prisoner in some secret place or had privately had him killed. The fury of the people grew to frenzy. There were new uprisings, and every few days the palace was attacked and searched again. But no trace of the prince was found. He had vanished as a star vanishes when it drops from its place in the sky. During a riot in the palace, when a last fruitless search was made, the king himself was killed.

In his place a powerful noble made himself king. From that time, the once splendid little kingdom was like a bone fought over by dogs. Its pastoral peace was forgotten. It was torn and shaken by stronger countries. It tore and worried itself with internal fights. It assassinated kings and created new ones. No man was sure in his youth what ruler he would live under in his maturity, or whether his children would die in useless fights, or through stress of poverty and cruel, useless laws.

There were no more shepherds who were poets, but on the mountainsides and in the valleys some of the old songs were sung. Those most beloved were songs about a Lost Prince whose name had been Ivor. If he had been king, he would have saved Samavia, the verses said, and all brave hearts believed that he would still return. In the modern cities, one of the cynical sayings was, "Yes, that will happen when Prince Ivor comes again."

In his more childish days, Marco had been bitterly troubled by the unsolved mystery. Where had he gone—the Lost Prince? Had he been killed, or had he been hidden away in a dungeon? The boy had invented for himself a dozen endings to the story.

"Did no one ever find his sword or his cap or hear anything or guess anything about him ever? Ever?" he would say restlessly again and again, but he knew the rest.

Almost a hundred years after the prince was lost, an old shepherd had gone out in the early morning on the mountainside and had found in the forest what he at first thought to be the dead body of a handsome, boyish, young huntsman. Some enemy had plainly attacked him from behind and believed he had killed him. The young huntsman was not quite dead, however, and the shepherd dragged him into a cave where he himself often took refuge from storms with his flocks. He was afraid to speak of what he had found; and by the time he discovered that he was harboring the prince, the king had already been killed, and an even worse man had taken possession of his throne.

To the terrified and simple peasant the safest thing was to get the wounded youth out of the country before there was any chance of his being discovered and murdered outright. The cave in which he was hidden was not far from the frontier, and while he was still so weak that he was hardly conscious of what befell him, he was smuggled away in a cart loaded with sheepskins and left with some kind churchmen who did not know his rank or name.

The shepherd went back to his flocks and his mountains, and lived and died among them, always in terror of the changing rulers and their savage battles with each other.

The mountaineers said among themselves, as the generations succeeded each other, that the Lost Prince must have died young, because otherwise he would have come back to his country and tried to restore its good, bygone days.

"Yes, he would have come," Marco said.

"He would have come *if* he had seen that he could help his people," his father had answered, as if he were not reflecting on a story that was probably only a legend. "But he was very young, and Samavia was in the hands of the new dynasty and filled with his enemies. He could not have crossed the frontier without an army. Still, I think he died young."

It was of this story that Marco was thinking as he walked, and perhaps the thoughts that filled his mind expressed themselves in his face in some way that attracted attention. As he was nearing Buckingham Palace, a distinguished looking well dressed man with clever eyes caught sight of him, and after looking at him keenly, slackened his pace as he approached him from the opposite direction. An observer might have thought he saw something that puzzled and surprised him. Marco didn't see him at all, and still moved forward, thinking of the shepherds and the prince. The well dressed man began to walk still more slowly. When he was quite close to Marco, he stopped and spoke to him—in the Samavian language.

"What is your name?" he asked.

Marco's training from his earliest childhood had been an extraordinary thing. His love for his father had made it simple and natural to him, and he had never questioned the reason for it. As he had been taught to keep silence, he had been taught to control the expression of his face and the sound of his voice, and above all, never to allow himself to look startled.

But for this he might have started at the extraordinary sound of the Samavian words suddenly uttered in a London street by an English gentleman. He might even have answered the question in Samavian himself. But he did not.

He courteously lifted his cap and replied in English, "Excuse me?"

The gentleman's clever eyes scrutinized him keenly. Then he also spoke in English. "Perhaps you do not understand? I asked your name because you are very like a Samavian I know," he said.

"I am Marco Loristan," the boy answered him.

The man looked straight into his eyes and smiled. "That is not the name," he said. "I beg your pardon, my boy."

He was about to go on and had indeed taken a couple of steps away, when he paused and turned to him again. "You may tell your father that you are a very well trained lad. I wanted to find out for myself." And he went on.

Marco felt that his heart beat a little quickly. This was one of several incidents that had happened during the last three years and made him feel that he was living among things so mysterious that their very mystery hinted at danger. But he himself had never before seemed involved in them. Why should it matter that he was well behaved? Then he remembered something. The man had not said "well behaved"; he had said "well trained." Well trained in what way?

He felt his forehead prickle slightly as he thought of the smiling, keen look that set itself so straight upon him. Had he spoken to him in Samavian for an experiment, to see if he would be startled into forgetting his training? But he had not forgotten. He had remembered well and was thankful that he had betrayed nothing.

Even exiles may be Samavian soldiers. I am one. You must be one, his father had said on that day long ago when Marco had taken his oath. Perhaps remembering his training *was* being a soldier. Never had Samavia needed help as she needed it today. The present king was a powerful man and had a great following of the worst and most self-seeking of the people. Neighboring countries had interfered for their own sake, and the newspapers had been full of stories of savage fighting and of starving peasants.

Marco had late one evening entered their lodgings to find his father walking to and fro like a lion in a cage, a paper crushed and torn in his hands, and his eyes blazing. Loristan had been reading of cruelties wrought upon innocent peasants and women and children.

Lazarus was standing staring at him with huge tears running down his cheeks. When Marco opened the door, the old soldier strode over to him, turned him about, and led him out of the room.

"Pardon, young sir, pardon," the servant sobbed. "No one must see him, not even you. He suffers so horribly."

He half pushed, half led Marco into his own small bedroom. The old man bent his grizzled head and wept like a beaten child.

"Dear God of those who are in pain, assuredly it is now the time to give back to us our Lost Prince!" Lazarus said.

Marco knew the words were a prayer and wondered at the frenzied intensity of it, because it seemed so wild a thing to pray for the return of a youth who had died five hundred years before.

When Marco reached the palace, he was still thinking of the man who had spoken to him. He was thinking of him even as he looked at the majestic gray stone building and counted the number of its stories and windows. He walked around it that he might make a note in his memory of its size and form and its entrances, and guess at the size of its gardens. This he did because it was part of his game and part of his strange training.

When he came back to the front, he saw in the great entrance court an elegant-looking closed carriage drawing up before the doorway. Marco stood and watched with interest to see who from the palace would come out and enter it. He knew that kings and emperors who were not on parade looked merely like well dressed private gentlemen and often chose to go out as simply and quietly as other men. So he thought that perhaps, if he waited, he might see one of those well-known faces.

I should like to be able to tell my father that I have seen the king and know his face, as I know the faces of the czar and the two emperors.

There was a little movement among the tall menservants in the royal scarlet liveries, and an elderly man descended the steps, attended by another who walked behind him. He entered the carriage, the other man followed him, the door was closed, and the carriage drove through the entrance gates where the sentries saluted.

Marco was near enough to see distinctly. The face of the first man was the face he had often seen in shop windows and newspapers. The boy made his quick, formal salute.

It was the king, and as he smiled and acknowledged his greeting, he spoke to his companion. "That fine lad salutes as if he belonged to the army," he said, though Marco could not hear him.

His companion leaned forward to look through the window. When he caught sight of Marco, a singular expression crossed his face. "He does belong to an army, sir, though he does not know it. His name is Marco Loristan."

Then Marco saw him plainly for the first time. He was the man with the keen eyes who had spoken to him in Samavian.

THE RAT

4

Marco would have wondered very much if he had heard the words, but as he did not hear them, he turned toward home. A man who was in attendance on a king must be a person of importance. He no doubt knew many things not only of his own ruler's country, but of the countries of other kings. And so few had really known anything of poor Samavia until the newspapers had begun to tell them of the horrors of its war. Who but a Samavian could speak its language? It would be an interesting thing to tell his father—that a man who knew the king had spoken to him in Samavian and had sent that curious message.

Later he found himself passing a side street and looked up it. It was so narrow, and on either side of it

were such old, tall, and sloping walled houses that it attracted his attention. It looked as if a bit of old London
had been left to stand while newer places grew up and
hid it from view. This was the kind of street he liked to
pass through for curiosity's sake. He could find his way
home from the other end of it. Then he heard a clamor
of boys' voices, and he wanted to see what they were
doing. Sometimes when he had reached a new place and
had that lonely feeling, he had followed some boyish
clamor and found a temporary friend or so.

Halfway to the street's end there was an arched brick
passage. The sound of the voices came from there—one
of them high and shriller than the rest. Marco tramped
up to the arch and looked down through the passage. It
opened onto a gray flagged space, shut in by the railings
of a black, deserted, and ancient graveyard. The boys
were not playing, but listening to one of their number
who was reading to them from a newspaper.

Marco walked down the passage and listened also,
standing in the dark arched outlet at its end and watching the boy who read. He was a strange little creature
with a big forehead and sharp eyes with a curious depth
of understanding. But this was not all. He had a hunchback. His legs seemed small and crooked. He sat crossed-
legged on a rough wooden platform set on low wheels on
which he evidently pushed himself about. Near him were
a number of sticks stacked together as if they were rifles.
One of the first things that Marco noticed was that he
had a savage little face marked with lines as if he had been
angry all his life.

"Hold your tongues, you fools!" he shrilled out to some boys who interrupted him. "Don't you want to know anything, you ignorant swine?"

He was as ill dressed as the rest of them, but he did not speak in the Cockney dialect. If he was of the riffraff of the streets, as his companions were, he was somehow different.

Then he saw Marco, who was standing in the arched end of the passage.

"What are you doing there listening?" he shouted and at once stooped to pick up a stone and threw it at him. The stone hit Marco's shoulder, but it did not hurt him much. What he did not like was that another lad should want to throw something at him before they had even exchanged greetings. He also did not like the fact that two other boys promptly took the matter up by bending down to pick up stones also.

He walked forward straight into the group and stopped close to the hunchback. "What did you do that for?" he asked in his rather deep young voice.

He was big and strong looking enough to suggest that he was not a boy it would be easy to dispose of, but that was not what made the group stand still a moment to stare at him. It was as if the stone had not mattered to him in the least. It had not made him feel angry or insulted—only rather curious. Because he was clean, and his hair and his shabby clothes were brushed, the first impression given by his appearance as he stood in the archway was that he was a young swell poking his nose where it was not wanted. But as he drew near, they saw that the well brushed clothes were worn, and there were patches on his shoes.

"What did you do that for?" he asked again, and he asked it merely as if he wanted to find out the reason.

"I'm not going to have you swells dropping into my club as if it was your own," said the hunchback.

"I'm not a swell, and I didn't know it was a club," Marco answered. "I heard boys, and I thought I'd come and look. When I heard you reading about Samavia, I wanted to hear."

He looked at the reader with his silent expressive eyes. "You needn't have thrown a stone. Men don't do that. I'll go away."

He turned about as if he were going, but before he had taken three steps, the hunchback hailed him unceremoniously.

"Hi!" he called out. "Hi, you!"

"What do you want?" said Marco.

"I bet you don't know where Samavia is, or what they're fighting about." The hunchback threw the words at him.

"Yes, I do. It's north of Beltrazo and east of Jiardasia, and they are fighting because one party has assassinated King Maran, and the other will not let them crown Nicola Iarovitch. And why should they? He's a bandit and hasn't a drop of royal blood in him."

"Oh," reluctantly admitted the hunchback. "You do know it, don't you? Come back here."

Marco turned back while the boys still stared. It was as if two leaders—generals—were meeting for the first time, and the rabble looking on wondered what would come of their encounter.

"The Samavians of the Iarovitch party are a bad lot and want only bad things," said Marco, speaking first. "They care nothing for Samavia. They only care for money and the power to make laws that will serve them and crush everybody else. They know that Nicola is a weak man and that if they can crown him king, they can make him do what they like."

The fact that he spoke first and that he somehow seemed to take it for granted that they would listen, made his place for him at once. Boys know a leader when they see him. The hunchback fixed glittering eyes on him. The rabble began to murmur.

"Rat! Rat!" several voices cried at once in good strong Cockney. "Get 'im some more, Rat!"

"Is that what they call you?" Marco asked the hunchback.

"It's what I called myself," he answered resentfully. "*The Rat.* Look at me. Crawling 'round on the ground like this. Look at me!"

He made a gesture ordering his followers to move aside and began to push himself rapidly with strange darts this side and that around the enclosure. He bent his head and body, and twisted his face, and made strange animal-like movements. He even uttered sharp squeaks as he rushed here and there—as a rat might have done were it being hunted. He did it as if he were displaying an accomplishment, and his followers' laughter was applause.

"Wasn't I like a rat?" he demanded, when he suddenly stopped.

"You made yourself like one on purpose," Marco answered. "You do it for fun."

"Not so much fun," said The Rat. "I feel like one. Everyone's my enemy. I'm vermin. I can't fight or defend myself unless I bite. I can bite though." And he showed two rows of fierce, strong, white teeth, sharper at the points than human teeth usually are. "I bite my father when he gets drunk and beats me. He hasn't tried it for three months—even when he was drunk—and he's always drunk." Then he laughed shrilly. "He's a gentleman, and I'm a gentleman's son. He was a master at a big school until he was kicked out. That was when I was four and my mother died. I'm thirteen now. How old are you?"

"I'm twelve," answered Marco.

The Rat twisted his face enviously. "I wish I was your size! Are you a gentleman's son? You look as if you were."

"I'm a very poor man's son," was Marco's answer. "My father is a writer."

"Then ten to one, he's a sort of gentleman," said The Rat. Then quite suddenly he threw another question at him. "What's the name of the other Samavian party?"

"The Maranovitch. The Maranovitch and the Iarovitch have been fighting with each other for five hundred years. First one dynasty rules, and then the other gets in when it has killed somebody as it killed King Maran," Marco answered without hesitation.

"What was the name of the dynasty that ruled before they began fighting? The first Maranovitch assassinated the last of them," The Rat asked him.

"The Fedorovitch," said Marco. "The last one was a bad king."

"His son was the one they never found again," said The Rat. "The one they call the Lost Prince."

Marco would have started but for his long training in exterior self-control. It was so strange to hear his hero spoken of in this back alley in a slum, and just after he had been thinking of him.

"What do you know about him?" Marco asked, and as he did so, he saw the group of vagabond lads draw nearer.

"Not much. I read something about him in a torn magazine I found in the street," The Rat answered. "The man that wrote about him said he was only part of a legend, and he laughed at people for believing in him. He said it was about time that he should turn up again if he intended to. I've invented things about him because these chaps like to hear me tell them. They're only stories."

"We likes 'im," a voice called out, "becos 'e wos the right sort; 'e'd fight, 'e would, if 'e was in Samavia now."

Marco rapidly asked himself how much he might say. He decided and spoke to them all. "He is not part of a *legend*. He's part of Samavian *history*," he said. "I know something about him too."

"How did you find it out?" asked The Rat.

"Because my father's a writer, he's obliged to have books and papers, and he knows things. I like to read, and I go into the free libraries. You can always get books and papers there. Then I ask my father questions. All the newspapers are full of things about Samavia just now." Marco felt that this was an explanation that betrayed nothing. It was true that no one could open a newspaper at this period without seeing news and stories of Samavia.

The Rat saw possible vistas of information opening up before him. "Sit down here," he said, "and tell us what you know about him. Sit down, you fellows."

There was nothing to sit on but the broken flagged pavement, but that was a small matter. Marco himself had sat on flags or bare ground often enough before, and so had the rest of the lads. He took his place near The Rat, and the others made a semicircle in front of them. The two leaders had joined forces, so to speak, and the followers fell into line at attention.

Then the newcomer began to talk. It was a good story, that of the Lost Prince, and Marco told it in a way that gave it reality. How could he help it? He knew—as they could not—that it was real. He had pored over maps of Samavia since his seventh year, had studied them with his father, knew every highway and byway, and in the capital city of Melzarr could almost have made his way blindfolded. He knew the palaces and the forts, the churches, the poor streets and the rich ones.

His father had once shown him a plan of the royal palace that they had studied together until the boy knew each apartment and corridor in it by heart. But of this he did not speak. He knew it was one of the things to be silent about.

He *could* speak of the mountains and the emerald velvet meadows climbing their sides. He could make pictures of the plains where herds of wild horses fed. He could describe where clear rivers ran and flocks of sheep pastured. He could speak of them because he could offer a good enough reason for his knowledge of them. It was not the only reason he had for his knowledge, but it was one that would serve well enough.

"That torn magazine you found had more than one article about Samavia in it," he said to The Rat. "The same man wrote four. I read them all in a free library. He had been to Samavia and knew a great deal about it. He said it was one of the most beautiful countries he had ever traveled in—and the most fertile. That's what they all say of it."

The group before him knew nothing of fertility or open country. They only knew London back streets and courts. Most of them had never traveled as far as the public parks, and in fact scarcely believed in their existence. They were a rough lot, and they continued to stare at Marco as he talked. When he told of the tall Samavians who had been like giants centuries ago, and who had hunted the wild horses and captured and trained them to obedience, their mouths fell open. This was the sort of thing to allure any boy's imagination.

When he told of the deep endless forests and of the shepherds who played on their pipes and made songs about high deeds and bravery, they grinned with pleasure without knowing they were grinning. When Marco pictured the Lost Prince tall and strong limbed and young, winning all the people when he rode smiling among them, the boys grinned again with unconscious pleasure.

"Wisht 'e 'adn't got lost!" someone cried out.

When they heard of the unrest and dissatisfaction of the Samavians, they began to get restless themselves. When Marco reached the part of the story in which the mob rushed into the palace and demanded their prince from the king, they exclaimed with boyish wrath, "Wisht the lot of us had been there then. Wisht we 'ad. We'd 'ave give 'im wot for anyway!"

It was a story that had a strange effect on them. It made them think they saw things; it fired their blood; it set them wanting to fight for ideals they knew nothing about—adventurous things, for instance, and high and noble young princes who were full of the possibility of great and good deeds. Sitting upon the broken flagstones on the bit of ground behind the deserted graveyard, they were suddenly dragged into the world of noble young princes. The great and good deeds became as real as the sunken gravestones—and far more interesting.

Marco told of the smuggling across the frontier of the unconscious prince in the bullock cart loaded with sheepskins. They held their breaths. Would the old shepherd get him past the line? Marco, who was lost in the recital himself, told it as if he had been present.

Indeed, he felt as if he had, and as this was the first time he had ever told it to thrilled listeners, his imagination got him in its grip, and his heart jumped in his breast as he was sure the old man's must have done when the guard stopped his cart and asked him what he was carrying out of the country. He knew he must have had to call up all his strength to force his voice into steadiness.

And then there was no more to tell—no more. There it broke off, and something like a low howl of dismay broke from the semicircle.

"Aw!" they protested, "it 'adn't ought to stop there! Ain't there no more? Is that all there is?"

"It's all that was ever known really. And that last part might only be a sort of story made up by somebody. But I believe it myself."

The Rat had listened with burning eyes. He had sat biting his fingernails, as was a trick of his when he was excited or angry.

"Tell you what!" The Rat exclaimed suddenly. "This was what happened. It was some of the Maranovitch fellows that tried to kill him. They meant to kill his father and make their own man king, and they knew the people wouldn't stand it if young Ivor was alive. They just stabbed him in the back, the fiends! I dare say they heard the old shepherd coming and left him for dead and ran."

"Right, oh! That was it," the lads agreed. "Yer right there, Rat!"

"When he got well," The Rat went on feverishly, still biting his nails, "he couldn't go back. He was only a boy. The other fellow had been crowned, and his followers felt strong because they'd just conquered the country. He could have done nothing without an army, and he was too young to raise one. Perhaps he thought he'd wait till he was old enough to know what to do. I dare say he went away and had to work for his living as if he'd never been a prince at all. Then perhaps sometime he married somebody and had a son, and told him as a secret who he was and all about Samavia."

The Rat began to look vengeful. "If I'd bin him, I'd have told him not to forget what the Maranovitch had done to me. I'd have told him that if I couldn't get back the throne, he must see what he could do when he grew to be a man. And I'd have made him swear if he got the throne back, to take it out on them or their children or their children's children in torture and killing. I'd have made him swear not to leave a Maranovitch alive. And I'd have told him that if he couldn't do it in his life, he must pass the oath on to his son and his son's son, as long as there was a Fedorovitch on earth. Wouldn't you?" he demanded hotly of Marco.

Marco's blood was also hot, but it was a different kind of blood, and he had talked too much to a very sane man. "No," he said slowly. "What would have been the use? It wouldn't have done Samavia any good, and it wouldn't have done him any good to torture and kill people. Better to keep them alive and make them do things for the country. If you're a patriot, you think of the country." He wanted to add *That's what my father says*, but he did not.

"Torture 'em first and then attend to the country," snapped The Rat. "What would you have told your son if you'd been Ivor?"

"I'd have told him to learn everything about Samavia—all the things kings have to know. Study things about laws and other countries—about keeping silent and about governing himself as if he were a general commanding soldiers in battle—so that he would never do anything he did not mean to do or could be ashamed of doing after it was over. And I'd have asked him to tell his son's sons to tell their sons to learn the same things. So, you see, however long the time was, there would always be a king getting ready for Samavia, when Samavia really wanted him. And he would be a *real* king."

He stopped himself suddenly and looked at the staring semicircle.

"I didn't make that up myself," he said. "I have heard a man who reads and knows things say it. I believe the Lost Prince would have had the same thoughts. If he had and told them to his son, then there has been a line of kings in training for Samavia for five hundred years. Perhaps one is walking about the streets of Vienna, or Paris, or London now, and he'd be ready if the people found out about him and called him."

"Wisht they would!" someone yelled.

"It would be a strange secret to know all the time when no one else knew it." The Rat communed with himself as it were. "Strange to know that you were a king, and you ought to be on a throne wearing a crown. I wonder if it would make a chap look different?"

He laughed his squeaky laugh and then turned in his sudden way to Marco, "But he'd be a fool to give up the vengeance. What is your name?"

"Marco Loristan. What's yours? It isn't *The Rat* really."

"It's Jem *Rat*cliffe. That's pretty near. Where do you live?"

"Number 7 Philibert Place."

"This club is a soldiers' club," said The Rat. "It's called the Squad. I'm the captain. 'Tention, you fellows! Let's show him."

The semicircle sprang to its feet. There were about twelve lads altogether, and when they stood upright, Marco saw at once that for some reason they were accustomed to obeying the word of command with military precision.

"Form in line!" ordered The Rat.

They did it at once and held their backs and legs straight and their heads up amazingly well. Each had seized one of the sticks that had been stacked together like guns.

The Rat himself sat up straight on his platform. There was actually something military in the bearing of his lean body. His voice lost its squeak, and its sharpness became commanding.

He put the dozen lads through the drill as if he had been a smart young officer. And the drill itself was prompt and smart enough to have done credit to practiced soldiers in barracks. It made Marco involuntarily stand very straight himself and watch with surprised interest.

"That's good!" he exclaimed when it was at an end. "How did you learn that?"

The Rat made a savage gesture. "If I'd had legs to stand on, I'd have been a soldier!" he said. "I'd have enlisted in any regiment that would take me. I don't care for anything else."

Suddenly his face changed, and he shouted a command to his followers. "Turn your backs!" he ordered.

And they did turn their backs and looked through the railings of the old churchyard. Marco saw that they were obeying an order that was not new to them. The Rat had thrown his arm up over his eyes and covered them. He held it there for several moments, as if he did not want to be seen. Marco turned his back as the rest had done. All at once he understood that, though The Rat was not crying, yet he was feeling emotion that another boy would possibly have broken down under.

"All right," he shouted presently and dropped his ragged sleeved arm and sat up straight again.

"I want to go to war," he said hoarsely. "I want to fight! I want to lead a lot of men into battle! But I haven't got any legs. Sometimes it takes the pluck out of me."

"You've not grown up yet," said Marco. "You might get strong. No one knows what is going to happen. How did you learn to drill the Squad?"

"I hang about barracks. I watch and listen. I follow soldiers. If I could get books, I'd read about wars. I can't go to libraries as you can. I can do nothing but scuffle about like a rat."

"I can take you to some libraries," said Marco. "There are places where boys can get in. And I can get some papers from my father."

"Can you?" said The Rat. "Do you want to join the club?"

"Yes," Marco answered. "I'll speak to my father about it."

He said it because the hungry longing for companionship in his own mind had found a sort of response in the hungry look in The Rat's eyes. He wanted to see him again. Strange creature as he was, there was attraction in him.

Scuffling about on his low-wheeled platform, he had drawn this group of rough lads to him and made himself their commander. They obeyed him; they listened to his stories and harangues about war and soldiering; they let him drill them and give them orders. Marco knew that, when he told his father about him, he would be interested. The boy wanted to hear what Loristan would say.

"I'm going home now," he said. "If you're going to be here tomorrow, I will try to come."

"We shall be here," The Rat answered. "It's our barracks."

Marco drew himself up smartly and made his salute as if to a superior officer. Then he wheeled about and marched through the brick archway, and the sound of his boyish tread was as regular and decided as if he had been a man keeping time with his regiment.

"He's been drilled himself," said The Rat. "He knows as much as I do." And he sat up and stared down the passage with new interest.

SILENCE IS STILL
THE ORDER

---— 5 —---

They were even poorer than usual just now, and
the supper Marco and his father sat down to was scant
enough. Lazarus stood upright behind his master's chair
and served him with strictest ceremony.

Their poor lodgings were always kept with a soldierly cleanliness and order. When an object could be
polished, it was forced to shine. No grain of dust was
allowed to lie undisturbed, yet this perfection was not
attained through the ministrations of a lodging house
servant. Lazarus made himself extremely popular by
taking the work of caring for his master's rooms entirely
out of the hands of the overburdened maids. He had
learned to do many things in his young days in barracks.
He carried about with him coarse bits of tablecloths and

towels, which he laundered as if they had been the finest linen. He mended, he patched, he darned, and in the hardest fight the poor must face—the fight with dirt and dinginess—he always held his own. They had nothing but dry bread and coffee this evening, but Lazarus had made the coffee and the bread was good.

As Marco ate, he told his father the story of The Rat and his followers. Loristan listened, as the boy had known he would, with the far-off, intently-thinking smile in his dark eyes.

It was a look that always fascinated Marco because it meant that he was thinking so many things.

"And they were talking about Samavia? He knew the story of the Lost Prince?" Loristan pondered. "Even in that place!"

"He wants to hear about wars. He wants to talk about them," Marco answered. "If he could stand and were old enough, he would go and fight for Samavia himself."

"It is a blood-drenched and sad place now," said Loristan. "The people are mad when they are not heart-broken and terrified."

Suddenly Marco struck the table with a sounding slap of his boy's hand. He did it before he realized any intention in his own mind.

"Why should either one of the Iarovitch or one of the Maranovitch be king?" he cried. "They were only savage peasants when they first fought for the crown hundreds of years ago. The most savage one got it, and they have been fighting ever since. Only the Fedorovitch were born kings. There is only one man in the world who has the right to the throne, and I don't know whether he is in the world or not. But I believe he is. I do!"

Loristan looked at Marco's hot twelve-year-old face with a reflective curiosity. He saw that the flame had leaped up in him without warning—just as a fierce heartbeat might have shaken him.

"You mean—?" he suggested softly.

"Ivor Fedorovitch. *King Ivor* he ought to be. The people would obey him, and the good days would come again."

"It is five hundred years since Ivor Fedorovitch left Samavia." Loristan still spoke softly.

"But, Father," Marco protested, "even The Rat said what you said—that he was too young to be able to come back while the Maranovitch were in power. He would have to work and have a home, and perhaps he is as poor as we are. But when he had a son, he would call him Ivor and *tell* him. And his son would call *his* son Ivor and tell *him*. And it would go on and on. They could never call their eldest sons anything but Ivor. And what you said about the training would be true. There would always be a king being trained for Samavia—ready to be called."

In the fire of his feelings he sprang from his chair and stood upright. "Why! There may be a king of Samavia in some city now who knows he is king, and when he reads about the fighting among his people, his blood gets red hot. They're his own people—his very own! He ought to go to them. He ought to go and tell them who he is. Don't you think he ought, Father?"

"It would not be as easy as it seems to a boy," Loristan answered. "There are many countries which would have something to say. Russia would have her word, and Austria, and Germany; and England never is silent. But if he were a strong man and knew how to make strong friends in silence, he might sometime be able to declare himself openly."

"But if he is anywhere, someone—some Samavian—ought to go and look for him. It ought to be a Samavian who is very clever and a patriot—" He stopped at a flash of recognition. "Father!" he cried out. "Father! You. You are the one who could find him if anyone in the world could. But perhaps—" and he stopped a moment again because new thoughts rushed through his mind. "Have *you* ever looked for him?" he asked hesitating.

Perhaps he had asked a stupid question. Perhaps his father had always been looking for him. Perhaps that was his secret and his work.

But Loristan did not look as if he thought him stupid. Quite the contrary. He kept his handsome eyes fixed on him still in that curious way, as if he were studying him—as if he were much more than twelve years old, and he were deciding to tell him something.

"Comrade at arms," he said, with the smile which always gladdened Marco's heart, "you have kept your oath of allegiance like a man. You were not seven years old when you took it. You are growing older. Silence is still the order, but you are man enough to be told more." He paused and looked down, and then looked up again, speaking in a low tone. "I have not looked for him," he said, "because . . . I believe I know where he is."

Marco caught his breath. "Father."

He said only that word. He could say no more. He
knew he must not ask questions. *Silence is still the order.* But
as they faced each other in their dingy room at the back
of the shabby house on the side of the roaring common
road, as Lazarus stood stock-still behind his father's
chair and kept his eyes fixed on the empty coffee cups
and the dry bread plate, and everything looked as poor
as things always did, there was a king of Samavia—an
Ivor Fedorovitch with the blood of the Lost Prince in
his veins—alive in some town or city this moment! And
Marco's own father knew where he was!

He glanced at Lazarus, but though the old soldier's
face looked as expressionless as if it were cut out of
wood, Marco realized that he knew this thing and had
always known it. He had been a comrade at arms all his
life. He continued to stare at the bread plate.

Loristan spoke again and in an even lower voice.
"The Samavians who are patriots and thinkers," he said,
"formed themselves into a secret party about eighty years
ago. They formed it when they had no reason for hope,
but they formed it because one of them discovered that
an Ivor Fedorovitch was living. He was head forester
on a great estate in the Austrian Alps. The nobleman
he served had always thought him a mystery because he
had the bearing and speech of a man who had not been
born a servant. His methods in caring for the forests
and game were those of a man who was educated and
had studied his subject. But he was never familiar or as-
suming, and he never professed superiority over any of
his fellows. He was a man of great stature and was extraordinarily brave and silent.

"The nobleman who was his master made a companion of him when they hunted together. Once he took him with him when he traveled to Samavia to hunt wild horses. He found that he knew the country strangely well, and that he was familiar with Samavian hunting and customs. Before he returned to Austria, the man obtained permission to go to the mountains alone. He went among the shepherds and made friends among them, asking many questions.

"One night around a camp fire he heard the old songs about the Lost Prince. The shepherds talked about Prince Ivor and told stories about him, and related the prophecy that he would come back and bring again Samavia's good days. He might come only in the body of one of his descendants, but it would be his spirit that came, because his spirit would never cease to love Samavia. One very old shepherd tottered to his feet and lifted his face to the myriad stars bestrewn like jewels in the blue sky above the forest trees, and he wept and prayed aloud that God would send their king to them. And the stranger huntsman stood upright also and lifted his face to the stars. And though he said no word, the shepherd nearest to him saw tears on his cheeks—great, heavy tears.

"The next day the stranger went to the church that had taken care of the Lost Prince. When he had left Samavia, the secret society was formed, and the members of it knew that an Ivor Fedorovitch had passed through his ancestors' country as the servant of another man. But the secret society was only a small one, and, though it has been growing ever since and it has done good deeds and good work in secret, the mysterious huntsman died an old man before the society was strong enough even to dare to tell Samavia what it knew."

"Had he a son?" cried Marco. "Had he a son?"

"Yes. He had a son. His name was Ivor. And he was trained as I told you. That part I knew to be true, though I would have believed it was true even if I had not known. There has always been a king ready for Samavia, even when he has labored with his hands and served others. Each one took the oath of allegiance."

"As I did?" said Marco, breathless with excitement. When one is twelve years old, to be so near a Lost Prince who might end wars is a thrilling thing.

"The same," answered Loristan.

Marco threw up his hand in salute. *"Here grows a man for Samavia! God be thanked!"* he quoted. "And he is some- where? And you know?"

Loristan bent his head in acquiescence. "For years much secret work has been done, and the Fedorovitch party has grown until it is much more powerful than the other parties dream. The larger countries are tired of the constant war and disorder in Samavia. They are deciding that they must have peace and laws that can be counted on. There have been Samavian patriots who have spent their lives in trying to bring this about by making friends in the most powerful capitals, and working secretly for the future good of their own land. Because Samavia is so small and uninfluential, it has taken a long time, but when King Maran and his family were assassinated and the war broke out, there were great powers that began to say that if some king of good blood and reliable charac- teristics were given the crown, he should be upheld."

"His blood," Marco's intensity made his voice drop almost to a whisper. "His blood has been trained for five hundred years, Father! If it comes true," though he laughed a little, he was obliged to wink his eyes hard because suddenly he felt tears rush into them, which no boy likes, "the shepherds will have to make a new song. It will have to be a shouting one about a prince going away and a king coming back."

"But the end is not yet," Loristan said. "The end is not yet. Sometimes it seems that perhaps it is near, but only God knows."

Then there leaped back upon Marco the story he had to tell, but which he had held back for the last—the story of the man who spoke Samavian and drove in the carriage with the king. He knew now that it might mean some important thing that he could not have before suspected.

"There is something I must tell you," he said.

He had learned to relate incidents in few, but clear, words when he related them to his father. It had been part of his training. Loristan had said that he might sometime have a story to tell when he had but few moments to tell it in—a story which meant life or death to someone. He told this one quickly and well. He made Loristan see the well dressed man with the deliberate manner and the keen eyes, and he made him hear his voice when he said, "Tell your father that you are a very well trained lad."

"I am glad he said that. He is a man who knows what training is," said Loristan. "He is a person who knows what all Europe is doing, and almost all that it will do.

He is an ambassador from a powerful and great country. If he saw that you are a well trained and fine lad, it might . . . it might even be good for Samavia."

"Would it matter that I was well trained? Could it matter to Samavia?" Marco pondered.

Loristan paused for a moment, watching him gravely and looking him over, his big, well-built boy's frame, his shabby clothes, and his eagerly burning eyes.

He smiled one of his slow wonderful smiles. "Yes. It might even matter to Samavia," he answered.

The Drill and the Secret Party

6

Loristan did not forbid Marco to pursue his acquaintance with The Rat and his followers.

"You will find out for yourself whether they are friends for you or not," he said. "You will know in a few days, and then you can make your own decision. You have known lads in various countries, and you are a good judge of them, I think. You will soon see whether they are going to be men or mere rabble. The Rat now— how does he strike you?" And the handsome eyes held their keen look of questioning.

"He'd be a brave soldier if he could stand," said Marco, thinking him over. "But he might be cruel."

"A lad who might make a brave soldier cannot be disdained, but a man who is cruel is a fool. Tell him that from me," Loristan answered. "He wastes force—his own and the force of the one he treats cruelly. Only a fool wastes force."

"May I speak of you sometimes?" asked Marco.

"Yes. You will know how. You will remember the things about which silence is the order."

"I never forget them," said Marco. "I have been trying not to for such a long time."

"You have succeeded well, comrade," returned Loristan, from his writing table.

A strong impulse overpowered the boy. He marched over to the table and stood very straight, making his soldierly young salute, his whole body glowing.

"Father," he said, "you don't know how I love you! I wish you were a general and I might die in battle for you. When I look at you, I long to do something for you a boy could not do. I would die of a thousand wounds rather than disobey you—or Samavia."

He seized Loristan's hand and knelt on one knee and kissed it. An English boy could not have done such a thing from unaffected natural impulse. But he was of warm southern blood.

"I took my oath of allegiance to you, Father, when I took it to Samavia. It seems as if you were Samavia too," he said.

Loristan had turned toward him with one of the movements that were full of dignity and grace. Marco, looking up at him, felt that there was always a certain remote stateliness in him that made it seem quite natural that anyone should bend the knee and kiss his hand.

A sudden great tenderness glowed in his father's face as he raised the boy and put his hand on his shoulder. "Comrade," he said, "you don't know how much I love you, and what reason there is that we should love each other. You don't know how I have been watching you and thanking God each year that here grew a man for Samavia. I know that you are a man, though you have lived but twelve years. Twelve years may grow a man or prove that a man will never grow, though he may remain for ninety years. This year may be full of strange things for both of us. We cannot know what I may have to ask you to do for me . . . and for Samavia. Perhaps such a thing as no twelve-year-old boy has ever done before."

"Every night and every morning," said Marco, "I shall pray that I may be called to do it, and that I may do it well."

"You will do it well, comrade, if you are called. That I could promise," Loristan answered him.

The Squad had collected in the enclosure behind the church when Marco appeared at the arched end of the passage. The boys were drawn up with their rifles, but they all wore a rather dogged and sullen look. The explanation that darted into Marco's mind was that this was because The Rat was in a bad humor. He sat crouched together on his platform biting his nails fiercely, his elbows on his up drawn knees, his face twisted into a hideous scowl. He did not look around or even look up from the cracked flagstone on which his eyes were fixed.

Marco went forward with military step and stopped opposite to him with prompt salute. "Sorry to be late, sir," he said, as if he had been a private speaking to his colonel.

"It's 'im, Rat! 'E's come, Rat!" the Squad shouted. "Look at 'im!"

But The Rat would not look and did not even move.

"What's the matter?" said Marco with less ceremony than a private would have shown. "There's no use in my coming here if you don't want me."

" 'E's got a grouch on 'cos you're late," called out the head of the line. "No doin' nothin' when 'e's got a grouch on."

"I shan't try to do anything," said Marco, his face setting itself into good stubborn lines. "That's not what I came here for. I came to drill. I've been with my father. He comes first. I can't join the Squad if my father doesn't come first. We're not on active service, and we're not in barracks."

Then The Rat moved sharply and turned to look at him. "I thought you weren't coming at all!" he snapped and growled at once. "My father said you wouldn't. He said you were a young swell for all your patched clothes. He said your father would think he was a swell too, and he wouldn't let you have anything to do with a vagabond and a nuisance. Nobody begged you to join."

"Don't you speak in that way about my father," said Marco, quite quietly, "because I can't knock you down."

"I'll get up and let you!" began The Rat, immediately white and raging. "I can stand up with two sticks. I'll get up and let you!"

"No, you won't," said Marco. "If you want to know what my father said, I can tell you. He said I could come as often as I liked . . . till I found out whether we should be friends or not. He says I shall find that out for myself."

It was a strange thing The Rat did. It must always be remembered of him that his wretched father, who had each year sunk lower and lower, had been a gentleman once, a man who had been familiar with good manners and had been educated in the customs of good breeding. Sometimes when he was drunk, and sometimes when he was partly sober, he talked to The Rat of many things the boy would never have heard of otherwise. That was why the lad was different from the other vagabonds.

He suddenly altered the whole situation by doing a strange and unexpected thing. He utterly changed his expression and voice, fixing his sharp eyes shrewdly on Marco's. It was almost as if he were asking him a riddle. The Rat knew it would have been one to most boys of the class he appeared outwardly to belong to. Marco would either know the answer or he wouldn't.

"I beg your pardon," The Rat said.

That was the puzzle. It was what a gentleman and an officer would have said, if he felt he had been mistaken or rude. He had heard that from his drunken father.

"I beg yours . . . for being late," said Marco.

That was the right answer. It was the one another officer and gentleman would have made. It settled the matter at once, and it settled more than was apparent at the moment. It decided that Marco was one of those who knew the things The Rat's father had once known—the things gentlemen do and say and think. Not another word was said. It was all right. Marco slipped into line with the Squad, and The Rat sat erect with his military bearing and began his drill:

"Squad!

" 'Tention!

"Number!

"Slope arms!

"Form fours!

"Right!

"Quick march!

"Halt!

"Left turn!

"Order arms!

"Stand at ease!

"Stand easy!"

They did it so well that it was quite wonderful when one considered the limited space at their disposal. They had evidently done it often, and The Rat had been not only a smart, but a severe, officer. This morning they repeated the exercise a number of times, and even varied it with review drill with which they seemed just as familiar.

"Where did *you* learn it?" The Rat asked when the arms were stacked again and Marco was sitting by him as he had sat the previous day.

"From an old soldier. And I like to watch it as you do."

"If you were a young swell in the guards, you couldn't be smarter at it," The Rat said. "The way you hold yourself. The way you stand. You've got it! Wish I was you! It comes natural to you."

"I've always liked to watch it and try to do it myself. I did when I was a little fellow," answered Marco.

"I've been trying to kick it into these chaps for more than a year," said The Rat. "A nice job I had of it. It nearly made me sick at first."

The semicircle in front of him only giggled or laughed outright. The members of it seemed to take very little offense at his cavalier treatment of them. He had evidently something to give them which was entertaining enough to make up for his tyranny and indifference. The Rat thrust his hand into one of the pockets of his ragged coat and drew out a piece of newspaper.

"My father brought this home wrapped around a loaf of bread," he said. "See what it says there."

He handed it to Marco, pointing to some words printed in large letters at the head of a column. Marco looked at it and sat very still. The words he read were: "The Lost Prince."

Silence is still the order was the first thought that flashed through his mind. *Silence is still the order.*

"What does it mean?" he said aloud.

"There isn't much of it. I wish there was more," The Rat said fretfully. "Read and see. Of course they say it mayn't be true, but I believe it is. They say that people think someone knows where he is—at least where one of his descendants is. It'd be the same thing. He'd be the real king. If he'd just show himself, it might stop all the fighting. Just read."

Marco read, and his skin prickled as the blood went racing through his body. But his face did not change. There was a sketch of the story of the Lost Prince to begin with. It had been regarded by most people, the article said, as a sort of legend. Now there was a definite rumor that it was not a legend at all, but a part of the long history of Samavia. It was said that through the centuries there had always been a party secretly loyal to the memory of this lost Fedorovitch. It was even said that from father to son, generation after generation, had descended the oath of allegiance to him and his descendants. The people had made a hero of him, and now, romantic as it seemed, it was beginning to be an open secret that some persons believed that a descendant had been found—a Fedorovitch worthy of his young ancestor—and that a certain secret party also held that if he were called back to the throne of Samavia, the interminable wars and bloodshed would reach an end.

The Rat had begun to bite his nails fast. "Do you believe he's found?" he asked feverishly. "*Do you?* I do!"

"I wonder where he is, if it's true? I wonder. Where?" exclaimed Marco. He could say that, and he might seem as eager as he felt.

The Squad all began to jabber at once. The Rat continued to bite his nails. "He might be anywhere," he said, his small fierce face glowing. "That's what I like to think about. He might be passing in the street outside there. He might be up in one of those houses," jerking his head over his shoulder toward the backs of the inclosing dwellings. "Perhaps he knows he's a king, and perhaps he doesn't. He'd know if what you said yesterday was true, about the king always being made ready for Samavia."

"Yes, he'd know," put in Marco.

"Well, it'd be finer if he did," went on The Rat. "However poor and shabby he was, he'd know the secret all the time. And if people sneered at him, I dare say he'd walk tremendously straight and hold his head up. If I was him, I'd like to make people suspect a bit that I wasn't like the common lot o' them." He put out his hand and pushed Marco excitedly. "Let's work out plots for him. That'd be a splendid game. Let's pretend we're the Secret Party!"

He was tremendously excited. Out of the ragged pocket he fished a piece of chalk. Then he leaned forward and began to draw something quickly on the flagstones closest to his platform. The Squad leaned forward also, quite breathlessly, and Marco leaned forward. The chalk was sketching a roughly outlined map, and he knew what map it was before The Rat spoke.

"That's a map of Samavia," he said. "It was in that piece of magazine I told you about—the one where I read about Prince Ivor. I studied it until it fell to pieces. But I could draw it myself by that time, so it didn't matter. I could draw it with my eyes shut. That's the capital city," pointing to a spot. "It's called Melzarr. The palace is there. It's the place where the first of the Maranovitch killed the last of the Fedorovitch—the bad chap that was

Ivor's father. It's the palace Ivor wandered out of singing the shepherds' song that early morning. It's where the throne is that his descendant would sit upon to be crowned. That he's *going* to sit upon. I believe he is! Let's promise he shall!" He flung down his piece of chalk and sat up. "Give me two sticks. Help me to get up."

Two of the Squad sprang to their feet and came to him. Each snatched one of the sticks from the stacked rifles, evidently knowing what he wanted. Marco rose too and watched with keen curiosity. He had thought that The Rat could not stand up, but it seemed that he could in a fashion of his own, and he was going to do it. The boys lifted him by his arms, set him against the stone coping of the iron railings of the churchyard, and put a stick in each of his hands. They stood at his side, but he supported himself.

" 'E could get about if 'e 'ad the money to buy crutches," said one whose name was Cad, and he said it quite proudly. The queer thing that Marco had noticed was that the ragamuffins were proud of The Rat and regarded him as their master.

" 'E could get about an' stand as well as anyone," added the other, and he said it in the tone of one who boasts. His name was Ben.

"I'm going to stand now, and so are the rest of you," said The Rat. "Squad! 'Tention! You at the head of the line," he said to Marco. They were in line in a moment—straight, shoulders back, chins up. And Marco stood at the head.

"We're going to take an oath," said The Rat. "It's an oath of allegiance. Allegiance means faithfulness to a thing—a king or a country. Ours means allegiance to the King of Samavia. We don't know where he is, but we swear to be faithful to him, to fight for him, to plot for him, to **die** for him, and to bring him back to his throne!" The way in which he flung up his head when he said the word *die* was very fine indeed. "We are the Secret Party. We will work in the dark and find out things—and run risks—and collect an army no one will know anything about until it is strong enough to suddenly rise at a secret signal and overwhelm the Maranovitch and Iarovitch, and seize their forts and citadels. No one even knows we are alive. We are a silent, secret thing that never speaks aloud."

Silent and secret as they were, however, they spoke aloud at this juncture. It was such a grand idea for a game, and so full of possible larks, that the Squad broke into a howl of an exultant cheer.

"Hooray!" they yelled. "Hooray for the oath of 'legiance! 'Ray! 'Ray! 'Ray!"

"Shut up, you swine!" shouted The Rat. "Is that the way you keep yourself secret? You'll call the police in, you fools. Look at *him*!" pointing to Marco. "He's got some sense."

Marco, in fact, had not made any sound.

"Come here, you Cad and Ben, and put me back on my wheels," raged the Squad's commander. "I'll not make up the game at all. It's no use with a lot of raw recruits like you."

The line broke and surrounded him in a moment, pleading and urging. "Aw, Rat! We forgot. It's the primest game you've ever thought out, Rat. Rat! Don't get a grouch on. We'll keep still, Rat. Primest lark of all 'll be the sneakin' about an' keepin' quiet. Aw, Rat. Keep it up."

"Keep it up yourselves," snarled The Rat.

"Not another one of us could do it but you. Not one! There's no other fellow could think it out. You're the only chap that can think out things. You thought out the Squad. That's why you're captain!"

This was true. He was the one who could invent entertainment for them, these street lads who had nothing. Out of that nothing he could create what excited them and give them something to fill empty, useless, often cold and foggy hours. That made him their captain and their pride.

The Rat began to yield, though grudgingly. He pointed again to Marco, who had not moved, but stood still at attention.

"Look at him," he said. "He knows enough to stand where he's put until he's ordered to break line. He's a soldier. He is not a raw recruit that don't know the goose step. He's been in barracks before."

But after this outburst, he deigned to go on.

"Here's the oath," he said. "We swear to stand any torture and submit in silence to any death rather than betray our secret and our king. We will obey in silence and in secret. We will swim through seas of blood and fight our way through lakes of fire, if we are ordered. Nothing shall bar our way. All we do and say and think is for our country and our king. If any of you have anything to say, speak out before you take the oath."

He saw Marco move a little, and he made a sign to him.

"You," he said. "Have you something to say?"

Marco turned to him and saluted. "Here stand ten men for Samavia. God be thanked," he said. He dared say that much, and he felt as if his father himself would have told him that they were the right words.

The Rat thought they were. Somehow he felt that they struck home. He reddened with a sudden emotion. "Squad!" he said. "I'll let you give three cheers on that. It's the last time. We'll begin to be quiet afterward."

And to the Squad's exultant relief he led the cheer, and they were allowed to make as much uproar as they liked. They liked to make a great deal, and when it was at an end, it had done them good and made them ready for business.

The Rat opened the drama at once. Surely there had never before been heard a conspirator's whisper as hollow as his.

"Secret ones," he said, "it is midnight. We meet in the depths of darkness. We dare not meet by day. When we meet in the daytime, we pretend not to know each other. We are meeting now in a Samavian city where there is a fortress. We shall have to take it when the secret sign is given and we make our rising. We are getting everything ready so that when we find the king, the secret sign can be given."

"What is the name of the city we are in?" whispered Cad.

"It is called Larrina. It is an important seaport. We must take it as soon as we rise. The next time we meet I will bring a lantern and draw a map and show it to you."

It would have been a great advantage to the game if Marco could have drawn for them the map he could have made, a map that would have shown every fortress—every stronghold and every weak place. Being a boy, he knew what excitement would have thrilled each breast, how they would lean forward and pile question on question, pointing to this place and to that. He had learned to draw the map before he was ten, and he had drawn it again and again because there had been times when his father had told him that changes had taken place.

Oh, yes! He could have drawn a map that would have moved them to a frenzy of joy. But he sat silent and listened, only speaking when he asked a question, as if he knew nothing more about Samavia than The Rat did. What a Secret Party they were! They drew themselves together in the closest of circles; they spoke in unearthly whispers.

"A sentinel ought to be posted at the end of the passage," Marco whispered.

"Ben, take your gun," commanded The Rat.

Ben rose stealthily, and shouldering his weapon, crept on tiptoe to the opening. There he stood on guard.

"My father says there's been a Secret Party in Samavia for a hundred years," The Rat whispered.

"Who told him?" asked Marco.

"A man who has been in Samavia," answered The Rat. "He said it was the most wonderful Secret Party in the world, because it has worked and waited so long, and never given up, though it has had no reason for hoping. It began among some shepherds and charcoal burners who bound themselves by an oath to find the Lost Prince and bring him back to the throne. There were too few of them to do anything against the Maranovitch, and when the first lot found they were growing old, they made their sons take the same oath. It has been passed on from generation to generation, and in each generation the band has grown.

"No one really knows how large it is now, but they say that there are people in nearly all the countries in Europe who belong to it in dead secret and are sworn to help it when they are called. They are only waiting. Some are rich people who will give money, and some are poor ones who will slip across the frontier to fight or to help to smuggle in arms. They even say that for all these years there have been arms made in caves in the mountains and hidden there year after year. There are men who are called Forgers of the Sword, and they, and their fathers, and grandfathers, and great-grandfathers have always made swords and stored them in caverns no one knows of—hidden caverns underground."

Marco spoke aloud the thought that had come into his mind as he listened, a thought which brought fear to him. "If the people in the streets talk about it, they won't be hidden long."

"It isn't common talk, my father says. Only very few have guessed, and most of them think it is part of the Lost Prince legend," said The Rat. "The Maranovitch

and Iarovitch laugh at it. They have always been great
fools. They're too full of their own swagger to think
anything can interfere with them."

"Do you talk much to your father?" Marco asked.

The Rat showed his sharp white teeth in a grin.
"I know what you're thinking of," he said. "You're
remembering that I said he was always drunk. So he is,
except when he's only *half* drunk. And when he's half
drunk, he's the most splendid talker in London. He
remembers everything he has ever learned or read or
heard since he was born. I get him going, then listen.
He wants to talk, and I want to hear. I found out almost
everything I know in that way. He didn't know he was
teaching me, but he was. He goes back into being a
gentleman when he's half drunk."

"If you care about the Samavians, you'd better ask
him not to tell people about the Secret Party and the
Forgers of the Sword," suggested Marco.

The Rat started a little. "That's true," he said.
"You're sharper than I am. It oughtn't to be blabbed
about, or the Maranovitch might hear enough to make
them stop and listen. I'll get him to promise. There's
one odd thing about him," he added very slowly, as if he
were thinking it over. "I suppose it's part of the gentleman that's left in him. If he makes a promise, he never
breaks it—drunk or sober."

"Ask him to make one," said Marco. The next
moment he changed the subject because it seemed the
best thing to do. "Go on and tell us what our own Secret
Party is to do. We're forgetting," he whispered.

The Rat took up his game with renewed zeal. It was
a game that attracted him immensely because it called
upon his imagination and held his audience spellbound
besides plunging him into war and strategy.

"We're preparing for the rising," he said. "It must
come soon. We've waited so long. The caverns are
stacked with arms. The Maranovitch and the Iarovitch
are fighting and using all their soldiers, and now is our
time." He stopped and thought, his elbows on his knees.
He began to bite his nails again.

"The secret signal must be given," he said. Then he
stopped again, and the Squad held its breath and pressed
nearer with a softly shuffling sound. "Two of the Secret
Ones must be chosen by lot and sent forth," he went on;
and the Squad almost brought ruin and disgrace upon
itself by wanting to cheer again, and only just stopping
itself in time.

"Must be chosen by lot," The Rat repeated, looking
from one face to another. "Each one will take his life in
his hand when he goes forth. He may have to die a thousand deaths, but he must go. He must steal in silence
and disguise from one country to another. Wherever
there is one of the Secret Party, whether he is in a hovel
or on a throne, the messengers must go to him in darkness and stealth and give him the sign. It will mean, *The
hour has come. God save Samavia!*"

"God save Samavia," whispered the Squad excitedly.
And because they saw Marco raise his hand to his forehead, every one of them saluted.

They all began to whisper at once. "Let's draw lots
now. Let's draw lots, Rat. Don't let's 'ave no waitin'."

The Rat began to look about him with dread anxiety. He seemed to be examining the sky. "The darkness is not as thick as it was," he whispered. "Midnight has passed. The dawn of day will be upon us. If anyone has a piece of paper or a string, we will draw the lots before we part."

Cad had a piece of string, and Marco had a knife that could be used to cut it into lengths. This The Rat did himself. Then after shutting his eyes and mixing them, he held them in his hand ready for the drawing.

"The Secret One who draws the longest lot is chosen. The Secret One who draws the shortest is chosen," he said solemnly.

The drawing was as solemn as his tone. Each boy wanted to draw either the shortest lot or the longest one. The heart of each thumped somewhat as he drew his piece of string.

When the drawing was at an end, each showed his lot. The Rat had drawn the shortest piece of string, and Marco had drawn the longest one.

"Comrade," said The Rat, taking his hand. "We will face death and danger together!"

"God save Samavia," answered Marco.

And the game was at an end for the day. The finest thing, the Squad said, The Rat had ever made up for them. " 'E wos a wonder, he wos!"

The Lamp
is Lighted!

7

On his way home, Marco thought of nothing
but the story he must tell his father, the story that the
stranger who had been to Samavia had told The Rat's
father. He felt that it must be a true story and not
merely an invention. The Forgers of the Sword must be
real men, and the hidden subterranean caverns stacked
through the centuries with arms must be real too. And
if they were real, surely his father was one of those who
knew the secret.

His thoughts ran very fast. The Rat's boyish invention of the rising was only part of a game, but how
natural it would be that sometime—perhaps before
long—there would be a real rising!

He longed to reach home and tell his father at once all he had heard. He recalled to mind, word for word, all that The Rat had been told, and even all he had added in his game, because . . . well, because that seemed so real too, so real that it actually might be useful.

When he reached Number 7 Philibert Place, he found Loristan and Lazarus very much absorbed in work. The door of the back sitting room was locked when he first knocked on it, and locked again as soon as he had entered. There were many papers on the table, and they were evidently studying them. Several of them were maps. Some were road maps, some maps of towns and cities, and some of fortifications; but they were all maps of places in Samavia. They were usually kept in a strongbox, and when they were taken out to be studied, the door was always kept locked.

Before they had their evening meal, these were all returned to the strongbox, which was pushed into a corner and had newspapers piled upon it.

"When he arrives," Marco heard Loristan say to Lazarus, "we can show him clearly what has been planned. He can see for himself."

His father spoke scarcely at all during the meal, and though it was not the habit of Lazarus to speak at such times unless spoken to, this evening it seemed to Marco that he *looked* more silent than he had ever seen him look before. They were plainly both thinking of deeply serious things. The story of the stranger who had been to Samavia must not be told yet; it was one that would keep.

Loristan did not say anything until Lazarus had removed the things from the table and made the room as neat as possible. While that was being done, he sat with his forehead resting on his hand, as if absorbed in thought. Then he made a gesture to Marco.

"Come here, comrade," he said.

Marco went to him.

"Tonight someone may come to talk with me about grave things," he said. "I think he will come, but I cannot be quite sure. It is important that he should know that when he comes, he will find me quite alone. He will come at a late hour, and Lazarus will open the door quietly that no one may hear. It is important that no one should see him. Someone must go and walk on the opposite side of the street until he appears. Then the one who goes to give warning must cross the pavement before him and say in a low voice, 'The Lamp is lighted!' and at once turn quietly away."

What boy's heart would not have leaped with joy at the mystery of it? Even a common and dull boy who knew nothing of Samavia would have felt jerky. Marco's voice almost shook with the thrill of his feeling.

"How shall I know him?" he said at once. Without asking at all, he knew he was the someone who was to go.

"You have seen him before," Loristan answered. "He is the man who drove in the carriage with the king."

"I shall know him," said Marco. "When shall I go?"

"Not until it is half past one o'clock. Go to bed and sleep until Lazarus calls you." Then he added, "Look well at his face before you speak. He will probably not be dressed as well as he was when you saw him first."

Marco went upstairs to his room and went to bed as he was told, but it was hard to go to sleep. The rattle and roaring of the road did not usually keep him awake, because he had lived in the poorer quarter of too many big cities not to be accustomed to noise. But tonight it seemed to him that, as he lay and looked out at the lamplight, he heard every bus and cab that went past. He could not help thinking of the people who were in them and of the people who were hurrying along on the pavement outside the broken iron railings. He was wondering what they would think if they knew that things connected with the battles they read of in the daily papers were going on in one of the shabby houses they scarcely gave a glance to as they went by. It must be something connected with the war, if a man who was a great diplomat and the companion of kings came in secret to talk alone with a patriot who was a Samavian.

Whatever his father was doing was for the good of Samavia, and perhaps the Secret Party knew he was doing it. His heart almost beat aloud under his shirt as he lay on the lumpy mattress thinking it over. He must indeed look well at the stranger before he even moved toward him. He must be sure he was the right man. The game he had amused himself with so long—the game of trying to remember pictures and people and places clearly and in detail—had been wonderful training. If he could draw, he knew he could have made a sketch of the keen-eyed, clever, aquiline face with the well cut and delicately closed mouth that looked as if it had been shut upon secrets always—always. If he could draw, he found himself saying again. He *could* draw, though perhaps only roughly. He had often amused himself by making sketches of things he wanted to ask questions about. He had even drawn people's faces in his untrained way, and his father had said that he had a crude gift for catching a likeness. Perhaps he could make a sketch of this face that would show his father that he knew and would recognize it.

He jumped out of bed and went to a table near the window. There was paper and a pencil lying on it. A streetlamp exactly opposite threw into the room quite enough light for him to see by. He half knelt by the table and began to draw. He worked for about twenty minutes steadily, and he tore up two or three unsatisfactory sketches. The poor drawing would not matter if he could catch that subtle look which was not slyness but something more dignified and important. It was not difficult to get the marked, aristocratic outline of the features. A common-looking man with less pronounced profile would have been less easy to draw in one sense. He gave his mind wholly to the recalling of every detail that had photographed itself on his memory through its trained habit. Gradually he saw that the likeness was becoming clearer. It was not long before it was clear enough to be a striking one. Anyone who knew the man would recognize it. He got up, drawing a long and joyful breath.

He did not put on his shoes, but crossed his room as noiselessly as possible, and just as noiselessly opened the door. He made not a sound when he went down the stairs. The woman who kept the lodging house had gone to bed, and so had the other lodgers and the maid. All the lights were out except the one he saw a glimmer of under the door of his father's room. When he had been a mere baby, he had been taught to make a special sign on the door when he wished to speak to Loristan. He stood still outside the back sitting room and made it now. It was a low scratching sound—two scratches and a soft tap. Lazarus opened the door and looked troubled.

"It is not yet time, sir," he said very low.

"I know," Marco answered. "But I must show something to my father."

Lazarus let him in, and Loristan turned round from his writing table questioningly.

Marco went forward and laid the sketch down before him. "Look at it," he said. "I remember him well enough to draw that. I thought of it all at once—that I could make a sort of picture. Do you think it is like him?"

Loristan examined it closely. "It is very like him," he answered. "You have made me feel entirely safe. Thanks, comrade. It was a good idea."

There was relief in the grip he gave the boy's hand, and Marco turned away with an exultant feeling. Just as he reached the door, Loristan said to him, "Make the most of this gift. It *is* a gift. And it is true your mind has had good training. The more you draw the better. Draw everything you can."

Neither the streetlamps, nor the noises, nor his thoughts kept Marco awake when he went back to bed. But before he settled himself upon his pillow, he gave himself certain orders. He had both read and heard Loristan say that the mind can control the body when once it finds out that it can do so. He had tried experiments himself and had found out some curious things. One was that if he told himself to remember a certain thing at a certain time, he usually found that he *did* remember it. Something in his brain seemed to remind him. He had often tried the experiment of telling himself to awaken at a particular hour and had awakened almost exactly at the moment by the clock.

"I will sleep until one o'clock," he said as he shut his eyes. "Then I will awaken and feel quite fresh. I shall not be sleepy at all."

He slept as soundly as a boy can sleep. And at one o'clock exactly he awakened and found the streetlamp still throwing its light through the window. He knew it was one o'clock, because there was a cheap little round clock on the table, and he could see the time. He was quite fresh and not at all sleepy. His experiment had succeeded again.

He got up and dressed. Then he went downstairs as noiselessly as before. He carried his shoes in his hands, as he meant to put them on only when he reached the street. He made his sign at his father's door, and it was Loristan who opened it.

"Shall I go now?" Marco asked.

"Yes. Walk slowly to the other side of the street. Look in every direction. We do not know where he will come from. After you have given him the sign, then come in and go to bed again."

Marco saluted as a soldier would have done on receiving an order. Then without a second's delay, he passed noiselessly out of the house.

Loristan turned back into the room and stood silently in the center of it. The long lines of his handsome body looked particularly erect and stately, and his eyes were glowing as if something deeply moved him. "There grows a man for Samavia," he said to Lazarus, who watched him. "God be thanked!"

Lazarus's voice was low and hoarse, and he saluted quite reverently. "Yes, sir," he said. "God save the prince!"

"Yes," Loristan answered, after a moment's hesitation, ". . . when he is found." And he went back to his table, smiling his beautiful smile.

The wonder of silence in the deserted streets of a great city after midnight is an almost unbelievable thing. A few hours ago, the tumult was rushing past; in a few hours more, it will be rushing past again. But now the street is a naked thing; a distant policeman's step on the bare pavement has a hollow and almost fearsome sound. It seemed especially so to Marco as he crossed the road.

Had it ever been so empty and deadly silent before? Was it so every night? Perhaps it was, when he was fast asleep on his lumpy mattress with the light from a streetlamp streaming into the room. He listened for the step of the policeman on night watch, because he did not wish to be seen. There was a jutting wall where he could stand in the shadow while the man passed. A policeman would stop to look questioningly at a boy who walked up and down the pavement at half past one in the morning. Marco could wait until he had gone by and then come out into the light and look up and down the road and the cross streets.

He heard his approaching footsteps in a few minutes and was safely in the shadows before he could be seen. When the policeman passed, he came out and walked slowly down the road, looking on each side, and now and then looking back. At first no one was in sight. Then a late cab came along, but the people in it were returning from some festivity and were laughing and talking, and noticed nothing but their own joking. Then there was silence again, and for a long time, as it seemed to Marco, no one was to be seen. It was not really so long as it appeared—only that he was anxious. Then a very early vegetable wagon on the way from the country to Covent Garden Market came slowly lumbering by with its driver almost asleep on his piles of potatoes and cabbages. After it had passed, there was stillness and emptiness once more until the policeman showed himself again on his beat, and Marco slipped into the shadow of the wall as he had done before.

When he came out into the light, he had begun to hope that the time would not seem long to his father. It had not really been long, he told himself. It had only seemed so. But his father's anxiousness would be greater than his own could be. Loristan knew all that depended on the coming of this great man who sat side by side with a king in his carriage and talked to him as if he knew him well.

It might be something which all Samavia is waiting to know—at least all the Secret Party, Marco thought. *The Secret Party* is *Samavia.* He started at the sound of footsteps. "Someone is coming," he said. "It is a man."

It was a man who was walking up the road on the same side of the pavement as his own. Marco began to walk toward him quietly but rather rapidly. He thought it might be best to appear as if he were some boy sent on a midnight errand—perhaps to call a doctor. Then, if it was a stranger he passed, no suspicion would be aroused. Was this man as tall as the one who had driven with the king? Yes, he was about the same height, but he was too far away to be recognizable otherwise. He drew nearer, and Marco noticed that he also seemed slightly to hasten his footsteps. Marco went on. A little nearer, and he would be able to make sure. Yes, now he was near enough. Yes, this man was the same height and not unlike in figure, but he was much younger. He was not the one who had been in the carriage with His Majesty. He was not more than thirty years old. He began swinging his cane and whistling softly as Marco passed him without changing his pace.

It was after the policeman had walked around his beat and disappeared for the third time, that Marco heard footsteps echoing at some distance down a cross street. After listening to make sure that they were approaching instead of receding in another direction, he placed himself at a point where he could watch the length of the thoroughfare. Yes, someone was coming. It was a man's figure again. He was able to place himself rather in the shadow so that the person approaching would not see that he was being watched. The solitary walker reached a recognizable distance in about two minutes' time. He was dressed in an ordinary suit of clothes that was rather shabby and quite unremarkable in its appearance. His common hat was worn so that it shaded his face. But even before he had crossed to

Marco's side of the road, the boy had clearly recognized him. It was the man who had driven with the king!

The man crossed at the exact place, which made it easy for the boy to step lightly from behind him, walk a few paces by his side, and then pass directly before him across the pavement. Marco glanced quietly up into his face and said in a low but distinct voice, "The Lamp is lighted." Then without pausing a second, he walked on his way down the road. He did not slacken his pace or look back until he was some distance away. Then he glanced over his shoulder and saw that the figure had crossed the street and was inside the railings. It was all right. His father would not be disappointed. The great man had come.

He walked for about ten minutes, and then went home and to bed. But he was obliged to tell himself to go to sleep several times before his eyes closed for the rest of the night.

An Exciting Game

8

Loristan referred only once during the next day to what had happened.

"You did your errand well. You were not hurried or nervous," he said. "The prince was pleased with your calmness."

No more was said. Marco knew that the quiet mention of the stranger's title had been made merely as a designation. If it was necessary to mention him again in the future, he could be referred to as "the prince." In various continental countries there were many princes who were not royal, but who were merely called princes as other nobles were called dukes or barons. Nothing special was revealed when a man was spoken of as a prince.

Though nothing was said on the subject of the incident, it was plain that much work was being done by Loristan and Lazarus. The sitting room door was locked, and the maps and documents, usually kept in the strongbox, were being used.

Marco went to the Tower of London and spent part of the day in living again the stories which centuries past had enclosed within the massive and ancient stone walls. In this way he had throughout boyhood become intimate with people who to most boys seemed only the unreal creatures who professed to be alive in school-books of history. He had learned to know them as men and women because he had stood in the palaces they had been born in and had played in as children. He had seen the dungeons they had been imprisoned in, the thrones they had sat upon, the crowns they had worn, and the jeweled scepters they had held. He had stood before their portraits and had gazed curiously at their "Robes of Investiture," sewn with tens of thousands of seed pearls. To look at a man's face and feel his pictured eyes follow you as you move away from him is to realize that history is not a mere lesson in a schoolbook, but is a relation of the life stories of men and women who saw strange and splendid days and sometimes suffered strange and terrible things.

There were only a few people who were being led about sightseeing. The man in the ancient beefeaters' costume, who was their guide, was good-natured and evidently fond of talking. He was a stout man, with a large face and small, merry eyes. He was rather like pictures of Henry the Eighth, himself. He was especially talkative when he stood by the tablet that marks the spot where stood the block on which Lady Jane Grey had laid her young head. One of the sightseers who knew little of English history had asked some questions about the reasons for her execution.

"If her father-in-law, the Duke of Northumberland, had left that young couple alone—she and her husband, Lord Guildford Dudley—they'd have kept their heads on. He was bound to make her a queen, and Mary Tudor was bound to be queen herself. The duke wasn't clever enough to manage a conspiracy and work up the people. These Samavians we're reading about in the papers would have done it better. And they're half savages."

"They had a big battle outside Melzarr yesterday," said the sightseer standing next to Marco. "Thousands of 'em killed. I saw it in big letters on the boards as I rode on the top of the bus. They're just slaughtering each other, that's what they're doing."

The talkative beefeater heard him. "They can't even bury their dead fast enough," he said. "There'll be some sort of plague breaking out and sweeping into the countries nearest them. It'll end by spreading all over Europe as it did in the Middle Ages. What the civilized countries have got to do is to make them choose a decent king and begin to behave themselves."

I'll tell my father that too, Marco thought. *It shows that everybody is thinking and talking of Samavia, and that even the common people know it must have a real king. This must be the time!*

What he meant was that this must be the time for which the Secret Party had waited and worked so long— the time for the rising.

But his father was out when he went back to
Philibert Place, and Lazarus looked more silent than
ever as he stood behind Marco's chair and waited on
him through his insignificant meal. However plain and
scant the food they had to eat, it was always served with as
much care and ceremony as if it had been a banquet.

"A man can eat dry bread and drink cold water as if
he were a gentleman," his father had said long ago. "It
is easy to form careless habits; yet even if one is hungry
enough to feel ravenous, a man who has been well bred
will not allow himself to look so. A dog may; a man may
not. Just as a dog may howl when he is angry or in pain,
and a man may not."

It was only one of the small parts of the training
which had quietly made the boy, even as a child, self-
controlled and courteous, had taught him ease and
grace of boyish carriage, the habit of holding his body
well and his head erect, and had given him a certain look
of young distinction which, though it assumed nothing,
set him apart from boys of carelessly awkward bearing.

"Is there a newspaper here which tells of the battle,
Lazarus?" he asked after he had left the table.

"Yes, sir," was the answer. "Your father said that you
might read it. It is a black tale," he added, as he handed
him the paper.

It was a black tale. As he read, Marco felt as if he
could scarcely bear it. It was as if Samavia swam in blood,
and as if the other countries must stand aghast before
such furious cruelties.

"Lazarus," he said, springing to his feet at last, his
eyes burning, "something must stop it! There must be

something strong enough. The time has come. The time has come." And he walked up and down the room because he was too excited to stand still.

How Lazarus watched him! What a strong and glowing feeling there was in his own restrained face.

"Yes, sir. Surely the time has come," he answered. But that was all he said, and he turned and went out of the shabby back sitting room at once. It was as if he felt it was wiser to go before he lost power over himself and said more.

Marco made his way to the meeting place of the Squad, to which The Rat had in the past given the name of the Barracks. The Rat was sitting among his followers, and he had been reading the morning paper to them, the one that contained the account of the battle of Melzarr. The Squad had become the Secret Party, and each member of it was thrilled with the spirit of dark plot and adventure. They all whispered when they spoke.

"This is not the Barracks now," The Rat said. "It is a subterranean cavern. Under the floor of it thousands of swords and guns are buried, and it is piled to the roof with them. We crawl in through a hole, and the hole is hidden by bushes."

To the rest of the boys this was only an exciting game, but Marco knew that to The Rat it was more. Though The Rat knew none of the things he knew, he saw that the whole story seemed real to him. The struggles of Samavia, as he had heard and read of them in the newspapers, had taken possession of him. His passion for soldiering and warfare and his curiously mature brain had led him into following every detail he could lay hold of. He had listened to all he had heard with remarkable results. He remembered things older people forgot after they had mentioned them. He forgot nothing. He had drawn on the flagstones a map of Samavia that Marco saw was actually correct, and he had made a rough sketch of Melzarr and the battle that had had such disastrous results.

"The Maranovitch had possession of Melzarr," he explained with feverish eagerness. "And the Iarovitch attacked them from here," pointing with his finger. "That was a mistake. I would have attacked them from a place where they would not have been expecting it. They expected attack on their fortifications, and they were ready to defend them. I believe the enemy could have stolen up in the night and rushed in here," pointing again.

Marco thought he was right. The Rat had argued it all out and had studied Melzarr as he might have studied a puzzle or an arithmetic problem. He was very clever and as sharp as his curious face looked.

"I believe you would make a good general if you were grown up," said Marco. "I'd like to show your maps to my father and ask him if he doesn't think your strategy would have been a good one."

"Does he know much about Samavia?" asked The Rat.

"He has to read the newspapers because he writes things," Marco answered. "And everyone is thinking about the war. No one can help it."

The Rat drew a dingy, folded paper out of his pocket and looked it over with an air of reflection.

"I'll make a clean one," he said. "I'd like a grownup man to look at it and see if it's all right. My father was more than half drunk when I was drawing this, so I couldn't ask him questions. He'll kill himself before long. He had a sort of fit last night."

"Tell us, Rat, wot you an' Marco'll 'ave ter do. Let's 'ear wot you've made up," suggested Cad. He drew closer, and so did the rest of the circle, hugging their knees with their arms.

"This is what we shall have to do," began The Rat in the hollow whisper of the Secret Party. "*The hour has come. To all the Secret Ones in Samavia,* and to the friends of the Secret Party in every country, the sign must be carried. It must be carried by someone who could not be suspected. Who would suspect two boys—and one of them a cripple? The best thing of all for us is that I am a cripple. Who would suspect me? When my father is drunk and beats me, he does it because I won't go out and beg in the streets and bring him the money I get. He says that people will nearly always give money to a cripple. I won't be a beggar for him, but I will be one for Samavia and the Lost Prince. Marco shall pretend to be my brother and take care of me. I say," speaking to Marco with a sudden change of voice, "can you sing anything? It doesn't matter how you do it."

"Yes, I can sing," Marco replied.

"Then Marco will pretend he is singing to make people give him money. I'll get a pair of crutches some-where, and part of the time I will go on crutches and part of the time on my platform. We'll live like beggars and go wherever we want to. I can whiz past a man and give the sign and no one will know. Some times Marco can give it when people are dropping money into his cap. We can pass from one country to another and rouse everybody who is of the Secret Party. We'll work our way into Samavia, and we'll be only two boys—and one a cripple—and nobody will think we could be doing anything. We'll beg in great cities and on the high road."

"Where'll you get the money to travel?" said Cad.

"The Secret Party will give it to us, and we shan't need much. We could beg enough for that matter. We'll sleep under the stars, or under bridges, or archways, or in dark corners of streets. I've done it myself many a time when my father drove me out-of-doors. If it's cold weather, it's bad enough; but if it's fine weather, it's better than sleeping in the kind of place I'm used to. Comrade," he said to Marco, "are you ready?"

He said "comrade" as Loristan did, and somehow Marco did not resent it, because he was ready to labor for Samavia. It was only a game, but it made them comrades. And was it really only a game, after all? His excited voice and his strange, lined face made it singularly unlike one.

"Yes, comrade, I am ready," Marco answered him.

"We shall be in Samavia when the fighting for the Lost Prince begins." The Rat carried on his story with fire. "We may see a battle. We might do something to help. We might carry messages under a rain of bullets . . . **a rain of bullets!**" The thought so elated him that he forgot his whisper and his voice rang out fiercely. "Boys have been in battles before. We might find the Lost King—no, the *Found* King—and ask him to let us be his servants. He could send us where he couldn't send bigger people. I could say to him, 'Your Majesty, I am called The Rat, because I can creep through holes and into corners and dart about. Order me into any danger. and I will obey you. Let me die like a soldier if I can't live like one.' "

Suddenly he threw his ragged coat sleeve up across his eyes. He had wrought himself up tremendously with the picture of the rain of bullets. And he felt as if he saw the king who had at last been found. The next moment he uncovered his face.

"That's what we've got to do," he said. "Just that, if you want to know. And a lot more. There's no end to it."

Marco's thoughts were in a whirl. It ought to be more than a game. He grew quite hot all over. If the Secret Party wanted to send messengers no one would think of suspecting, who could be more harmless look-ing than two vagabond boys wandering about picking up their living as best they could, not seeming to belong to anyone? And one a cripple. It was true, yes, it was true as The Rat said, that his being a cripple made him look safer than anyone else. Marco actually put his forehead in his hands and pressed his temples.

"What's the matter?" exclaimed The Rat. "What are you thinking about?"

"I'm thinking what a general you would make. I'm thinking that it might all be real. Every word of it. It mightn't be a game at all," said Marco.

"No, it mightn't," The Rat answered. "If I knew where the Secret Party was, I'd like to go and tell them about it. What's that?" he said, suddenly turning his head toward the street. "What are they calling out?"

Some newsboy with a particularly shrill voice was shouting out something at the topmost of his lungs.

Tense and excited, no member of the circle stirred or spoke for a few seconds. The Rat listened, Marco listened, and the whole Squad listened, pricking up their ears.

"Startling news from Samavia," the newsboy was shrilling out. "Amazing story! Descendant of the Lost Prince found! Descendant of the Lost Prince found!"

"Any chap got a penny?" snapped The Rat, beginning to move toward the arched passage.

"I have," answered Marco, following him.

"Come on," The Rat yelled. "Let's go and get a paper!" And he whizzed down the passage with his swiftest ratlike dart, while the Squad followed him, shouting and tumbling over each other.

It Is Not a Game

9

Loristan walked slowly up and back down the sitting room and listened to Marco, who sat by the small fire and talked.

"Go on," he said, whenever the boy stopped. "I want to hear it all. He's a strange lad, and it is a splendid game."

Marco was telling him the story of his second and third visits to the enclosure behind the deserted churchyard. He had begun at the beginning, and his father had listened with a deep interest.

"Go on," he said. "He has thought it out well. The lad is a born soldier."

"It is not a game to him," Marco said, "and it is not a game to me. The Squad is only playing, but with him it's quite different. He knows he'll never really get what he wants, but he feels as if this was something near it. He said I might show you the map he made. Father, look at it."

He gave Loristan the clean copy of The Rat's map of Samavia. The city of Melzarr was marked with certain signs. They were to show at what points The Rat—if he had been a Samavian general—would have attacked the capital. As Marco pointed them out, he explained The Rat's reasons for his planning.

Loristan held the paper for some minutes. He fixed his eyes on it curiously, and his black brows drew themselves together.

"This is very wonderful!" he said at last. "He is quite right. They might have got in there, and for the very reasons he hit on. How did he learn all this?"

"He thinks of nothing else now," answered Marco. "He has always thought of wars and made plans for battles. He's not like the rest of the Squad. His father is nearly always drunk, but he is very well educated, and when he is only half drunk, he likes to talk. The Rat asks him questions then, until he finds out a great deal. Then he begs old newspapers, and he hides himself in corners and listens to what people are saying. He says he lies awake at night thinking it out, and he thinks about it all the day. That was why he got up the Squad."

Loristan had continued examining the paper. "Tell him," he said, when he refolded and handed it back, "that I studied his map, and he may be proud of it. You may also tell him," and he smiled quietly as he spoke, "that in my opinion he is right. The Iarovitch would have held Melzarr today if he had led them."

Marco was full of exultation. "I thought you would say he was right. I felt sure you would. That is what makes me want to tell you the rest," he hurried on. "If you think he is right about the rest too—" He stopped awkwardly because of a sudden wild thought that rushed upon him. "I don't know what you will think," he stammered. "Perhaps it will seem to you as if the game—as if that part of it could . . . could only be a game."

He was so fervent in spite of his hesitation that Loristan began to watch him with sympathetic respect, as he always did when the boy was trying to express something he was not sure of. One of the great bonds between them was that Loristan was always interested in Marco's boyish mental processes, in the way in which his thoughts led him to any conclusion.

"Go on," he said again. "I am like The Rat, and I am like you. It has not seemed quite like a game to me so far."

He sat down at the writing table and Marco in his eagerness drew nearer and leaned against it, resting on his arms and lowering his voice. It was always their habit to speak at such a pitch that no one outside the room they were in could distinguish what they said.

"It is The Rat's plan for giving the signal for a rising," he said.

Loristan made a slight movement. "Does he think there will be a rising?" he asked.

"He says that must be what the Secret Party has been preparing for all these years. And it must come soon.

The other nations see that the fighting must be put an end to even if they have to stop it themselves."

"And The Rat has a plan for giving the signal?" Loristan said.

Marco forgot his first feeling of hesitation. He began to see the plan again as he had seen it when The Rat talked. He began to speak as The Rat had spoken, forgetting that it was a game. He made an even clearer picture than The Rat had made of the two vagabond boys—one of them a cripple—making their way from one place to another, quite free to carry messages or warnings where they chose, because they were so insignificant and poor looking that no one could think of them as anything but waifs and strays. He felt as if he wanted to convince his father that the plan was a possible one. He did not quite know why he felt so anxious to win his approval of the scheme—as if it were real—as if it could actually be done. But this feeling was what inspired him to enter into new details and suggest possibilities.

"A boy who was a cripple and one who was only a street singer and a sort of beggar could get almost anywhere," Marco said. "Soldiers would listen to a singer if he sang good songs, and they might not be afraid to talk before him. A strolling singer and a cripple would perhaps hear a great many things it might be useful for the Secret Party to know. They might even hear important things. Don't you think so?"

Before he had gone far with his story, the faraway look had fallen upon Loristan's face. He sat turned a little sidewise from the boy, his elbow resting on the table and his forehead on his hand. He looked down at the worn carpet at his feet, and so he looked as he listened to the end. It was as if some new thought were slowly growing in his mind as Marco went on talking and enlarging on The Rat's plan. He did not even look up or change his position as he answered, "Yes. I think so."

But because of the deep and growing thought in his face, Marco's courage increased. His first fear that this part of the planning might seem so bold and reckless that it would only appear to belong to a boyish game gradually faded away for some strange reason. His father had said that the first part of The Rat's imaginings had not seemed quite like a game to him, and now—even now—he was not listening as if he were listening to the details of mere exaggerated fancies. It was as if the thing he was hearing was not wildly impossible. Marco's knowledge of continental countries and of methods of journeying helped him to enter into much detail and give realism to his plans.

"Sometimes we could pretend we knew nothing but English," he said. "Then, though The Rat could not understand, I could. I would always understand in each country. I know the cities and the places we would want to go to. I know how boys like us live, and so we would not do anything that would make the police angry or make people notice us. If anyone asked questions, I would let them believe that I had met The Rat by chance, and we had made up our minds to travel together because people gave more money to a boy who sang if he was with a cripple. There was a boy who used to play the guitar in the streets of Rome, and he always had a lame girl with him, and everyone knew it was for that reason.

When he played, people looked at the girl and were sorry for her and gave her coins. You remember."

"Yes, I remember. And what you say is true," Loristan answered.

Marco leaned forward across the table so that he came closer to him. The tone in which the words were said made his courage leap like a flame. To be allowed to go on with this boldness was to feel that he was being treated almost as if he was a man. If his father had wished to stop him, he could have done it with one quiet glance, without uttering a word. For some wonderful reason he did not wish him to cease talking. He was willing to hear what he had to say. He was even interested.

You are growing older, he had said the night he had revealed the marvelous secret. *Silence is still the order, but you are man enough to be told more.*

Was he man enough to be thought worthy to help Samavia in any small way—even with boyish fancies which might contain a germ of some thought which older and wiser minds might make useful? Was he being listened to because the plan—made as part of a game—was not an impossible one if two boys who could be trusted could be found? He caught a deep breath as he went on, drawing still nearer and speaking so low that his tone was almost a whisper.

"If the men of the Secret Party have been working and thinking for so many years, they have prepared everything. They know by this time exactly what must be done by the messengers who are to give the signal. They can tell them where to go and how to know the secret friends who must be warned. If the orders could be written and given to . . . to someone who has . . . who has learned to remember things." He had begun to breathe so quickly that he stopped for a moment.

Loristan looked up. He looked directly into Marco's eyes. "Someone who has been *trained* to remember things?" he said.

"Someone who has been trained," Marco went on, catching his breath again, "someone who does not forget—who would never forget. Never! That one, even if he were only twelve—even if he were only ten—could go and do as he was told."

Loristan put his hand on his shoulder. "Son, you are speaking as if you were ready to go yourself."

Marco's eyes looked bravely straight into his, but he said not one word.

"Do you know what it would mean?" his father went on. "You are right. It is not a game. And you are not thinking of it as one. But have you thought how it would be if something betrayed you, and you were set up against a wall to be shot?"

Marco stood up quite straight. He tried to believe he felt the wall against his back.

"If I were shot, I should be shot for Samavia," he said. "And for you, Father."

Even as he was speaking, the front doorbell rang and Lazarus evidently opened it. He spoke to someone, and then they heard his footsteps approaching the back sitting room.

"Open the door," said Loristan, and Marco opened it.

"There is a boy who is a cripple here, sir," the old soldier said. "He asked to see Master Marco."

"If it is The Rat," said Loristan, "bring him in here. I wish to see him."

Marco went down the passage to the front door. The Rat was there, but he was not upon his platform. He was leaning upon an old pair of crutches, and Marco thought he looked wild and strange. He was white, and somehow the lines of his face seemed twisted in a new way. Marco wondered if something had frightened him, or if he felt ill.

"Rat," he began, "my father—"

"I've come to tell you about *my* father," The Rat broke in without waiting to hear the rest, and his voice was as strange as his pale face. "I don't know why I've come, but I . . . I just wanted to. He's dead."

"Your father?" Marco stammered. "He's—"

"He's dead," The Rat answered shakily. "I told you he'd kill himself. He had another fit, and he died in it. I knew he would one of these days. I told him so. He knew he would himself. I stayed with him till he was dead, and then I got a bursting headache, and I felt sick, and I thought about you."

Marco made a jump at him because he saw he was suddenly shaking as if he were going to fall. He was just in time, and Lazarus, who had been looking on from the back of the passage, came forward. Together they held him up.

"I'm not going to faint," he said weakly, "but I felt as if I was. It was a bad fit, and I had to try and hold him.

I was all by myself. The people in the other attic thought he was only drunk, and they wouldn't come in. He's lying on the floor there, dead."

"Come and see my father," Marco said. "He'll tell us what do. Lazarus, help him."

"I can get on by myself," said The Rat. "Do you see my crutches? I did something for a pawnbroker last night, and he gave them to me for pay."

But though he tried to speak carelessly, it was plain that he had been horribly shaken and overwrought. His face was yellowish-white still, and he was trembling a little.

Marco led the way into the back sitting room. In the midst of its shabby gloom and under the dim light, Loristan was standing in one of his still, attentive attitudes. He was waiting for them.

"Father, this is The Rat," the boy began. The Rat stopped short and rested on his crutches, staring at the tall, calm figure with widened eyes.

"Is that your father?" he said to Marco. And then added with a jerky half laugh, "He's not much like mine, is he?"

The Rat
and Samavia

10

What The Rat thought when Loristan began to
speak to him, Marco wondered. Suddenly he stood in
an unknown world, and it was Loristan who made it
so because its poverty and shabbiness had no power to
touch him. He looked at the boy with calm and clear
eyes. He asked him practical questions gently, and it was
plain that he understood many things without asking
questions at all. He seemed to know the awfulness of the
night through which The Rat had passed. He made him
sit down, and he ordered Lazarus to bring him some hot
coffee and simple food.

"Haven't had a bite since yesterday," The Rat said,
still staring at him. "How did you know I hadn't?"

"You have not had time," Loristan answered.

Afterward he made him lie down on the sofa.

"Look at my clothes," said The Rat.

"Lie down and sleep," Loristan replied, putting his hand on his shoulder and gently forcing him toward the sofa. "You will sleep a long time. You must tell me how to find the place where your father died, and I will see that the proper authorities are notified."

"What are you doing it for?" The Rat asked, and then he added, "sir."

"Because I am a man, and you are a boy, and this is a terrible thing," Loristan answered him.

He went away without saying more, and The Rat lay on the sofa staring at the wall and thinking about it until he fell asleep. But before this happened, Marco had quietly left him alone. So, as Loristan had told him he would, he slept deeply and long; in fact, he slept through all the night.

When he awakened, it was morning, and Lazarus was standing by the side of the sofa looking down at him.

"You will want to make yourself clean," he said. "It must be done."

"Clean!" said The Rat, with his squeaky laugh. "I couldn't keep clean when I had a room to live in, and now where am I to wash myself?" He sat up and looked about him. "Give me my crutches. I've got to go. They've let me sleep here all night. They didn't turn me into the street. I don't know why they didn't. Marco's father—he's the right sort. He looks like a swell."

"The master," said Lazarus, with a rigid manner, "the master is a great *gentleman*. He would turn no tired creature into the street. He and his son are poor, but they are of those who give. He desires to see and talk to you again. You are to have bread and coffee with him and the young master. But it is I who tell you that you cannot sit at table with them until you are clean. Come with me," and he handed him his crutches. His manner was authoritative, but it was the manner of a soldier. His somewhat stiff and erect movements were those of a soldier also, and The Rat liked them because they made him feel as if he were in barracks. He did not know what was going to happen, but he got up and followed him on his crutches.

Lazarus took him to a closet under the stairs where a battered tin bath was already full of hot water, which the old soldier himself had brought in pails. There were soap and coarse, clean towels on a wooden chair, and also there was a worn but clean suit of clothes.

"Put these on when you have bathed," Lazarus ordered, pointing to them. "They belong to the young master and will be large for you, but they will be better than your own." And then he went out of the closet and shut the door.

It was a new experience for The Rat. So long as he remembered, he had washed his face and hands—when he had washed them at all—at an iron tap set in the wall of a back street in some slum. His father and himself had long ago sunk into the world where to wash one's self is not a part of everyday life. They had lived amid dirt and foulness, and when his father had been in a sentimental state, he had sometimes cried and talked of the long past days when he had shaved every morning and put on a clean shirt.

To sit even in the most battered of tin baths full of clean hot water and to splash and scrub with a big piece of flannel and plenty of soap was a marvelous thing. The Rat's tired body responded to the novelty with a curious feeling of freshness and comfort.

"I dare say swells do this every day," he muttered. "I'd do it myself if I was a swell. Soldiers have to keep themselves so clean they shine."

After making the most of his soap and water, he came out of the closet under the stairs. He was as fresh as Marco himself; and though his clothes had been built for a more stalwart body, his recognition of their cleanliness filled him with pleasure. He wondered if by any effort he could keep himself clean when he went out into the world again and had to sleep in any hole the police did not order him out of.

He wanted to see Marco again, but he wanted more to see the tall man with the soft dark eyes and that odd look of being a swell in spite of his shabby clothes and the dingy place he lived in. There was something about him which made you keep on looking at him and wanting to know what he was thinking of and why you felt as if you'd take orders from him as if you were a soldier. He looked somehow like a soldier, but as if he were something more—as if people had taken orders from him all his life and always would take orders from him. And yet he had that quiet voice and those fine, easy movements, and he was not a soldier at all, but only a poor man who wrote things for papers that did not pay him well enough to give him and his son a comfortable living.

Through all the time of his seclusion with the battered bath and the soap and water, The Rat thought of
Marco's father, and longed to have another look at him
and hear him speak again. He did not see any reason
why he should have let him sleep on his sofa or why he
should give him a breakfast before he turned him out to
face the world. It was first-rate of him to do it.

The Rat felt that when he was turned out, after he
had had the coffee, he would want to hang about the
neighborhood just on the chance of seeing him pass by
sometimes. He did not know what he was going to do.
The parish officials would by this time have taken his
dead father, and he would not see him again. He did
not want to see him again. He had never seemed like a
father. They had never cared anything for each other.
He had only been a wretched outcast whose best hours
had been when he had drunk too much to be violent and
brutal. Perhaps, The Rat thought, he would be driven to
going about on his platform on the pavements and beg-
ging as his father had tried to force him to do. Could he
sell newspapers? What could a crippled lad do unless he
begged or sold papers?

Lazarus was waiting for him in the passage. The Rat
held back a little.

"Perhaps they'd rather not eat their breakfast with
me," he hesitated. "I'm not—I'm not the kind they are.
I could swallow the coffee out here and carry the bread
away with me. And you could thank him for me. I'd
want him to know I thanked him."

Lazarus also had a steady eye. The Rat realized that
he was looking him over as if he were summing him up.

"You may not be the kind they are, but you may be of a kind the Master sees good in. If he did not see something, he would not ask you to sit at his table. You are to come with me."

The Squad had seen good in The Rat, but no one else had. Policemen had moved him on whenever they set eyes on him; the wretched women of the slums had regarded him as they regarded his father. Loafing or busy men had seen in him a young nuisance to be kicked or pushed out of the way. But the Squad had not called *good* what they saw in him. They would have yelled with laughter if they had heard anyone else call it so. *Goodness* was not considered an attraction in their world.

The Rat grinned a little and wondered what was meant, as he followed Lazarus into the back sitting room.

It was as dingy and gloomy as it had looked the night before, but by the daylight The Rat saw how rigidly neat it was, how well swept and free from any speck of dust, how the poor windows had been cleaned and polished, and how everything was set in order. The coarse linen cloth on the table was fresh and spotless, so was the cheap crockery and the spoons that shone with brightness.

Loristan was standing on the hearth, and Marco was near him. They were waiting for their vagabond guest as if he had been a gentleman.

The Rat hesitated and shuffled at the door for a moment, and then it suddenly occurred to him to stand as straight as he could and salute. When he found himself in the presence of Loristan, he felt as if he ought to do something, but he did not know what.

Loristan's recognition of his gesture and his expression as he moved forward lifted from The Rat's shoulders a load which he himself had not known lay there. Somehow he felt as if something new had happened to him, as if he were not mere vermin after all, as if he need not be on the defensive. The mere straight and far-seeing look of this man's eyes seemed to make a place somewhere for what he looked at. And yet what he said was quite simple.

"This is well," he said. "You have rested. We will have some food, and then we will talk together." He made a slight gesture in the direction of the chair at the right hand of his own place.

The Rat hesitated again. What a man he was! With that wave of the hand he made you feel as if you were a fellow like himself, and he was doing you some honor.

"I'm not—" The Rat broke off and jerked his head toward Marco. "He knows," he ended. "I've never sat at a table like this before."

"There is not much on it." Loristan made the slight gesture toward the right-hand seat again and smiled. "Let us sit down."

The Rat obeyed him, and the meal began. There were only bread and coffee and a little butter before them. But Lazarus presented the cups and plates on a small tray as if it were a golden platter. When he was not serving, he stood upright behind his master's chair, as though he wore a royal uniform of scarlet and gold. To the boy who had gnawed a bone or munched a crust wherever he found them, and with no thought but of the appeasing of his own wolfish hunger, to watch the two with whom he sat eat their simple food was a new thing. He knew nothing of the everyday decencies of civilized people.

The Rat liked to look at them, and he found himself trying to hold his cup as Loristan did, and to sit and move as Marco was sitting and moving, taking his bread or butter, when it was held at his side by Lazarus, as if it were a simple thing to be waited upon. Marco had had things handed to him all his life, and it did not make him feel awkward. The Rat knew that his own father had once lived like this. In a few minutes Loristan began to talk about the copy of the map of Samavia. Then The Rat forgot everything else and was ill at ease no more.

He found himself telling all that he had read or overheard or thought as he lay awake in his garret. He had thought out a great many things in a way not at all like a boy's. His strangely concentrated and overly mature mind had been full of military schemes that Loristan listened to with curiosity and also with amazement. He himself had become extraordinarily clever in one direction because he had fixed all his mental powers on one thing, but it seemed scarcely natural that an untaught vagabond lad should know so much and reason so clearly. There had been no skirmish, no attack, no battle which The Rat had not led and fought in his own imagination, and he had made scores of rough plans of all that had been or should have been done.

Lazarus listened as attentively as his master, and once Marco saw him exchange a startled, rapid glance with Loristan. It was at a moment when The Rat was sketching with his finger on the cloth an attack that ought to have been made but was not. And Marco knew at once that the quickly exchanged look meant *He is right! If it had been done, there would have been victory instead of disaster!*

It was a wonderful meal, though it was only of bread and coffee. The Rat knew he would never be able to forget it.

Afterward Loristan told him of what he had done the night before. He had seen the parish authorities and all had been done that a city government provides in the case of a pauper's death.

His father would be buried in the usual manner. "We will follow him," Loristan said in the end. "You and I and Marco and Lazarus."

The Rat's mouth fell open. "You . . . and Marco . . . and Lazarus!" he exclaimed, staring. "And me! Why should any of us go? I don't want to. He wouldn't have followed me if I'd been the one."

Loristan remained silent for a few moments. "When a life has counted for nothing, the end of it is a lonely thing," he said at last. "If it has forgotten all respect for itself, pity is all that one has left to give." He said the last brief sentence after a pause. "One would like to give *something* to anything so lonely."

"Let us go," Marco said suddenly, and he caught The Rat's hand.

The Rat's own movement was sudden. He slipped from his crutches to a chair and sat and gazed at the worn carpet as if he were not looking at it at all, but at something a long way off. After a while he looked up at Loristan. "Do you know what I thought of all at once?" he said in a shaky voice. "I thought of that Lost Prince.

He only lived once. Perhaps he didn't live a long time. Nobody knows. But it was five hundred years ago. And just because he was the kind he was, everyone that remembers him thinks of something fine. It's odd, but it does you good just to hear his name. And if he has been training kings for Samavia all these centuries, they may have been poor and nobody may have known about them, but they've been *kings*. That's what *he* did . . . just by being alive a few years. When I think of him and then think of . . . my father . . . there's such an awful difference that . . . yes, I'm sorry. For the first time. I'm his son, and I can't care about him, but he's too lonely. I want to go."

So it was that when the forlorn derelict was carried to the graveyard where nameless burdens on the city were given to the earth, a curious funeral procession followed him. There were two tall and soldierly looking men and two boys, one of whom walked on crutches, and behind them were ten other boys who walked two by two.

These ten were a ragged lot; but they had respectfully sober faces, held their heads and their shoulders well, and walked with a remarkably regular marching step. It was the Squad, but they had left their rifles at home.

Come with Me

II

When they came back from the graveyard, The Rat was silent all the way. He was thinking of what had happened and of what lay before him. He was in fact thinking chiefly that nothing lay before him. Nothing. The certainty of that gave his sharp, lined face new lines and sharpness which made it look pinched and hard.

He had nothing before but a corner in a bare garret in which he could find little more than a leaking roof over his head, when he was not turned out into the street. Before when policemen asked him where he lived, he could say he lived in Bone Court with his father. Now he couldn't even say that.

He got along very well on his crutches, but he was rather tired when they reached the turn in the street that led in the direction of his old haunts. But they were haunts he knew, and he belonged to them more than he belonged elsewhere. The Squad stopped at this particular corner because it led to such homes as they possessed. They stopped in a body and looked at The Rat, and The Rat stopped also. He swung himself to Loristan's side, touching his hand to his forehead.

"Thank you, sir," he said. "Line and salute, you chaps!" And the Squad stood in line and raised their hands also. "Thank you, sir. Thank you, Marco. Goodbye."

"Where are you going?" Loristan asked.

"I don't know yet," The Rat answered, biting his lip.

He and Loristan looked at each other a few moments in silence. Both of them were thinking very hard. In The Rat's eyes there was a kind of desperate adoration. He did not know what he should do when this man turned and walked away from him. It would be as if the sun itself had dropped out of the heavens—and The Rat had not thought of what the sun meant before.

But Loristan did not turn and walk away. He looked deep into the lad's eyes as if he were searching to find some certainty. Then he said in a low voice, "You know how poor I am."

"I don't care," said The Rat. "You . . . you're like a king to me. I'd stand up and be shot to bits if you told me to do it."

"I am so poor that I am not sure I can give you enough dry bread to eat—always. Marco and Lazarus and I are often hungry. Sometimes you might have nothing to sleep on but the floor. But I can find a place for you

if I take you with me," said Loristan. "Do you know what
I mean by *a place*?"

"Yes, I do," answered The Rat. "It's what I've never
had before . . . sir."

What he knew was that it meant some bit of space,
out of all of the world, where he would have a sort of
right to stand, however poor and bare it might be.

"I'm not used to beds or to food enough," he said.
But he did not dare to insist too much on that place. It
seemed too great a thing to be true.

Loristan took his arm. "Come with me. We won't
part. I believe you are to be trusted."

The Rat turned quite white in a sort of anguish
of joy. He had never cared for anyone in his life. And
during the last twelve hours he had plunged into a tumultuous ocean of boyish hero-worship. What Loristan
had said and done the day before, in what had been The
Rat's hours of extremity after that appalling night, the
way he had looked into his face and understood it all,
his silent companionship as they followed the pauper
hearse together, these things were enough to make the
lad longingly ready to be any sort of servant or slave to
him if he might see and be spoken to by him even once
or twice a day.

The Squad wore a look of dismay for a moment,
and Loristan saw it. "I am going to take your captain
with me," he said, "but he will come back to barracks. So
will Marco."

"Will yer go on with the game?" asked Cad, as eager
spokesman. "We want to go on being the Secret Party."

"Yes, I'll go on," The Rat answered. "I won't give it up. There's a lot in the papers today."

So they were pacified and went on their way, and Loristan and Lazarus and Marco and The Rat went on theirs also.

Odd thing is, The Rat thought as they walked together, *I'm a bit afraid to speak to him unless he speaks to me first. Never felt that way before with anyone.*

He had jeered at policemen and had impudently chaffed swells, but he felt a sort of secret awe of this man and actually liked the feeling.

It's as if I was a private and he was commander in chief, he thought. *That's it.*

Loristan talked to him as they went. He was simple enough in his statements of the situation. There was an old sofa in Marco's bedroom. It was narrow and hard, as Marco's bed itself was, but The Rat could sleep upon it. They would share what food they had. There were newspapers and magazines to be read. There were papers and pencils to draw new maps and plans of battles. There was even an old map of Samavia of Marco's that the two boys could study together as an aid to their game. The Rat's eyes began to have points of fire in them.

"If I could see the papers every morning, I could fight the battles on paper by night," he said, panting at the incredible vision of splendor. Were all the kingdoms of the earth going to be given to him? Was he going to sleep without a drunken father near him? Was he going to have a chance to wash himself and to sit at a table and hear people say "Thank you" and "I beg pardon" as if they were using the most ordinary of speech? His own father, before he had sunk into the depths, had lived and spoken in this way.

"When I have time, we will see who can draw up the best plans," Loristan said.

"Do you mean that you'll look at mine then? When you have time?" asked The Rat, hesitatingly. "I wasn't expecting that."

"Yes," answered Loristan, "I'll look at them, and we'll talk them over."

As they went on, he told him that he and Marco could do many things together. They could go to museums and galleries, and Marco could show him what he himself was familiar with.

"My father said you wouldn't let him come back to barracks when you found out about it," The Rat said, hesitating again and growing hot because he remembered so many ugly past days. "But I promise I won't do him any harm, sir. I won't."

"When I said I believed you could be trusted, I meant several things," Loristan answered him. "That was one of them. You're a new recruit. You and Marco are both under a commanding officer." He said the words because he knew they would elate him and stir his blood.

ONLY TWO BOYS

12

The words did elate him, and they stirred his blood every time they returned to his mind. He remembered them through the days and nights that followed. He sometimes awakened from his deep sleep on the hard and narrow sofa in Marco's room and found that he was saying them half aloud to himself. The hardness of the sofa did not prevent his resting as he had never rested before in his life. By contrast with the past he had known, this poor existence was comfort that verged on luxury. He got into the battered tin bath every morning, he sat at the clean table, and could look at Loristan and speak to him and hear his voice. He could not bear to lose a look or a movement.

At the end of the second day, he found his way with some trouble to Lazarus's small back room. "Will you let me come in and talk a bit?" he said.

When he went in, he was obliged to sit on the top of Lazarus's wooden box because there was nothing else for him.

"I want to ask you," he plunged into his talk at once, "isn't there anything—anything you'd let me do for him? It wouldn't matter what it was. And he needn't know you are not doing it. I know you wouldn't be willing to give up anything particular. But you wait on him night and day. Couldn't you give up something to me?"

Lazarus pierced him with keen eyes. He did not answer for several seconds. "Now and then," he said gruffly at last, "I'll let you brush his boots. But not every day. Perhaps once a week."

"When will you let me have my first turn?" The Rat asked.

Lazarus reflected. His shaggy eyebrows drew them-selves down over his eyes as if this were a question of state. "Next Saturday," he conceded. "Not before. I'll tell him when you brush them."

"You needn't," said The Rat. "It's not that I want him to know. I want to know myself that I'm doing something for him. I'll find out things that I can do without interfering with you. I'll think them out."

"Anything anyone else did for him would be inter-fering with me," said Lazarus.

It was The Rat's turn to reflect now, and his face twisted itself into new lines and wrinkles. "I'll tell you before I do anything," he said, after he had thought it over. "You served him first."

"I have served him ever since he was born," said Lazarus.

"He's . . . he's yours," said The Rat, still thinking deeply.

"I am his," was Lazarus's stern answer. "I am his . . . and the young master's."

"That's it," The Rat said. Then a squeak of a half laugh broke from him. "I've never been anybody's," he added. His sharp eyes caught a passing look on Lazarus's face. Such a disturbed look. Could he be rather sorry for him? Perhaps the look meant something like that.

"If you stay near him long enough—and it needn't be long—you will be his too. Everybody is."

The Rat sat up as straight as he could. "When it comes to that," he blurted out, "I'm his now, in my way. I was his two minutes after he looked at me with his handsome eyes. They get you, and you want to follow him. I'm going to follow."

That night Lazarus recounted to his master the story of the scene. He simply repeated word for word what had been said, and Loristan listened gravely.

"We have not had time to learn much of him yet," he commented. "But that is a faithful soul, I think."

A few days later Marco missed The Rat soon after their breakfast hour. He had gone out without saying anything to the household. He did not return for several hours, and when he came back he looked tired. In the afternoon he fell asleep on his sofa in Marco's room and slept heavily. No one asked him any questions as he volunteered no explanation. The next day he went out again in the same mysterious manner, and the next and the next. For an entire week he went out and returned with the tired look, but he did not explain until one morning as he lay on his sofa before getting up.

He said to Marco, "I'm practicing walking with my crutches. I don't want to go about like a rat anymore. I mean to be as near like other people as I can. I walk farther every morning. I began with two miles. If I practice every day, my crutches will be like legs."

"Shall I walk with you?" asked Marco.

"Wouldn't you mind walking with a cripple?"

"Don't call yourself that," said Marco. "We can talk together and try to remember everything we see as we go along."

"I want to learn to remember things. I'd like to train myself in that way too," The Rat answered. "I'd give anything to know some of the things your father taught you. I've got a good memory. I remember a lot of things I don't want to remember. Will you go this morning?"

That morning they went, and Loristan was told the reason for their walk. But though he knew one reason, he did not know all about it. When The Rat was allowed his turn at the boot brushing, he told more to Lazarus.

"What I want to do," he said, "is not only walk as fast as other people do, but faster. Acrobats train themselves to do anything. It's training that does it. There might come a time when he might need someone to go on an errand quickly, and I'm going to be ready. I'm going to train myself until he needn't think of me as if I were only a cripple who can't do things and has to be taken care of. I want him to know that I'm really as strong as Marco, and where Marco can go, I can go."

He was what he always said, and Lazarus always understood without explanation.

"*The master* is your name for him," The Rat had explained at the beginning. "And I can't call him just *Mister* Loristan. If he was called General or Colonel, I could stand it, though it wouldn't be quite right. Someday I shall find a name. When I speak to him, I say *sir*."

The walks were taken every day, and each day were longer. Marco found himself silently watching The Rat with amazement at his determination and endurance. He knew that he must not speak of what he could not fail to see as they walked. He must not tell him that he looked tired and pale and sometimes desperately fatigued. He had inherited from his father the tact that sees what people do not wish to be reminded of. He knew that for some reason of his own The Rat had determined to do this thing at any cost to himself. Sometimes his face grew white and worn and he breathed hard, but he never rested more than a few minutes and never turned back or shortened a walk they had planned.

"Tell me something about Samavia, something to remember," he would say, when he looked his worst. "When I try to remember, I forget . . . other things."

So as they went on their way, they talked, and The Rat committed things to memory. He was quick at it and grew quicker every day. They invented a game of

remembering faces they passed. Both would learn them
by heart, and on their return home Marco would draw
them. They went to the museums and galleries and
learned things there, making from memory lists and descriptions which at night they showed to Loristan when
he was not too busy to talk to them.

As the days passed, Marco saw that The Rat was
gaining strength. This exhilarated him greatly. They
often went to Hampstead Heath and walked in the wind
and sun. The Rat would go through curious exercises
that he believed would develop his muscles. He began
to look less tired during and after his journey. There
were even fewer wrinkles on his face, and his sharp eyes
looked less fierce. The talks between the two boys were
long and curious. Marco soon realized that The Rat
wanted to learn—learn—learn.

"Your father can talk to you almost as if you were
twenty years old," he said once. "He knows you can understand what he's saying. If he were to talk to me, he'd
always have to remember that I was only a rat that had
lived in gutters and seen nothing else."

They were talking in their room, as they nearly
always did after they went to bed and the streetlamp
shone in and lighted their bare little room. They often
sat up clasping their knees, Marco on his poor bed, The
Rat on his hard sofa, but neither of them conscious
either of the poorness or hardness, because to each one
the long unknown sense of companionship was such a
satisfying thing. Neither of them had ever talked con-
fidentially to another boy, and now they were together
day and night. They told each other things it had never
before occurred to either to think of telling anyone.

In fact they found out about themselves as they talked. Things they had not quite known before. Marco had gradually discovered that the admiration The Rat had for his father was an impassioned and curious feeling that possessed him entirely. So when he spoke of Loristan's knowing him to be only a rat of the gutter, Marco felt he was fortunate in remembering something he could say.

"My father said yesterday that you had a big brain and a strong will," he answered from his bed. "He said that you had a wonderful memory that only needed exercising. He said it after he looked over the list you made of the things you had seen in the Tower."

The Rat shuffled on his sofa. "He did, did he?"

He rested his chin upon his knees for a few minutes and stared straight before him. Then he turned to the bed.

"Marco," he said, in a rather hoarse voice, "are you jealous?"

"Jealous?" said Marco. "Why?"

"Are you ever jealous of Lazarus because he's always with your father—because he's with him oftener than you are—and knows about his work and can do things for him you can't? I mean, are you jealous of . . . your father?"

Marco lay down flat on his pillow. "No, I'm not. The more people love and serve him, the better. The only thing I care for is him. Lazarus does too. Don't you?"

The Rat was greatly excited internally. He had been thinking of this thing a great deal. The thought had sometimes terrified him. He might as well have it out now if he could. If he could get at the truth, everything would be easier. But would Marco really tell him?

"Don't you mind?" he said, still hoarse and eager, "don't you mind how much I care for him? Could it ever make you feel savage? Could it ever set you thinking I was nothing but what I am? That it was daring of me to push myself in and fasten onto a gentleman who only took me up for charity? Here's the living truth," he ended in an outburst, "if I were you and you were me, I should be so jealous that I should just rage."

He had wrought himself up to such a passion of feeling that he set Marco thinking that what he was hearing meant strange and strong emotions such as he himself had never experienced. The Rat had been thinking over all this in secret for some time, it was evident.

Marco lay still a few minutes and thought it over. "You might, if you hadn't found out that it is such a mistake to think in that way. But, you see, if you were I, you would have lived with my father, and he'd have told you what he knows—what he's been finding out all his life."

"What's he found out?"

"It's like this," said Marco, lying flat and cool on his hard pillow and looking at the reflection of the streetlamp on the ceiling. "He knows the simple laws of nature. You have to be either on one side or the other, like an army. You choose your side. You either build up or tear down. You either keep in the light where you can see, or you stand in the dark and fight everything that comes near you, because you can't see and you think it's an enemy. No, you wouldn't have been jealous if you'd been I and I'd been you."

"And you're not?" The Rat's sharp voice was almost hollow. "You'll promise you're not?"

"I'm not," said Marco.

The Rat's excitement even increased a shade as he poured forth his confession.

"I was afraid," he said. "I've been afraid every day since I came here. I'll tell you straight out. It seemed just natural that you and Lazarus wouldn't stand me, just as I wouldn't have stood you. It seemed just natural that you'd work together to throw me out. I knew how I would have worked myself. Marco—I said I'd tell you straight out—I'm jealous of you. I'm jealous of Lazarus. It makes me wild when I see you both knowing all about him and fit and ready to do anything he wants done. I'm not ready, and I'm not fit."

"You'd do anything he wanted done, whether you were fit and ready or not," said Marco. "He knows that."

"Does he? Do you think he does?" cried The Rat. "I wish he'd try me. I wish he would."

Marco turned over on his bed and rose up on his elbow so that he faced The Rat on his sofa.

"Let us wait," he said in a whisper, "for him to find out that we're fit to be tried. Don't you see what fools we would be if we spent our time in being jealous, either of us? We're only two boys. Suppose he saw we were only two silly fools."

The Rat caught his breath and threw his arms up over his eyes. "Oh, if only I'd lived near him always as you have. If I just had."

"We're both living near him now," said Marco. "And here's something to think of," leaning more forward on his elbow, "the kings who were being made ready for Samavia have waited all these years. We can make ourselves ready and wait so that, if just two boys are wanted to do something—just two boys—we can step out of the ranks when the call comes and say 'Here!' Now let's lie down and think of it until we go to sleep."

LORISTAN MEETS
THE SQUAD

13

The Squad was not forgotten. It found that Loristan himself would have regarded neglect as a breach of military duty.

"You must remember your men," he said, two or three days after The Rat became a member of his household. "You must keep up their drill. Marco tells me it was very smart. Don't let them get slack."

His men! The Rat felt what he could not have put into words.

He knew he had worked, and that the Squad had worked, in their hidden holes and corners. Only hidden holes and corners had been possible for them because they had existed in spite of the protest of their world and the vigilance of its policemen. But somehow this man knew that there had evolved from it something more than mere noisy play, that he, The Rat, had *meant* order and discipline.

His men! It made him feel as if he had the Victoria Cross fastened on his coat. He had brain enough to see many things, and he knew that it was in this way that Loristan was finding him his place. He knew how.

When they went to the Barracks, the Squad greeted them with a tumultuous welcome that expressed a great sense of relief. Privately the members had been filled with fears that they had talked over together in deep gloom. Marco's father, they decided, was too big a swell to let the two come back after he had seen the sort the Squad was made up of. He might be poor just now, swells sometimes lost their money for a bit, but you could see what he was, and fathers like him weren't going to let their sons make friends with "such as us." He'd stop the drill and the Secret Society game. That's what he'd do!

But The Rat came swinging in on his secondhand crutches looking as if he had been made a general, and Marco came with him. The drill the Squad was put through was stricter and finer than any drill they had ever known.

"I wish my father could have seen that," Marco said to The Rat.

The Rat turned red and white and then red again, but he said not a single word. The mere thought was like a flash of fire passing through him. But no fellow could hope for a thing as big as that. The Secret Party in its subterranean cavern, surrounded by its piled arms, sat down to read the morning paper.

The war news was bad to read. The Maranovitch held the day for the moment, and while they suffered and wrought cruelties in the capital city, the Iarovitch suffered and wrought cruelties in the country outside. So fierce and dark was the record that Europe stood aghast.

The Rat folded his paper when he had finished and sat biting his nails. Having done this for a few minutes, he began to speak in his dramatic and hollow Secret Party whisper.

"The hour has come," he said to his followers. "The messengers must go forth. They know nothing of what they go for; they only know that they must obey. If they were caught and tortured, they could betray nothing because they know nothing but that at certain places they must utter a certain word. They carry no papers. All commands they must learn by heart. When the sign is given, the Secret Party will know what to do—where to meet and where to attack."

He drew plans of the battle on the flagstones, and he sketched an imaginary route that the two messengers were to follow. But his knowledge of the map of Europe was not worth much, and he turned to Marco.

"You know more about geography than I do. You know more about everything," he said. "I only know Italy is at the bottom and Russia is at one side and England's at the other. How would the secret messengers go to Samavia? Can you draw the countries they'd have to pass through?"

Because any schoolboy who knew the map could
have done the same thing, Marco drew them. He also
knew the stations the secret two would arrive at and leave
by when they entered a city, the streets they would walk
through and the very uniforms they would see; but of
these things he said nothing. The reality his knowledge
gave to the game was, however, a thrilling thing. He
wished he could have been free to explain to The Rat the
things he knew. Together they could have worked out
so many details of travel and possible adventure that it
would have been almost as if they had set out on their
journey in fact.

As it was, the mere sketching of the route fired The
Rat's imagination. He forged ahead with the story of
adventure and filled it with such mysterious purpose and
design that the Squad at times gasped for breath. In his
glowing version the secret two entered cities by midnight
and sang and begged at palace gates where kings driving
outward paused to listen and were given the Sign.

"Though it would not always be kings," he said.
"Sometimes it would be the poorest people. Sometimes
they might seem to be beggars like ourselves, when they
were only Secret Ones disguised. A great lord might
wear poor clothes and pretend to be a workman, and
we should only know him by the signs we had learned
by heart. When we were sent to Samavia, we should be
obliged to creep in through some back part of the country where no fighting was being done and where no one
would attack. Their generals are not clever enough to
protect the parts that are joined to friendly countries,
and they have not forces enough. Two boys could find a
way in if they thought it out."

He became possessed by the idea of thinking it out on the spot. He drew his rough map of Samavia on the flagstones with his chalk.

"Look here," he said to Marco, who with the elated and thrilled Squad bent over it in a close circle of heads. "Beltrazo is here, and Carnolitz is here. Here is Jiardasia. Beltrazo and Jiardasia are friendly, though they don't take sides. All the fighting is going on in the country about Melzarr. There is no reason why they should prevent single travelers from coming in across the frontiers of friendly neighbors. They're not fighting with the countries outside; they are fighting with themselves." He paused a moment and thought.

"The article in that magazine said something about a huge forest on the eastern frontier. That's here. We could wander into a forest and stay there until we'd planned all we wanted to do. Even the people who had seen us would forget about us. What we have to do is to make people feel as if we were nothing—nothing."

They were in the very midst of it, crowded together, leaning over, stretching necks and breathing quickly with excitement, when Marco lifted his head. Some mysterious impulse made him do it in spite of himself.

"There's my father," he said.

The chalk dropped, everything dropped, even Samavia. The Rat was up and on his crutches as if some magic force had swung him there. How he gave the command, or if he gave it at all, not even he himself knew. But the Squad stood at salute.

Loristan was standing at the opening of the archway as Marco had stood that first day. He raised his right hand in return salute and came forward.

"I was passing the end of the street and remembered the Barracks was here," he explained. "I thought I should like to look at your men, Captain."

He smiled, but it was not a smile that made his words really a joke. He looked down at the chalk map drawn on the flagstones.

"You know that map well," he said. "Even I can see that it is Samavia. What is the Secret Party doing?"

"The messengers are trying to find a way in," answered Marco.

"We can get in there," said The Rat, pointing with a crutch. "There's a forest where we could hide and find out things."

"Reconnoiter," said Loristan, looking down. "Yes. Two stray boys could be very safe in a forest. It's a good game."

That he should be there! That he should have cared enough even to look up the Barracks was what The Rat was thinking. A batch of ragamuffins they were and nothing else, and he standing looking at them with his fine smile. There was something about him that made him seem so splendid. The Rat's heart thumped with startled joy.

"Father," said Marco, "will you watch The Rat drill us? I want you to see how well it is done."

"Captain, will you do me that honor?" Loristan said to The Rat, and to even these words he gave the right tone, neither jesting nor too serious. Because it was so right a tone, The Rat's pulses beat only with exultation. This hero of his had looked at his maps, he had talked of his plans, he had come to see the soldiers who were his work! The Rat began his drill as if he had been reviewing an army.

What Loristan saw was wonderful in its mechanical exactness.

The Squad moved like the perfect parts of a perfect machine. That they could so do it in such space, and that they should have accomplished such precision, was an extraordinary testimonial to the military efficiency and curious qualities of this one hunchbacked, vagabond officer.

"That is magnificent," the spectator said, when it was over. "It could not be better done. Allow me to congratulate you."

He shook The Rat's hand as if it had been a man's, and after he had shaken it, he put his own hand lightly on the boy's shoulder and let it rest there as he talked a few minutes to them all.

He kept his talk within the game, and his clear comprehension of it added a flavor that even the dullest member of the Squad was elated by. Sometimes you couldn't understand swells when they tried being friendly, but you could understand him, and he stirred up your spirits. He didn't make jokes with you either, as if a chap had to be kept grinning. After the few minutes were over, he went away. Then they sat down again in their circle and talked about him, because they could talk and think about nothing else. They stared at Marco furtively, feeling as if he were a creature of another world because he had lived with this man. They stared at The Rat in a new way also. The wonderful-looking hand had rested on his shoulder, and he had been told that what he had done was magnificent.

"When you said you wished your father could have seen the drill," said The Rat, "you took my breath away. I'd never have had the courage to think of it myself. I'd never have dared to let you ask him, even if you wanted to do it. And he came himself! It struck me dumb."

"If he came," said Marco, "it was because he wanted to see it."

When they had finished talking, it was time for Marco and The Rat to go on their way. Loristan had given The Rat an errand. At a certain hour he was to present himself at a certain shop and receive a package.

"Let him do it alone," Loristan said to Marco. "He will be better pleased. His desire is to feel that he is trusted to do things alone."

So they parted at a street corner, Marco to walk back to Number 7 Philibert Place, The Rat to execute his commission. Marco turned into one of the better streets, through which he often passed on his way home. It was not a fashionable quarter, but it contained some respectable houses in whose windows here and there were to be seen neat cards bearing the word "Apartments," which meant that the owner of the house would rent to lodgers his drawing room or sitting room suite.

As Marco walked up the street, he saw someone come out of the door of one of the houses and walk quickly and lightly down the pavement. It was a young woman wearing an elegant dress and a hat that looked as if it had been bought in Paris. She had a slightly foreign air, and it was this which made Marco look at her long enough to see that she was also a graceful and lovely person. He wondered what her nationality was. Even at some distance he could see that she had long dark eyes and a curved mouth which seemed to be smiling to itself. He thought she might be Spanish or Italian.

He was trying to decide which of the two countries she belonged to, as she drew near to him. But quite suddenly the curved mouth ceased smiling as her foot seemed to catch in a break in the pavement, and she so lost her balance that she would have fallen if he had not leaped forward and caught her.

She was light and slender, and he was a strong lad and managed to steady her. An expression of sharp momentary anguish crossed her face.

"I hope you are not hurt," Marco said.

She bit her lip and clutched his shoulder very hard with her slim hand. "I have twisted my ankle," she answered. "I am afraid I have twisted it badly. Thank you for saving me. I should have had a bad fall."

Her long, dark eyes were very sweet and grateful. She tried to smile, but there was such distress under the effort that Marco was afraid she must have hurt herself very much.

"Can you stand on your foot at all?" he asked.

"I can stand a little now," she said, "but I might not be able to stand in a few minutes. I must get back to the house while I can bear to touch the ground with it. I am so sorry. I am afraid I shall have to ask you to go with me. Fortunately it is only a few yards away."

"Yes," Marco answered. "I saw you come out of the house. If you will lean on my shoulder, I can soon help you back. I am glad to do it. Shall we try now?"

She had a gentle and soft manner that would have appealed to any boy. Her voice was musical and her enunciation exquisite.

Whether she was Spanish or Italian, it was easy to imagine her a person who did not always live in London lodgings, even of the better class.

"If you please," she answered him. "It is very kind of you. You are very strong, I see. But I am glad to have only a few steps to go."

She rested on his shoulder as well as on her umbrella, but it was plain that every movement gave her intense pain. She caught her lip with her teeth, and Marco thought she turned white. He could not help liking her. She was so lovely and gracious and brave. He could not bear to see the suffering in her face.

"I am so sorry," he said, as he helped her, and his boy's voice had something of the wonderful sympathetic tone of Loristan's. The beautiful lady herself marked it and thought how unlike it was to the ordinary boy voice.

"I have a key," she said, when they stood on the step.

She found the key in her purse and opened the door. Marco helped her into the entrance hall. She sat down at once in a chair near the hat stand. The place was quite plain and old-fashioned inside.

"Shall I ring the front doorbell to call someone?" Marco inquired.

"I am afraid that the servants are out," she answered. "They had a holiday. Will you kindly close the door? I shall be obliged to ask you to help me into the sitting room at the end of the hall. I shall find all I want there—if you will kindly hand me a few things. Someone may come in presently, perhaps one of the other lodgers, and even if I am alone for an hour or so, it will not really matter."

"Perhaps I can find the landlady," Marco suggested.

The beautiful lady smiled. "She has gone to her sister's wedding. That is why I was going out to spend the day myself. I arranged the plan to accommodate her. I shall be quite comfortable directly, really. I can get to my easy chair in the sitting room now I have rested a little."

Marco helped her to her feet, and her sharp, involuntary exclamation of pain made him wince internally. Perhaps it was a worse sprain than she knew.

The house was of the early Victorian London order: a front lobby with a dining room on the right hand, and a back lobby after the foot of the stairs was passed, out of which opened the basement kitchen staircase, and a sitting room looking out on a gloomy flagged backyard enclosed by high walls. The sitting room was rather gloomy itself, but there were a few luxurious things among the ordinary furnishings. There was an easy chair with a small table near it, and on the table were a silver lamp and some rather elegant trifles. Marco helped his charge to the easy chair and put a cushion from the sofa under her foot. He did it very gently, and as he rose after doing it, he saw that the long, soft dark eyes were looking at him in a curious way.

"I must go away now," he said, "but I do not like to leave you. May I go for a doctor?"

"How dear you are!" she exclaimed. "But I do not want one, thank you. I know exactly what to do for a sprained ankle. And perhaps mine is not really a sprain. I am going to take off my shoe and see."

"May I help you?" Marco asked, and he kneeled down again and carefully unfastened her shoe and withdrew it from her foot. It was a slender and delicate foot in a silk stocking, and she bent and gently touched and rubbed it.

"No," she said, when she raised herself, "I do not think it is a sprain. Now that the shoe is off and the foot rests on the cushion, it is much more comfortable. Thank you, thank you. If you had not been passing, I might have had a dangerous fall."

"I am very glad to have been able to help you," Marco answered, with an air of relief. "Now I must go, if you think you will be all right."

"Don't go yet," she said, holding out her hand. "I should like to know you a little better, if I may. I am so grateful. I should like to talk to you. You have such beautiful manners for a boy," she ended, with a pretty, kind laugh, "and I believe I know where you got them from."

"You are very kind to me," Marco answered, wondering if he did not redden a little. "But I must go because my father will—"

"Your father would let you stay and talk to me," she said, with even a prettier kindliness than before. "It is from him you have inherited your beautiful manner. He was once a friend of mine. I hope he is my friend still, though perhaps he has forgotten me."

All that Marco had ever learned and all that he had ever trained himself to remember quickly rushed back upon him now, because he had a clear and rapidly working brain and had not lived the ordinary boy's life. Here was a beautiful lady of whom he knew nothing at all but that she had twisted her foot in the street and he had helped her back into her house. If silence was still the order, it was not for him to know things or ask questions or answer them. She might be the loveliest lady in the world and his father her dearest friend, and if this were so, he could best serve them both by obeying her commands with all courtesy yet forgetting no instruction his father had given.

"I do not think my father ever forgets anyone," he answered.

"No, I am sure he does not," she said softly. "Has he been to Samavia during the last three years?"

Marco paused a moment. "Perhaps I am not the boy you think I am," he said. "My father has never been to Samavia."

"He has not? But—you are Marco Loristan?"

"Yes. That is my name."

Suddenly she leaned forward and her long lovely eyes filled with fire. "Then you are a Samavian, and you know of the disasters overwhelming us. You know all the

barbarity of what is being done. Your father's son must
know it all!"

"Everyone knows it," said Marco.

"But it is your country—your own! Your blood must
burn in your veins!"

Marco stood quite still and looked at her. His eyes
told whether his blood burned or not, but he did not
speak. His look was answer enough, since he did not
wish to say anything.

"What does your father think? I am a Samavian
myself, and I think night and day. What does he think
of the rumor about the descendant of the Lost Prince?
Does he believe it?"

Marco was thinking very rapidly. Her beautiful face
was glowing with emotion, her beautiful voice trembled.
That she should be a Samavian, and love Samavia, and
pour her feeling forth even to a boy, was deeply moving
to him. But however one was moved, one must remember that silence was still the order. When one was very
young, one must remember orders first of all.

"It might be only a newspaper story," he said. "He
says one cannot trust such things. If you know him, you
know he is very calm."

"Has he taught you to be calm too?" she said patheti-
cally. "You are only a boy. Boys are not calm. Neither
are women when their hearts are wrung. Oh, my
Samavia! Oh, my poor little country. My brave, tortured
country." And with a sudden sob she covered her face
with her hands.

A great lump mounted to Marco's throat. Boys could not cry, but he knew what she meant when he said her heart was wrung.

When she lifted her head, the tears in her eyes made them softer than ever. "If I were a million Samavians instead of one woman, I would know what to do!" she cried. "If your father were a million Samavians, he would know too. He would find Ivor's descendant, if he is on the earth, and he would end all this horror!"

"Who would not end it if they could?" cried Marco, quite fiercely.

"But men like your father, men who are Samavians, must think night and day about it as I do," she impetuously insisted. "You see, I cannot help pouring my thoughts out even to a boy—because he is a Samavian. Only Samavians care. Samavia seems so little and unimportant to other people. They don't even seem to know that the blood she is pouring forth pours from human veins and beating human hearts. Men like your father must think and plan and feel that they must—must find a way. Even a woman feels it. Even a boy must. Stefan Loristan cannot be sitting quietly at home, knowing that Samavian hearts are being shot through and Samavian blood poured forth. He cannot think and say nothing!"

Marco started in spite of himself. He felt as if his father had been struck in the face. How dare she say such words! Big as he was, suddenly he looked bigger, and the beautiful lady saw that he did.

"He is my father," he said slowly.

She was a clever person and saw that she had made a great mistake. "You must forgive me," she exclaimed. "I used the wrong words because I was excited. That is the way with women. You must see that I meant that I knew he was giving his heart and strength, his whole being, to Samavia, even though he must stay in London."

She started and turned her head to listen to the sound of someone using the key and opening the front door. The someone came in with the heavy step of a man.

"It is one of the lodgers," she said. "I think it is the one who lives in the third floor sitting room."

"Then you won't be alone when I go," said Marco. "I am glad someone has come. I will say good morning. May I tell my father your name?"

"Tell me that you are not angry with me for expressing myself so awkwardly," she said.

"You couldn't have meant it. I know that," Marco answered boyishly. "You couldn't."

"No, I couldn't," she repeated, with the same emphasis on the words.

She took a card from a silver case on the table and gave it to him. "Your father will remember my name," she said. "I hope he will let me see him and tell him how you took care of me."

She shook his hand warmly and let him go. But just as he reached the door she spoke again. "Oh, may I ask you to do one thing more before you leave me?" she said suddenly. "I hope you won't mind. Will you run upstairs into the drawing room and bring me the purple book from the small table? I shall not mind being alone if I have something to read."

"A purple book? On a small table?" said Marco.

"Between the two long windows," she said.

Marco ran up lightly.

Marco Does
Not Answer

14

By the time he turned the corner of the stairs, the beautiful lady had risen from her seat in the back room and walked into the dining room at the front. A heavily built, dark-bearded man was standing inside the door as if waiting for her.

"I could do nothing with him," she said at once in her soft voice, speaking quite prettily and gently, as if what she said was the most natural thing in the world. "I managed the little trick of the sprained foot really well and got him into the house. He is an amiable boy with perfect manners, and I thought it might be easy to surprise him into saying more than he knew he was saying. You can generally do that with children and young things. But he either knows nothing or has been trained to hold his tongue. He's not stupid, and he's of a high spirit. I made a pathetic little scene about Samavia, because I saw he could be worked up. It did work him up. I tried him with the Lost Prince rumor; but if there is truth in it, he does not or will not know. I tried to make him lose his temper and betray something in defending his father, whom he thinks a hero, by the way. But I made a mistake. I saw that. It's a pity. Boys can sometimes be made to tell anything." She spoke very quickly under her breath.

The man spoke quickly too. "Where is he?" he asked.

"I sent him up to the drawing room to look for a book. He will look for a few minutes. Listen. He's an innocent boy. He sees me only as a gentle angel. Nothing will shake him so much as to hear me tell him the truth suddenly. It will be such a shock to him that perhaps you can do something with him then. He may lose his hold on himself. He's only a boy."

"You're right," said the bearded man. "And when he finds out he is not free to go, it may alarm him, and we may get something worthwhile."

"If we could find out what is true or what Loristan thinks is true, we would have a clue to work from," she said.

"We have not much time," the man whispered. "We are ordered to Bosnia at once. Before midnight we must be on the way."

"Let us go into the other room. He is coming."

When Marco entered the room, the heavily built man with the pointed dark beard was standing by the easy chair.

"I am sorry I could not find the book," he apologized. "I looked on all the tables."

"I shall be obliged to go and search for it myself," said the lady. She rose from her chair and stood up smiling. And at her first movement Marco saw that she was not disabled in the least.

"Your foot!" he exclaimed. "It's better?"

"It wasn't hurt," she answered in her softly pretty voice and with her softly pretty smile. "I only made you think so."

It was part of her plan to spare him no shock in her sudden transformation. Marco felt his breath leave him for a moment.

"I made you believe I was hurt because I wanted you to come into the house with me," she added. "I wished to find out certain things I am sure you know."

"They were things about Samavia," said the man. "Your father knows them, and you must know something of them at least. It is necessary that we should hear what you can tell us. We shall not allow you to leave the house until you have answered certain questions I shall ask you."

Then Marco began to understand. He had heard his father speak of political spies, men and women who were paid to trace the people that certain governments or political parties desired to have followed and observed. He knew it was their work to search out secrets, to disguise themselves and live among innocent people as if they were merely ordinary neighbors.

They must be spies who were paid to follow his father because he was a Samavian and a patriot. He did not know that they had taken the house two months before and had accomplished several things during their apparently innocent stay in it. They had discovered Loristan and had learned to know his outgoings and incomings, and also the outgoings and incomings of Lazarus, Marco, and The Rat. But they meant, if possible, to learn other things. If the boy could be startled and terrified into unconscious revelations, it might prove well worth their while to have played this bit of melodrama before they locked the front door behind them and hastily crossed the Channel, leaving their landlord to discover for himself that the house had been vacated.

In Marco's mind strange things were happening. They were spies! But that was not all. The lady had been right when she said that he would receive a shock. His strong young chest swelled. In all his life, he had never come face to face with black treachery before. He could not grasp it. This gentle and friendly being with the grateful soft voice and grateful soft eyes had betrayed . . . *betrayed* him! It seemed impossible to believe it, and yet the smile on her curved mouth told him that it was true. When he had sprung to help her, she had been playing a trick! When he had been sorry for her pain and had winced at the sound of her low exclamation, she had been deliberately laying a trap to harm him. For a few seconds he was stunned. Perhaps if he had not been his father's son, he might have been stunned only. But he was more. When the first seconds had passed, there arose slowly within him a sense of something like high, remote disdain. It grew in his deep boy's eyes as he gazed directly into the pupils of the long soft dark ones. His body felt as if it were growing taller.

"You are very clever," he said slowly. Then, after a second's pause, he added, "I was too young to know that there was anyone so . . . clever . . . in the world."

The lady laughed, but she did not laugh easily. She spoke to her companion. "A grand lord," she said. "As one looks at him, one half believes it is true."

The man with the beard was looking very angry. His eyes were savage and his dark skin reddened. Marco thought that he looked at him as if he hated him and was made fierce by the mere sight of him for some mysterious reason.

"Two days before you left Moscow," he said, "three men came to see your father. They looked like peasants. They talked to him for more than an hour. They brought with them a roll of parchment. Is that not true?"

"I know nothing," said Marco.

"Before you went to Moscow, you were in Budapest. You went there from Vienna. You were there for three months, and your father saw many people. Some of them came in the middle of the night."

"I know nothing," said Marco.

"You have spent your life in traveling from one country to another," persisted the man. "You know the European languages as if you were a courier or the porter in a Viennese hotel. Do you not?"

Marco did not answer.

The lady began to speak to the man rapidly in Russian.

"A spy and an adventurer Stefan Loristan has always been and always will be," she said. "We know what he is. The police in every capital in Europe know him as a swindler and a vagabond as well as a spy. And yet with all his cleverness, he does not seem to have money. What did he do with the bribe the Maranovitch gave him for betraying what he knew of the old fortress? The boy doesn't even suspect him. Perhaps it's true that he knows nothing. Or perhaps it is true that he has been so ill treated and flogged from his babyhood that he dare not speak. There is a cowed look in his eyes in spite of his childish swagger. He's been both starved and beaten."

The outburst was well done. She did not look at Marco as she poured forth her words. She spoke with the abruptness and impetuosity of a person whose feelings had got the better of her. If Marco was sensitive about his father, she felt sure that his youth would make his face reveal something if his tongue did not—if he understood Russian, which was one of the things it would be useful to find out, because it was a fact which would verify many other things.

Marco's face disappointed her. No change took place in it, and the blood did not rise to the surface of his skin. He listened with an uninterested air, blank and cold and polite. Let them say what they chose.

The man twisted his pointed beard and shrugged his shoulders. "We have a good little wine cellar downstairs," he said. "You are going down into it, and you will probably stay there for some time if you do not make up your mind to answer my questions. You think that nothing can happen to you in a house in a London street where policemen walk up and down. But you are mistaken. If you yelled now, even if anyone chanced to hear you, they would only think you were a lad getting a thrashing he deserved. You can yell as much as you like in the black little wine cellar, and no one will hear at all. We only took this house for three months, and we shall leave it tonight without mentioning the fact to anyone. If we choose to leave you in the wine cellar, you will wait there until somebody begins to notice that no one goes in and out and chances to mention it to the landlord— which few people would take the trouble to do. Did you come here from Moscow?"

Marco said nothing.

"You might remain in the good little black cellar an unpleasantly long time before you are found," the man went on, quite coolly. "Do you remember the peasants who came to see your father two nights before you left?"

"I know nothing," said Marco.

"By the time it is discovered that the house was empty and people came in to make sure, you might be too weak to call out and attract their attention. Did you go to Budapest from Vienna, and were you there for three months?" asked the inquisitor.

Marco said nothing.

"You are too good for the little black cellar," put in the lady. "I like you. Don't go into it."

"I know nothing," Marco answered, but the eyes that were like Loristan's gave her just such a look as Loristan would have given her, and she felt it. It made her uncomfortable.

"I don't believe you were ever ill treated or beaten," she said. "I tell you, the little black cellar will be a hard thing. Don't go there!"

And this time Marco said nothing, but looked at her still as if he were some great young noble who was very proud.

He knew that every word the bearded man had spoken was true, that to cry out would be of no use. If they went away and left him behind them, there was no knowing how many days would pass before the people of the neighborhood would begin to suspect that the place had been deserted, or how long it would be before it occurred to someone to give warning to the owner. And in the meantime, neither his father nor Lazarus nor The Rat would have the faintest reason for guessing where he was. And he would be sitting alone in the dark in the wine cellar. He did not know in the least what to do about this thing. He only knew that silence was still the order.

"It is a jet black hole," the man said. "You might crack your throat in it, and no one would hear. Did men come to talk with your father in the middle of the night when you were in Vienna?"

"I know nothing," said Marco.

"He won't tell," said the lady. "I am so sorry for this boy."

"He may tell after he has sat in the good little black wine cellar for a few hours," said the man with the pointed beard. "Come with me."

He put his powerful hand on Marco's shoulder and pushed him before him. Marco made no struggle. He remembered what his father had said about the game not being a game. It wasn't a game now, but somehow he had a strong haughty feeling of not being afraid.

He was taken through the hallway toward the rear and down the commonplace flagged steps that led to the basement. Then he was marched through a narrow, ill-lighted, flagged passage to a door in the wall. The door was not locked and stood a trifle ajar. His companion pushed it farther open and showed part of a wine cellar which was so dark that it was only the shelves nearest the door that Marco could faintly see. His captor pushed him in and shut the door. It was as black a hole as he had described. Marco stood still in the midst of darkness like black velvet. His guard turned the key.

"The peasants who came to your father in Moscow spoke Samavian and were big men. Do you remember them?" he asked from outside.

"I know nothing," answered Marco.

"You are a young fool," the voice replied. "And I believe you know even more than we thought. Your father will be greatly troubled when you do not come home. I will come back to see you in a few hours, if it is possible. I will tell you, however, that I have had disturbing news that might make it necessary for us to leave the house in a hurry. I might not have time to come down here again before leaving."

Marco stood with his back against a bit of wall and remained silent.

There was stillness for a few minutes, and then there was to be heard the sound of footsteps marching away.

When the last distant echo died, all was quite silent, and Marco drew a long breath. Unbelievable as it may appear, it was in one sense almost a breath of relief. In the rush of strange feeling which had swept over him when he found himself facing the astounding situation upstairs, it had not been easy to realize what his thoughts really were; there were so many of them and they came so fast. How could he quite believe the evidence of his eyes and ears? A few minutes, only a few minutes, had changed the beautiful lady into a subtle and cunning creature whose love for Samavia had been part of a plot to harm it and to harm his father.

What did she and her companion want to do? What could they do if they knew the things they were trying to force him to tell?

Marco braced his back against the wall stoutly. "What will it be best to think about first?"

This he said because one of the most absorbingly fascinating things he and his father talked about together was the power of the thoughts which human beings allow to pass through their minds—the strange strength of them.

He waited a few minutes for the right thought to come to him.

"I am not afraid," Marco said aloud. "I shall not be afraid. In some way I shall get out."

This was the image he wanted most to keep steadily in his mind—that nothing could make him afraid and that in some way he would get out of the wine cellar.

He thought of this for some minutes and said the words over several times. He felt more like himself when he had done it.

"When my eyes are accustomed to the darkness, I shall see if there is any little glimmer of light anywhere," he said next.

He waited with patience, and it seemed for some time that he saw no glimmer at all. He put out his hands on either side of him and found that on the side of the wall against which he stood, there seemed to be no shelves. Perhaps the cellar had been used for other purposes than the storing of wine, and if that was true, there might be somewhere some opening for ventilation. The air was not bad, but then the door had not been shut tightly when the man opened it.

"I am not afraid," he repeated. "I shall not be afraid. In some way I shall get out."

He would not allow himself to stop and think about his father waiting for his return. He knew that would only rouse his emotions and weaken his courage. He began to feel his way carefully along the wall. It reached farther than he had thought it would.

The cellar was not so very small. He crept around it gradually, and when he had crept around it, he made his way across it, keeping his hands extended before him and setting down each foot cautiously. Then he sat down on the stone floor and thought again that there was a way out of this place for him, and he would somehow find it and before too long be walking in the street again.

It was while he was thinking in this way that he felt a startling thing. It seemed almost as if something touched him. It made him jump, though the touch was so light and soft that it was scarcely a touch at all. In fact he could not be sure that he had not imagined it. He stood up and leaned against the wall again. Perhaps the suddenness of his movement placed him at some angle he had not reached before, or perhaps his eyes had become more completely accustomed to the darkness, for as he turned his head to listen, he made a discovery. Above the door there was a place where the velvet blackness was not so dense. There was something like a slit in the wall, though as it did not open upon daylight but upon the dark passage, it was not light it admitted so much as a lesser shade of darkness. But even that was better than nothing, and Marco drew another long breath.

"That is only the beginning. I shall find a way out," he said. "I *shall*."

He remembered reading a story of a man who, being shut by accident in a safety vault, passed through such terrors before his release that he believed he had spent two days and nights in the place when he had been there only a few hours.

"His thoughts did that. I must remember. I will sit down again and begin thinking of all the pictures in the Art History Museum in Vienna. It will take some time, and then there are the others," he said.

It was a good plan. While he could keep his mind upon the game which had helped him to pass so many dull hours, he could think of nothing else, as it required close attention. Perhaps as the day went on, his captors would begin to feel that it was not safe to run the risk of doing a thing as desperate as this would be. They might think better of it before they left the house at least. In any case, he had learned enough from Loristan to realize that only harm could come from letting one's mind run wild.

"A mind is either an engine with broken and flying gears, or a giant power under control," was what he had said.

Marco had walked in imagination through three of the gallery rooms and was turning mentally into a fourth, when he found himself starting again quite violently. This time it was not at a touch but at a sound. Surely it was a sound. And it was in the cellar with him. But it was the tiniest possible noise, a ghost of a squeak and a suggestion of a movement. It came from the opposite side of the cellar, the side where the shelves were. He looked across in the darkness and saw a light that there could be no mistake about. It *was* a light. Two lights indeed. Two round phosphorescent greenish balls. They were two eyes staring at him. And then he heard another sound. Not a squeak this time, but something so homely and comfortable that he actually burst out laughing. It was a cat purring, a nice warm cat! And she was curled up on one of the lower shelves purring to some newborn kittens.

He knew there were kittens because it was plain now what the tiny squeak had been, and it was made plainer by the fact that he heard another much more distinct one. They had all been asleep when he had come into the cellar. If the mother had been awake, she had probably been very much afraid. Afterward she had perhaps come down from her shelf to investigate and had passed close to him. The feeling of relief that came upon him at this simple discovery was wonderful. It was so natural and comfortable an everyday thing that it seemed to make spies and criminals unreal and only natural things possible. With a mother cat purring away among her kittens, even a dark wine cellar was not so black. He got up and kneeled by the shelf. The greenish eyes did not shine in an unfriendly way. He could feel that the owner of them was a nice big cat, and he counted four round little balls of kittens. It was a curious delight to stroke the soft fur and talk to the mother cat. She answered with purring, as if she liked the sense of friendly human nearness. Marco laughed to himself.

"What a difference it makes," he said. "It is almost like finding a window."

The mere presence of these harmless living things was companionship. He sat down close to the low shelf and listened to the motherly purring, now and then speaking and putting out his hand to touch the warm fur. The phosphorescent light in the green eyes was a comfort in itself.

"We shall get out of this—both of us," he said. "We shall not be here very long, Puss-cat."

He was not troubled by the fear of being really hungry for some time. He was so used to eating scantily from necessity and to passing long hours without food during his journeys that he had proved to himself that fasting is not, after all, such a desperate ordeal as most people imagine. If you begin by expecting to feel famished and by counting the hours between your meals, you will begin to be ravenous. But he knew better.

The time passed slowly. But he had known it would pass slowly, and he had made up his mind not to watch it nor ask himself questions about it. He was not a restless boy, but, like his father, could stand or sit or lie still. Now and then he could hear distant rumblings of carts and vans passing in the street. There was a certain degree of companionship in these also. He kept his place near the cat and his hand where he could occasionally touch her. He could lift his eyes now and then to the place where the dim glimmer of something like light showed itself.

Perhaps the stillness, perhaps the darkness, perhaps the purring of the mother cat, probably all three, caused his thoughts to begin to travel through his mind slowly and more slowly. At last they ceased, and he fell asleep. The mother cat purred for some time, and then fell asleep herself.

A Sound
in a Dream

$$15$$

Marco slept peacefully for several hours. There was nothing to awaken him during that time. But at the end of it, his sleep was penetrated by a definite sound. He had dreamed of hearing a voice at a distance, and as he tried in his dream to hear what it said, a brief metallic ringing sound awakened him outright. It was over by the time he was fully conscious, and at once he realized that the voice of his dream had been a real one and was speaking still. It was the lady's voice, and she was speaking rapidly, as if she were in the greatest haste. She was speaking through the door.

"You will have to search for it," was all he heard. "I have not a moment!"

And as he listened to her hurriedly departing feet, there came to him with their hastening echoes the words, "You are too good for the cellar. I like you!"

He sprang to the door and tried it, but it was still locked. The feet ran up the cellar steps and through the upper hall, and the front door closed with a bang. The two people had gone away, as they had threatened. The voice had been excited as well as hurried. Something had happened to frighten them, and they had left the house in great haste.

Marco turned and stood with his back against the door. The cat had awakened and she was gazing at him with her green eyes. She began to purr encouragingly. He was thinking with all his might and trying to remember.

"What did she come for? She came for something," he said to himself. "What did she say? I only heard part of it, because I was asleep. The voice in the dream was part of it. The part I heard was, *You will have to search for it. I have not a moment.* And as she ran down the passage, she called back, *You are too good for the cellar. I like you.*" He said the words over and over again and tried to recall exactly how they had sounded, and also to recall the voice which had seemed to be part of a dream but had been a real thing.

What did she come for? It was certain that she was in too great a hurry to be able, without a reason, to spare the time to come. What was the reason? She had said she liked him. Then she came because she liked him. If she liked him, she came to do something that was not un-friendly. The only good thing she could do for him was something that would help him to get out of the cellar.

She had said twice that he was too good for the cellar. If he had been awake, he would have heard all she said and have understood what she wanted him to do or meant to do for him. He must not stop even to think of that. The first words he had heard—what had they been? But he thought he was sure that they had been, *You will have to search for it.* Search for it. For what? He thought and thought. What must he search for?

He sat down on the floor of the cellar and held his head in his hands, pressing his eyes so hard that curious lights floated before them.

And in a few minutes, he recalled something that seemed so much a part of his sleep that he had not been sure that he had not dreamed it. The ringing sound! He sprang up on his feet with a little gasping shout. The ringing sound! It had been the ring of metal, striking as it fell. She had thrown something made of metal into the cellar. She had thrown it through the slit in the bricks near the door. She liked him and said he was too good for his prison. She had thrown to him the only thing that could set him free—the *key* to the cellar!

For a few minutes the feelings which surged through him were so full of strong excitement that they set his brain in a whirl. He knew what his father would say. That would not do. If he was to think, he must hold himself still and not let even joy overcome him. The key was in the cellar, and he must find it in the dark. Even the woman who liked him enough to give him a chance of freedom knew that she must not open the door and let him out. There must be a delay. He would have to find the key himself, and it would be sure to take time.

The chances were that they would be at a safe enough
distance before he could get out.

"I will kneel down and crawl on my hands and
knees," he said.

"I will crawl back and forth and go over every inch
of the floor with my hands until I find it. If I go over
every inch, I shall find it."

So he kneeled down and began to crawl, and the cat
watched him and purred.

"We shall get out, Puss-cat," he said to her. "I told
you we should."

He crawled from the door to the wall at the side
of the shelves, and then he crawled back again. The key
might be quite a small one, and it was necessary that
he should pass his hands over every inch, as he had
said. The difficulty was to be sure, in the darkness, that
he did not miss an inch. Sometimes he was not sure
enough, and then he went over the ground again. He
crawled backward and forward, and he crawled forward
and backward. He crawled crosswise and lengthwise. He
crawled diagonally, and he crawled round and round.
But he did not find the key. If he had had only a little
light, but he had none. He was so absorbed in his search
that he did not know he had been engaged in it for several hours, and that it was the middle of the night. But
at last he realized that he must stop for a rest, because
his knees were beginning to feel bruised, and the skin of
his hands was sore as a result of the rubbing on the flags.
The cat and her kittens had gone to sleep and awakened
again two or three times.

"But it is somewhere!" he said obstinately. "It is inside the cellar. I heard something fall which was made of metal. That was the ringing sound that awakened me."

When he stood up, he found his body ached, and he was very tired. He stretched himself and exercised his arms and legs.

"I wonder how long I have been crawling about," he thought. "But the key is in the cellar. It is in the cellar."

He sat down near the cat and her family, and laying his arm on the shelf above her, rested his head on it. And he fell asleep, sound and fast.

He did not know that he slept all the rest of the night, but he did. When he awakened, it was daylight in the streets, and the milk carts were beginning to jingle about, and the early postmen were knocking big double knocks at front doors. The cat may have heard the milk carts, but the actual fact was that she herself was hungry and wanted to go in search of food. Just as Marco lifted his head from his arm and sat up, she jumped down from her shelf and went to the door. She had expected to find it ajar as it had been before. When she found it shut, she scratched at it and was disturbed to find this of no use. Because she knew Marco was in the cellar, she felt she had a friend who would assist her, and she meowed appealingly.

This reminded Marco of the key.

"I will when I have found it," he said. "It is inside the cellar."

The cat meowed again, this time very anxiously indeed. The kittens heard her and began to squirm and squeak piteously.

He put his hand out toward the kittens, and it touched something lying not far from them. It must have been lying near his elbow all night while he slept.

It was the key! It had fallen upon the shelf and not on the floor at all.

He found his way to the door and fumbled until he found the keyhole and got the key into it. Then he turned it and pushed the door open, and the cat ran out into the passage before him.

The Rat
to the Rescue

16

Marco walked through the passage and into the kitchen part of the basement. The doors were all locked, and they were solid doors. He ran up the flagged steps and found the door at the top shut and bolted also, and that too was a solid door. His jailers had plainly made sure that it would take time enough for him to make his way into the world, even after he got out of the wine cellar.

The cat had run away to some part of the place where mice were plentiful. Marco was by this time rather gnawingly hungry himself. If he could get into the kitchen, he might find some fragments of food left in a cupboard; but there was no moving the locked door. Then he saw near it a smaller door. It was evidently the entrance to the coal cellar under the pavement. This was proved by the fact that trodden coal dust marked the flagstones, and near it stood a scuttle with coal in it.

This coal scuttle was the thing that might help him! Above the area door was a small window that was supposed to light the entry. He could not reach it, and if he reached it, he could not open it. He could throw pieces of coal at the glass and break it, and then he could shout for help when people passed by. They might not notice or understand where the shouts came from at first, but, if he kept them up, someone's attention would be attracted in the end.

He picked a large solid piece of coal out of the heap in the scuttle and threw it with all his force against the grimy glass. It smashed through and left a big hole. He threw another, and the entire pane was splintered and fell outside into the area. Then he saw it was broad daylight and guessed that he had been shut up a good many hours. There was plenty of coal in the scuttle, and he had a strong arm and a good aim. He smashed pane after pane, until only the framework remained. When he shouted, there would be nothing between his voice and the street. No one could see him, but if he could do something that would make people slacken their pace to listen, then he could call out that he was in the basement of the house with the broken window.

"Hallo!" he shouted. "Hallo! Hallo! Hallo! Hallo!"

But vehicles were passing in the street, and the passersby were absorbed in their own business. If they heard a sound, they did not stop to inquire into it.

"Hallo! Hallo! I am locked in!" yelled Marco, at the topmost power of his lungs. "Hallo! Hallo!"

After half an hour's shouting, he began to think that he was wasting his strength.

"They think it is only a boy shouting," he said. "Someone will notice in time. At night, when the streets are quiet, I might make a policeman hear. But my father does not know where I am. He will be trying to find me—so will Lazarus—so will The Rat. One of them might pass through this very street, as I did. What can I do?"

A new idea flashed light upon him.

"I will begin to sing a Samavian song, and I will sing it very loud. People nearly always stop a moment to listen to music and find out where it comes from. And if any of my own people came near, they would stop at once. Now and then I will shout for help."

Once when they had stopped to rest on Hampstead Heath, he had sung a valiant Samavian song for The Rat. The Rat had wanted to hear how he would sing when they went on their secret journey. He wanted him to sing for the Squad some day, to make the thing seem real. The Rat had been greatly excited and had begged for the song often. It was a stirring martial thing with a sort of trumpet call of a chorus. Thousands of Samavians had sung it together on their way to the battlefield, hundreds of years ago.

He drew back a step or so, and putting his hands on his hips, began to sing, throwing his voice upward that it might pass through the broken window. He had a splendid and vibrant young voice, though he knew nothing of its fine quality. Just now he wanted only to make it loud.

In the street outside very few people were passing. An irritable old gentleman who was taking an invalid walk quite jumped with annoyance when the song suddenly trumpeted forth. Boys had no right to yell in that manner. He hurried his step to get away from the sound. Two or three other people glanced over their shoulders, but had not time to loiter. A few others listened with pleasure as they drew near and passed on.

"There's a boy with a fine voice," said one.

"What's he singing?" said his companion. "It sounds foreign."

"Don't know," was the reply as they went by. But at last a young man who was a music teacher going to give a lesson, hesitated and looked about him. The song was very loud and spirited just at this moment. The music teacher could not understand where it came from and paused to find out. The fact that he stopped attracted the attention of the next comer, who also paused.

"Who's singing?" he asked. "Where is he singing?"

"I can't make that out," the music teacher laughed. "Sounds as if it came out of the ground."

And because it was odd that a song should seem to be coming out of the ground, a peddler stopped, and then a little boy, and then a lady.

There was quite a little group when another person turned the corner of the street. He was a shabby boy on crutches, and he had a frantic look on his face.

And Marco actually heard, as he drew near to the group, the *tap-tap-tap* of crutches.

It might be, he thought. *It might be!*

And he sang the trumpet call of the chorus as if it were meant to reach the skies, and he sang it again and again. And at the end of it shouted, "Hallo! Hallo! Hallo! Hallo! Hallo!"

The Rat swung himself into the group and looked as if he had gone crazy. He hurled himself against the people.

"Where is he? Where is he?" he cried, and he poured out some breathless words. It was almost as if he sobbed them out.

"We've been looking for him all night!" he shouted. "Where is he? Marco! Marco! No one else sings it but him. Marco! Marco!" And out of the area, as it seemed, came a shout of answer.

"Rat! Rat! I'm here in the cellar—locked in. I'm here!" and a big piece of coal came hurtling through the broken window and fell crashing on the area flags.

The Rat got down the steps into the area as if he had not been on crutches but on legs, and banged on the door, shouting back, "Marco! Marco! Here I am! Who locked you in? How can I get the door open?"

Marco was close against the door inside. It was The Rat! It was The Rat! And he would be in the street again in a few minutes. "Call a policeman!" he shouted through the keyhole. "The people locked me in on purpose and took away the keys."

Then the group of lookers on began to get excited and press against the area railings and ask questions. They could not understand what had happened to cause the boy with the crutches to look as if he were crazy with terror and relief at the same time.

Yet the boy ran delightedly to fetch a policeman and found one in the next street, and with some difficulty, persuaded him that it was his business to come and get a door open in an empty house where a boy who was a street singer had got locked up in a cellar.

It Is a
Very Bad Sign

17

The policeman was not so much excited as out of temper. He did not know what Marco knew or what The Rat knew. Some common lad had got himself locked up in a house, and someone would have to go to the landlord and get a key from him. He had no intention of laying himself open to the law by breaking into a private house with his club as The Rat expected him to do.

"He got himself in through some of his larks, and he'll have to wait till he's got out without smashing locks," he growled, shaking the area door. "How did you get in there?" he shouted.

It was not easy for Marco to explain through a keyhole that he had come in to help a lady who had met with an accident. The policeman thought this mere

boy's talk. As to the rest of the story, Marco knew that
it could not be related at all without saying things that
could not be explained to anyone but his father. He
quickly made up his mind that he must let it be believed
that he had been locked in by some accident. It must be
supposed that the people had not remembered in their
haste that he had not yet left the house.

When the young clerk from the house agency came
with the keys, he was much disturbed and bewildered
after he got inside.

"They've made a bolt of it," he said. "That happens
now and then, but there's something strange about this.
Why did they lock these doors in the basement and the
one on the stairs? What did they say to you?" he asked
Marco, staring at him suspiciously.

"They said they were obliged to go suddenly,"
Marco answered.

"What were you doing in the basement?"

"The man took me down."

"And left you there and bolted? He must have been
in a hurry."

"The lady said they had not a moment's time."

"Her ankle must have got well in short order," said
the young man.

"I knew nothing about them," answered Marco. "I
had never seen them before."

"The police were after them," the young man said.
"That's what I should say. They paid three months' rent
in advance, and they have only been here two. Some of

these foreign spies lurking about London—that's what they were."

The Rat had not waited until the keys arrived. He had swung himself at his swiftest pace back through the streets to Number 7 Philibert Place. People turned and stared at his wild pale face as he almost shot past them.

He had left himself barely breath enough to speak with when he reached the house and banged on the door with his crutch to save time.

Both Loristan and Lazarus came to answer.

The Rat leaned against the door gasping. "He's found!" he panted. "He's all right! Someone had locked him in a house and left him. They've sent for the keys. I'm going back. Brandon Terrace, Number 10."

Loristan and Lazarus exchanged glances. Both of them were at the moment as pale as The Rat.

"Help him into the house," said Loristan to Lazarus. "He must stay here and rest. We will go." The Rat knew it was an order.

He did not like it, but he obeyed.

"This is a bad sign, Master," said Lazarus, as they went out together.

"It is a very bad one," answered Loristan.

"God of the right, defend us!" Lazarus prayed.

"Amen," said Loristan. "Amen!"

The group had become a small crowd by the time they reached Brandon Terrace. Marco had not found it easy to leave the place because he was being questioned. Neither the policeman nor the agent's clerk seemed willing to relinquish the idea that he could give them some information about the absconding pair.

The entrance of Loristan produced its usual effect. The agent's clerk lifted his hat, and the policeman stood straight and made salute. Neither of them realized that the tall man's clothes were worn and threadbare. They felt only that a personage was before them and that it was not possible to question his air of absolute and serene authority. He laid his hand on Marco's shoulder and held it there as he spoke. When Marco looked up at him and felt the closeness of his touch, it seemed as if it were an embrace, as if he had caught him to his breast.

"My boy knew nothing of these people," he said. "That I can guarantee. He had seen neither of them before. His entering the house was the result of no boyish trick. He has been shut up in this place for nearly twenty-four hours and without food. I must take him home. This is my address." He handed the young man a card.

Then they went home together, and all the way to Philibert Place Loristan's firm hand held closely to his boy's shoulder as if he could not endure to let him go. But on the way they said very little.

"Father," Marco said, rather hoarsely, when they first got away from the house in the terrace, "I can't talk well in the street. For one thing, I am so glad to be with you again. It seemed as if . . . it might turn out badly."

"Beloved one," Loristan said the words in their own Samavian, "until you are fed and at rest, you shall not talk at all."

Afterward, when he was himself again and was allowed to tell his strange story, Marco found that both his father and Lazarus had at once had suspicions when he had not returned. They knew no ordinary event could have kept him. They were sure that he must have been detained against his will, and they were also sure that, if he had been so detained, it could only have been for reasons they could guess at.

"This was the card that she gave me," Marco said, and he handed it to Loristan. "She said you would remember the name." Loristan looked at the lettering with an ironic half smile.

"I never heard it before," he replied. "She would not send me a name I knew. Probably I have never seen either of them. But I know the work they do. They are spies of the Maranovitch and suspect that I know something of the Lost Prince. They believed they could terrify you into saying things that would be a clue. Men and women of their class will use desperate means to gain their end."

"Might they have left me as they threatened?" Marco asked him.

"They would scarcely have dared, I think. Too great a hue and cry would have been raised by the discovery of such a crime. Too many detectives would have been set at work to track them."

But the look in his father's eyes as he spoke and the pressure of the hand he stretched out to touch him made Marco's heart thrill. He had won a new love and trust from his father. When they sat together and talked that night, they were closer to each other's souls than they had ever been before.

They sat in the firelight, Marco upon the worn hearth rug, and they talked about Samavia—about the war and its heart-rending struggles, and about how they might end.

"Do you think that some time we might be exiles no longer?" the boy said wistfully. "Do you think we might go there together and see it, you and I, Father?"

There was a silence for a while. Loristan looked into the sinking bed of red coal. "For years. For years I have made for my soul that image."

Cities and Faces

18

The hours of Marco's unexplained absence had been terrible to Loristan and to Lazarus. They had reason for fears that it was not possible for them to express. As the night drew on, the fears took stronger form. They forgot the existence of The Rat, who sat biting his nails in the bedroom, afraid to go out lest he might lose the chance of being given some errand to do but also afraid to show himself lest he should seem in the way.

"I'll stay upstairs," he had said to Lazarus. "If you just whistle, I'll come."

The anguish he passed through as the day went by and Lazarus went out and came in and he himself received no orders, could not have been expressed in any ordinary words. He writhed in his chair, he bit his nails to the quick, he wrought himself into a frenzy of misery by recalling one by one all the crimes his knowledge of London police courts supplied him with. He was doing nothing, yet he dare not leave his post. It was his post after all, though they had not given it to him. He must do something.

In the middle of the night Loristan opened the door of the back sitting room, because he knew he must at least go upstairs and throw himself upon his bed even if he could not sleep.

He started back as the door opened. The Rat was sitting huddled on the floor near it with his back against the wall. He had a piece of paper in his hand, and his twisted face was a weird thing to see.

"Why are you here?" Loristan asked.

"I've been here three hours, sir. I knew you'd have to come out sometime, and I thought you'd let me speak to you. Will you? *Will you?*"

"Come into the room," said Loristan. "I will listen to anything you want to say. What have you been drawing on that paper?"

The Rat got up in the wonderful way he had taught himself. The paper was covered with lines that showed it to be another of his plans. "Please look at it," he begged. "I daren't go out lest you might want to send me somewhere. I daren't sit doing nothing. I began remembering and thinking things out. I put down all the streets and squares he might have walked through on his way home. I've not missed one. If you'll let me start out and walk through every one of them and talk to the policemen on

the beat and look at the houses and think out things and
work at them. I'll not miss an inch. I'll not miss a brick
or a flagstone. I'll . . ." His voice had a hard sound but it
shook, and he himself shook.

Loristan touched his arm gently. "You are a good
comrade. It is well for us that you are here. You have
thought of a good thing."

"May I go now?" said The Rat.

"This moment, if you are ready," was the answer.
The Rat swung himself to the door.

Loristan said to him a thing that was like the sudden
lighting of a great light in the very center of his being.
"You are one of us. Now that I know you are doing this,
I may even sleep." And it was because he was following
this plan that The Rat had turned into Brandon Terrace
and heard the Samavian song ringing out from the
locked basement of Number 10.

"Yes, he is one of us," Loristan said when he told
this part of the story to Marco as they sat by the fire. "I
had not been sure before. I wanted to be very sure. Last
night I saw into the depths of him and *knew*. He may be
trusted."

From that day The Rat held a new place. Lazarus
himself, strangely enough, did not resent his holding
it. The boy was allowed to be near Loristan as he had
never dared to hope to be near. It was not merely that
he was allowed to serve him in many ways, but he was
taken into the intimacy that had before enclosed only
the three. Loristan talked to him as he talked to Marco,
drawing him within the circle that held so much that
was comprehended without speech. The Rat knew that

he was being trained and observed, and he realized it with exaltation. His hero had said that he was "one of them," and he was watching and putting him to tests so that he might find out how much he was one of them. And he was doing it for some grave reason of his own. This thought possessed The Rat's whole mind. Perhaps he was wondering if he should find out that he was to be trusted, as a rock is to be trusted. That he should even think that perhaps he might find that he was like a rock was inspiration enough.

"Sir," he said one night when they were alone together because The Rat had been copying a road map. His voice was very low, "Do you think that sometime you could trust me as you trust Marco? Could it ever be like that—ever?"

"The time has come," and Loristan's voice was almost as low as his own, though strong and deep feeling underlay its quiet. "The time has come when I can trust you with Marco—to be his companion—to care for him, to stand by his side at any moment. And Marco is . . . Marco is my son." That was enough to uplift The Rat to the skies. But there was more to follow.

"It may not be long before it may be his part to do work in which he will need a comrade—a comrade who can be trusted as a rock can be trusted."

He had said the very words The Rat's own mind had given to him.

"A Rock. A Rock!" the boy broke out. "Let me show you, sir. Send me with him for a servant. The crutches are nothing. You've seen that they're as good as legs, haven't you? I've trained myself."

"I know. I know, dear lad." He gave him a gracious smile that seemed as if it held a sort of fine secret. "You shall go as his aide-de-camp. It shall be part of the game."

Loristan had always encouraged the game, and during the last weeks had even found time to help them in their planning for the mysterious journey of the Secret Two. He had been so interested that once or twice he had called on Lazarus as an old soldier and Samavian to give his opinions of certain routes and of the customs and habits of people in towns and villages by the way. Through talk and stories The Rat began to know the country almost as Marco knew it. That was part of the game too, because it was always "the game" that they called it.

Another part was The Rat's training of his memory and bringing home his proof of improvement at night when he returned from his walk and could describe, or recite, or roughly sketch all he had seen in his passage from one place to another. Marco's part was to recall and sketch faces. Loristan one night gave him a number of photographs of people to commit to memory. Under each face was written the name of a place.

"Learn these faces," he said, "until you would know each one of them at once wherever you met it. Fix them upon your mind, so that it will be impossible for you to forget them. You must be able to sketch any one of them and recall the city or town or neighborhood connected with it."

Even this was still called "the game," but Marco began to know in his heart that it was so much more,

that his hand sometimes trembled with excitement as
he made his sketches over and over again. To make
each one many times was the best way to etch it in his
memory. The Rat knew too, though he had no reason
for knowing, but mere instinct. He used to lie awake in
the night and think it over and remember what Loristan
had said of the time coming when Marco might need
a comrade in his work. What was his work to be? It was
to be something like the game. And they were being
prepared for it. And though Marco often lay awake on
his bed when The Rat lay awake on his sofa, neither boy
spoke to the other of the thing his mind dwelt on.

Marco worked as he had never worked before. The
game was very exciting when he could prove his prowess.
The four gathered together at night in the back sitting
room. Lazarus was obliged to be with them because a
second judge was needed. Loristan would mention the
name of a place, perhaps a street in Paris or a hotel in
Vienna, and Marco would at once make a rapid sketch
of the face under whose photograph the name of the
locality had been written. It was not long before he
could begin his sketch without more than a moment's
hesitation. And yet even when this had become the case,
they still played the game night after night. There was
a great hotel near the Place de la Concorde in Paris of
which Marco felt he should never hear the name during
all his life without there starting up before his mental
vision a tall woman with fierce black eyes and a delicate
high-bridged nose across which the strong eyebrows
almost met. In Vienna there was a palace that would
always bring back at once a pale cold-faced man with a
heavy blonde lock which fell over his forehead. A certain

street in Munich meant a stout genial old aristocrat with a sly smile; a village in Bavaria, a peasant with a vacant and simple countenance. A curled and smoothed man who looked like a hairdresser brought up a place in an Austrian mountain town. He knew them all as he knew his own face and Number 7 Philibert Place.

But still, night after night the game was played.

Then came a night when out of a deep sleep he was awakened by Lazarus touching him. He had so long been secretly ready to answer any call that he sat up straight in bed at the first touch.

"Dress quickly and come downstairs," Lazarus said. "The prince is here and wishes to speak with you."

Marco made no answer but got out of bed and began to slip on his clothes.

Lazarus touched The Rat.

The Rat was as ready as Marco and sat upright as he had done.

"Come down with the young master," he commanded. "It is necessary that you should be seen and spoken to." And having given the order, he went away.

No one heard the shoeless feet of the two boys as they stole down the stairs.

An elderly man in ordinary clothes, but with an unmistakable face, was sitting quietly talking to Loristan, who with a gesture called both forward.

"The prince has been much interested in what I have told him of your game," he said in his lowest voice. "He wishes to see you make your sketches, Marco."

Marco looked very straight into the prince's eyes that were fixed intently on him as he made his bow. "His Highness does me honor," he said, as his father might have said it. He went to the table at once and took from a drawer his pencils and pieces of cardboard.

"I should know he was your son and a Samavian," the prince remarked. Then his keen and deep-set eyes turned themselves on the boy with the crutches.

"This," said Loristan, "is the one who calls himself The Rat. He is one of us."

The Rat saluted. "Please tell him, sir," he whispered, "that the crutches don't matter."

"He has trained himself to an extraordinary activity," Loristan said. "He can do anything."

The keen eyes were still taking The Rat in. "They are an advantage," said the prince at last.

Lazarus had nailed together a light, rough easel that Marco used in making his sketches when the game was played. Lazarus was standing in state at the door, and he came forward, brought the easel from its corner, and arranged the necessary drawing materials upon it.

Marco stood near it and waited the pleasure of his father and his visitor. They were speaking together in low tones, and he waited several minutes. What The Rat noticed was what he had noticed before, that the big boy could stand still in perfect ease and silence. It was not necessary for him to say things or to ask questions, to look at people as if he felt restless if they did not speak to or notice him. He did not seem to require notice, and The Rat felt vaguely that, young as he was, this very freedom from any anxiety to be looked at or addressed made him somehow look like a great gentleman.

Loristan and the prince advanced to where he stood.

"L'Hotel de Marigny," Loristan said.

Marco began to sketch rapidly. He began the portrait of the handsome woman with the delicate high-bridged nose and the black brows that almost met. As he did it, the prince drew nearer and watched the work over his shoulder. It did not take very long and when it was finished, the inspector turned, and after giving Loristan a long and strange look, nodded twice.

"It is a remarkable thing," he said. "In that rough sketch she is not to be mistaken."

Loristan bent his head.

Then he mentioned the name of another street in another place, and Marco sketched again. This time it was the peasant with the simple face. The prince bowed again. Then Loristan gave another name, and after that another and another; and Marco did his work until it was at an end, and Lazarus stood near with a handful of sketches that he had silently taken charge of as each was laid aside.

"You would know these faces wherever you saw them?" said the prince. "If you passed one in Bond Street or in the Marylebone Road, you would recognize it at once?"

"As I know yours, sir," Marco answered.

Then followed a number of questions. Loristan asked them as he had often asked them before. They were questions as to the height and build of the originals of the pictures, of the color of their hair and eyes, and the order of their complexions. Marco answered them all. He knew all but the names of these people, and it was plainly not necessary that he should know them, as his father had never uttered them.

After this questioning was at an end, the prince pointed to The Rat who had leaned on his crutches against the wall, his eyes fiercely eager like a ferret's.

"And he?" the prince said. "What can he do?"

"Let me try," said The Rat. "Marco knows."

Marco looked at his father. "May I help him to show you?" he asked.

"Yes," Loristan answered, and then, as he turned to the prince, he said in his low voice, "He is one of us."

Then Marco began a new form of the game. He held up one of the pictured faces before The Rat, and The Rat named at once the city and place connected with it. He detailed the color of eyes and hair, the height, the build, all the personal details as Marco himself had detailed them. To these he added descriptions of the cities and points concerning the police system, the palaces, the people. His face twisted itself, his eyes burned, his voice shook, but he was amazing in his readiness of reply and his exactness of memory.

"I can't draw," he said at the end. "But I can remember. I didn't want anyone to be bothered with thinking I was trying to learn it, so only Marco knew."

This he said to Loristan with appeal in his voice.

"It was he who invented the game," said Loristan. "I showed you his strange maps and plans."

"It is a good game," the prince answered in the manner of a man extraordinarily interested and impressed. "They know it well. They can be trusted."

"No such thing has ever been done before," Loristan said. "It is as new as it is daring and simple."

"Therein lies its safety," the prince answered.

"Perhaps only boyhood," said Loristan, "could have dared to imagine it. The prince thanks you." After a few more words spoken aside to his visitor he said, "We both thank you. You may go back to your beds."

And the boys went.

THAT IS ONE

19

A week had not passed before Marco brought to The Rat in their bedroom an envelope containing a number of slips of paper on each of which was written something.

"This is another part of the game," he said gravely. "Let us sit down together by the table and study it."

They sat down and examined what was written on the slips. At the head of each was the name of one of the places with which Marco had connected a face he had sketched. Below were clear and concise directions as to how it was to be reached and the words to be said when each individual was encountered.

"This person is to be found at his stall in the market" was written of the vacant-faced peasant. "You will first attract his attention by asking the price of something. When he is looking at you, touch your left thumb lightly with the forefinger of your right hand. Then utter in a low distinct tone the words, *the Lamp is lighted*. That is all you are to do."

Sometimes the directions were not quite so simple, but they were all instructions of the same order. The originals of the sketches were to be sought out—always with precaution that should conceal that they were being sought at all and always in such a manner as would cause an encounter to appear to be mere chance. Then certain words were to be uttered, but always without attracting the attention of any bystander.

The boys worked at their task through the entire day. They concentrated all their powers upon it. They wrote and rewrote. They repeated to each other what they committed to memory as if it were a lesson. Marco worked with the greater ease and more rapidly, because exercise of this order had been his practice and entertainment from his babyhood. The Rat, however, almost kept pace with him, as he had been born with a phenomenal memory, and his eagerness and desire were a fury.

But throughout the entire day neither of them once referred to what they were doing as anything but "the game."

At night, it is true, each found himself lying awake and thinking. It was The Rat who broke the silence from his sofa.

"It is what the messengers of the Secret Party would be ordered to do when they were sent out to give the sign for the rising," he said. "I made that up the first day I invented the party, didn't I?"

"Yes," answered Marco.

After a third day's concentration they knew by heart everything given to them to learn. That night Loristan put them through an examination. "Can you write these things?" he asked, after each had repeated them and emerged safely from all cross-questioning.

Each boy wrote them correctly from memory.

"Write yours in French—in German—in Russian—in Samavian," Loristan said to Marco.

"All you have told me to do and to learn is part of myself, Father," Marco said in the end. "It is part of me, as if it were my hand or my eyes—or my heart."

"I believe that is true," answered Loristan.

Loristan was pale that night, and there was a shadow on his face. His eyes held a great longing as they rested on Marco. It was a yearning that had a sort of dread in it.

Lazarus also did not seem quite himself. He was red instead of pale, and his movements were uncertain and restless. He cleared his throat nervously at intervals and more than once left his chair as if to look for something.

It was almost midnight when Loristan, standing near Marco, put his arm around his shoulders.

"The game," he began, and then was silent a few moments while Marco felt his arm tighten its hold. Both Marco and The Rat felt a hard quick beat in their breasts, and because of this and because the pause seemed long, Marco spoke.

"The game? Yes, Father?" he said.

"The game is about to give you work to do. Both of you," Loristan answered.

Lazarus cleared his throat and walked to the easel in the corner of the room. But he only changed the position of a piece of paper on it and then came back.

"In two days you are to go to Paris, as you," to The Rat, "planned in the game."

"As I planned?" The Rat barely breathed the words.

"Yes," answered Loristan. "The instructions you have learned, you will carry out. There is no more to be done than to manage to approach certain persons closely enough to be able to utter certain words to them."

"Only two young strollers whom no man could suspect," put in Lazarus in an astonishingly rough and shaky voice. "They could pass near the emperor himself without danger. The young master . . ." His voice became so hoarse that he was obliged to clear it loudly. "The young master must carry himself less finely. It would be well to shuffle a little and slouch as if he were of the common people."

"Yes," said The Rat hastily. "He must do that. I can teach him. He holds his head and his shoulders like a gentleman. He must look like a street lad."

"I will look like one," said Marco with determination.

"I will trust you to remind him," Loristan said to
The Rat, and he said it with gravity. "That will be your
charge."

As he lay upon his pillow that night, it seemed
to Marco as if a load had lifted itself from his heart.
It was the load of uncertainty and longing. He had so
long borne the pain of feeling that he was too young to
be allowed to serve in any way. His dreams had never
been wild ones. They had in fact always been boyish
and modest. But now no dream that could have passed
through his brain would have seemed so wonderful as
this—that the hour had come. The hour had come and
that he, Marco, was to be its messenger. He was to do no
dramatic deed. He would not be announced by a flour-
ish of heralds. No one would know what he did. What he
achieved could only be attained if he remained obscure
and unknown and seemed to everyone only a common
ordinary boy who knew nothing whatever of important
things. But his father had given to him a gift so splendid
that he trembled with awe and joy as he thought of it. The
game had become real. He and The Rat were to carry with
them the Sign, and it would be like carrying a tiny lamp
to set aflame lights that would blaze from one mountaintop to another until half the world seemed on fire.

As he had awakened out of his sleep when Lazarus
touched him, so he awakened in the middle of the
night again. But he was not aroused by a touch. When
he opened his eyes, he knew it was a look that had penetrated his sleep—a look in the eyes of his father who was
standing by his side. In the road outside there was the
utter silence he had noticed the night of the prince's
first visit. The only light was that of the lamp in the

street, but he could see Loristan's face clearly enough to know that the mere intensity of his gaze had awakened him. The Rat was sleeping profoundly. Loristan spoke in Samavian and under his breath.

"Beloved one," he said. "You are very young. Because I am your father, just at this hour I can feel nothing else. I have trained you for this through all the years of your life. I am proud of your young maturity and strength but . . . Beloved . . . you are a child! Can I do this thing?"

For the moment, his face and his voice were scarcely like his own. He kneeled by the bedside, and as he did it, Marco half sitting up caught his hand and held it hard against his breast.

"Father, I know," he cried under his breath also. "It is true. I am a child, but am I not a man also? You your-self said it. I always knew that you were teaching me to be one—for some reason. It was my secret that I knew it. I learned well because I never forgot it. And I learned. Did I not?"

He was so eager that he looked more like a boy than ever. But his young strength and courage were splendid to see. Loristan knew him through and through and read every boyish thought of his.

"Yes," he answered slowly. "You did your part. And now if I drew back, you would feel that I had failed you."

"You," Marco breathed it proudly. "You could not fail even the weakest thing in the world."

There was a moment's silence in which the two pairs of eyes dwelt on each other with the deepest meaning, and then Loristan rose to his feet.

"The end will be all that our hearts most wish," he said. "Tomorrow you may begin the new part of the game. You may go to Paris."

When the train that was to meet the boat that crossed from Dover to Calais steamed out of the noisy Charing Cross Station, it carried two shabby boys in a third-class carriage. One of them would have been a handsome lad if he had not carried himself slouchingly and walked with a street lad's careless shuffling gait. The other was a cripple who moved slowly, and apparently with difficulty, on crutches. There was nothing remarkable or picturesque enough about them to attract attention. They sat in the corner of the carriage and neither talked much nor seemed to be particularly interested in the journey or each other. When they went on board the steamer, they were soon lost among the common passengers and in fact found for themselves a secluded place that was not fine enough to be wanted by anyone else.

"What can such a poor-looking pair of lads be going to Paris for?" someone asked his companion.

"Not for pleasure, certainly; perhaps to get work," was the casual answer.

In the evening they reached Paris, and Marco led the way to a small café in a side street where they got some cheap food. In the same side street they found a room they could share over a baker's shop.

The Rat was too much excited to be ready to go to bed early. He begged Marco to guide him about the brilliant streets. They went slowly along the broad

Avenue des Champs-Elysees under the lights glittering
among the horse chestnut trees. The Rat's sharp eyes
took it all in—the light of the cafés among the shelter-
ing trees, the many carriages rolling by, the people who
loitered and laughed or sat at little tables listening to
music, the broad stream of life that flowed on to the
Arch de Triomphe and back again.

"It's brighter and clearer than London," he said to
Marco. "The people look as if they were having more
fun than they do in England."

The Place de la Concorde spreading its stately
spaces held him as though by a fascination. He wanted
to stand and stare at it, first from one point of view and
then from another. It was bigger and more wonderful
than he had been able to picture when Marco had described it to him and told him of the part it had played
in the days of the French Revolution when the guillotine
had stood in it.

"I can see it all happening," he said at last, and he
pulled Marco away.

Before they returned home, they found their way
to a large house that stood in a courtyard. In the iron-
work of the handsome gates that shut it in was wrought a
gilded coronet. The gates were closed, and the house was
not brightly lighted.

They walked past it and around it without speaking,
but when they neared the entrance for the second time,
The Rat said in a low tone, "She is five feet seven, has
black hair, and a nose with a high bridge. Her eyebrows
are black and almost meet. She has pale olive skin and
holds her head proudly."

"That is the one," Marco answered.

They were a week in Paris, and each day passed this big house. There were certain hours when great ladies were more likely to go out and come in than they were at others. Marco knew this, and they managed to be within sight of the house or to pass it at these hours. For two days they saw no sign of the person they wished to see, but one morning the gates were thrown open, and they saw flowers and palms being taken in.

"She has been away and is coming back," said Marco. The next day they passed three times—once at the hour when fashionable women drive out to do their shopping, once at the time when afternoon visiting is most likely to begin, and once when the streets were brilliant with lights and the carriages had begun to roll by to dinner parties and operas.

Then as they stood at a little distance from the iron gates, a carriage drove through them and stopped before the big open door that was thrown open by two tall footmen in splendid livery.

"She is coming out," said The Rat.

They would be able to see her plainly when she came, because the lights over the entrance were so bright.

Marco slipped from under his coat sleeve a carefully made sketch.

He looked at it, and The Rat looked at it.

A footman stood erect on each side of the open door. The footman who sat with the coachman got down and was waiting by the carriage. Marco and The Rat glanced again with furtive haste at the sketch. A handsome woman appeared upon the threshold. She paused and gave some order to the footman who stood on the right. Then she came out in the full light and got into the carriage that drove out of the courtyard and quite near the place where the two boys waited.

When it was gone, Marco drew a long breath as he tore the sketch into very small pieces indeed. He did not throw them away but put them into his pocket.

The Rat drew a long breath also. "Yes," he said positively.

"Yes," said Marco.

When they were safely shut up in their room over the baker's shop, they discussed the chances of their being able to pass her in such a way as would seem accidental. Two common boys could not enter the courtyard. There was a back entrance for tradespeople and messengers. When she drove, she would always enter her carriage from the same place. Unless she sometimes walked, they could not approach her. What should be done? The thing was difficult. After they had talked some time, The Rat sat and gnawed his nails.

"Tomorrow afternoon," he broke out at last, "we'll watch and see if her carriage drives in for her. Then when she comes to the door, I'll go in and begin to beg. The servant will think I'm a foreigner and don't know what I'm doing. You can come after me to tell me to come away, because you know better than I do that I shall be ordered out. She may be a good-natured woman and listen to us. You might get near her."

"We might try it," Marco answered. "It might work. We will try it."

The Rat never failed to treat him as his leader. He had begged Loristan to let him come with Marco as his servant, and his servant he had been more than willing to be. When Loristan had said he should be his aide-de-camp, he had felt his trust lifted to a military dignity that uplifted him with it. As his aide-de-camp he must serve him, watch him, obey his lightest wish, and make everything easy for him. Sometimes Marco was troubled by the way in which he insisted on serving him, this once dictatorial and cantankerous lad who had begun by throwing stones at him.

"You must not wait on me," he said to him. "I must wait upon myself."

The Rat rather flushed. "He told me that he would let me come with you as your aide-de-camp," he said. "It . . . it's part of the game. It makes things easier if we keep up the game."

It would have attracted attention if they had spent too much time in the vicinity of the big house. So it happened that the next afternoon the great lady evidently drove out at an hour when they were not watching for her. They were on their way to try to carry out their plan when, as they walked together along the Rue Royale, The Rat suddenly touched Marco's elbow.

"The carriage stands before the shop with lace in the windows," he whispered hurriedly.

Marco saw and recognized it at once. The owner had evidently gone into the shop to buy something. This was a better chance than they had hoped for, and when they approached the carriage itself, they saw that there was another point in their favor. Inside were no less than three beautiful little Pekingese spaniels that looked exactly alike. They were all trying to look out of the window and were pushing against each other. They were so perfect and so pretty that few people passed by without looking at them. What better excuse could two boys have for lingering about a place?

They stopped and standing a little distance away began to look at and discuss them and laugh at their excited little antics. Through the shop window Marco caught a glimpse of the great lady.

"She does not look much interested. She won't stay long," he whispered, and added aloud, "that little one is the master. See how he pushes the others aside. He is stronger than the other two, though he is so small."

"He can snap too," said The Rat.

"She is coming now," warned Marco, and then laughed aloud as if at the Pekingese, which catching sight of their mistress at the shop door, began to leap and yelp for joy.

Their mistress herself smiled and was smiling as Marco drew near her.

"May we look at them, madame?" he said in French, and as she made an amiable gesture of acquiescence and moved toward the carriage with him, he spoke a few words, very low but very distinctly—in Russian.

"The Lamp is lighted," he said.

The Rat was looking at her keenly, but he did not see her face change at all. What he noticed most throughout their journey was that each person to whom they gave the Sign had complete control over his or her countenance if there were bystanders, and never betrayed by any change of expression that the words meant anything unusual.

The great lady merely went on smiling and spoke only of the dogs, allowing Marco and himself to look at them through the window of the carriage as the footman opened the door for her to enter.

"They are beautiful little creatures," Marco said, lifting his cap, and as the footman turned away, he uttered his few Russian words once more and moved off without even glancing at the lady again.

"That is *one*," he said to The Rat that night before they went to sleep, and with a match he burned the scraps of the sketch he had torn and put into his pocket.

Marco Goes
to the Opera

20

Their next journey was to Munich, but the night before they left Paris an unexpected thing happened.

To reach the narrow staircase that led to their bedroom, it was necessary to pass through the baker's shop itself.

The baker's wife was a friendly woman who liked the two boy lodgers who were so quiet and gave no trouble. More than once she had given them a hot roll or a freshly baked little tart with fruit in the center. When Marco came in this evening, she greeted him with a nod and handed him a small parcel as he passed through.

"This was left for you this afternoon," she said. "I see you are making purchases for your journey. My man and I are very sorry you are going."

"Thank you, madame. We also are sorry," Marco answered, taking the parcel. "They are not large purchases, you see."

But neither he nor The Rat had bought anything at all, though the ordinary looking little package was plainly addressed to him and bore the name of one of the big cheap shops. It felt as if it contained something soft.

When he reached their bedroom, The Rat was gazing out of the window, watching every living thing that passed in the street below. He who had never seen anything but London was absorbed by the spell of Paris and was learning it by heart.

"Something has been sent to us. Look at this," said Marco.

The Rat was at his side at once. "What is it? Where did it come from?"

They opened the package and at first sight saw only several pairs of quite common woolen socks. As Marco took up the sock in the middle of the parcel, he felt that there was something inside it—something laid flat and carefully. He put his hand in and drew out a number of five-franc notes—not new ones, because new ones would have betrayed themselves by crackling. These were old enough to be soft. But there were enough of them to amount to a substantial sum.

"It is in small notes because poor boys would have only small ones. No one will be surprised when we change these," The Rat said.

Each of them believed the package had been sent by the great lady, but it had been done so carefully that not the slightest clue was furnished.

To The Rat, part of the deep excitement of the game was the working out of the plans and methods of each person concerned. He could not have slept without working out some scheme that might have been used in this case. It thrilled him to contemplate the difficulties the great lady might have found herself obliged to overcome.

"Perhaps," he said, after thinking it over for some time, "when we left her, her carriage followed us at a distance to see where we stayed. Then she went to a big common shop dressed as if she were an ordinary woman and bought the socks and pretended she was going to carry them home herself. She would do that so that she could take them into some corner and slip the money in. Then, as she wanted to have them sent from the shop, perhaps she bought some other things and asked the people to deliver the packages to different places. The socks were sent to us, and the other things to some-one else. She would go to a shop where no one knew her and no one would expect to see her, and she would wear clothes that looked neither rich nor too poor."

The Rat created the whole episode with all its details and explained them to Marco. It fascinated him for the entire evening, and he felt relieved after it and slept well.

Even before they had left London, certain news-papers had swept out of existence the story of the descendant of the Lost Prince. This had been done by derision and light handling—by treating it as a romantic legend.

At first The Rat had resented this bitterly, but one day at a meal when he had been producing arguments to prove that the story must be a true one, Loristan somehow checked him by his own silence.

"If there is such a man," he said after a pause, "it is well for him that his existence should not be believed in—for some time at least."

The Rat came to a dead stop. He felt hot for a moment and then felt cold. He saw a new idea all at once. He had been making a mistake in tactics.

No more was said, but when they were alone after-wards, he poured himself forth to Marco.

"I was a fool!" he cried out. "Why couldn't I see it for myself? Shall I tell you what I believe has been done? There is someone who has influence in England and who is a friend to Samavia. They've got the newspapers to make fun of the story so that it won't be believed. If it was believed, both the Iarovitch and the Maranovitch would be on the lookout, and the Secret Party would lose their chances. What a fool I was not to think of it! There's someone watching and working here who is a friend to Samavia."

"But there is someone in Samavia who has begun to suspect that it might be true," Marco answered. "If there were not, I would not have been shut in the cellar.

Someone thought my father knew something. The spies had orders to find out what it was."

"Yes. Yes. That's true too," The Rat answered anxiously. "We shall have to be very careful."

In the lining of the sleeve of Marco's coat there was a slit into which he could slip any small thing he wished to conceal yet also wished to reach without trouble. In this pocket he had carried the sketch of the lady which he had torn up in Paris. When they walked in the streets of Munich, the morning after their arrival, he carried still another sketch. It was the one picturing the genial-looking old aristocrat with the sly smile.

One of the things they had learned about this one was that his chief characteristic was his passion for music. He was a patron of musicians, and he spent much time in Munich because he loved its musical atmosphere and the earnestness of its opera goers.

"The military band plays in the Feldherrnhalle at midday. When something very good is being played, sometimes people stop their carriages so that they can listen. We will go there," said Marco.

"It's a chance," said The Rat. "We mustn't lose anything like a chance."

The day was brilliant and sunny. The people passing through the streets looked comfortable and homely. The mixture of old streets and modern ones, of ancient corners and shops was picturesque and cheerful. The Rat swinging through the crowd on his crutches was full of interest and exhilaration. He had begun to grow, and the change in his face and expression that had begun in London had become more noticeable. He had been given his place and a work to do which entitled him to hold it.

No one could have suspected them of carrying a strange and vital secret with them as they strolled along together. They seemed only two ordinary boys who looked in at shop windows and talked over their contents, and who loitered with upturned faces in the Marienplatz before the ornate Gothic Rathaus to hear the eleven o'clock chimes play and see the painted figures of the king and queen watch the tournament procession with its trumpeters and tilting knights. When the show was over and the automatic cock broke forth into his lusty farewell crow, they laughed just as any other boys would have laughed. Sometimes it would have been easy for The Rat to forget that there was anything graver in the world than the new places and new wonders he was seeing, as if he were a wandering minstrel in a story.

But in Samavia bloody battles were being fought, and bloody plans were being wrought out, and in anguished anxiety the Secret Party and the Forgers of the Sword waited breathlessly for the Sign for which they had waited so long. Inside the lining of Marco's coat was hidden the sketched face, as the two unnoticed lads made their way to the Feldherrnhalle to hear the band play and see who might chance to be among the audience.

Because the day was sunny, and also because the band was playing an especially fine program, the crowd in the square was larger than usual. Several vehicles had stopped, and among them were one or two that were not merely hired cabs but were the carriages of private persons.

One of them had evidently arrived early, as it was drawn up in a good position when the boys reached the corner. It was a big open carriage and a grand one, luxuriously upholstered in green. The footman and coachman wore green and silver liveries and seemed to know that people were looking at them and their master.

He was a stout, genial-looking old aristocrat with a sly smile, though as he listened to the music, it almost forgot to be sly. In the carriage with him were a young officer and a little boy, and they also listened attentively. Standing near the carriage door were several people who were plainly friends or acquaintances, as they occasionally spoke to him. Marco touched The Rat's coat sleeve as the two boys approached.

"It would not be easy to get near him," he said. "Let us go and stand as close to the carriage as we can get without pushing. Perhaps we may hear someone say something about where he is going after the music is over."

Yes, there was no mistaking him. He was the right man. Each of them knew by heart the creases on his stout face and the sweep of his gray moustache. But there was nothing noticeable in a boy looking for a moment at a piece of paper, and Marco sauntered a few steps to a bit of space left bare by the crowd and took a last glance at his sketch. His rule was to make sure at the final moment. The music was very good, and the group about the carriage was evidently enthusiastic. There was talk and praise and comment, and the old aristocrat nodded his head repeatedly in applause.

"The chancellor is music mad," a looker-on near the boys said to another. "At the opera every night unless serious affairs keep him away! There you may see him nodding his old head and bursting his gloves with applause when a good thing is done. He ought to have led an orchestra or played a cello. He is too big for first violin."

There was a group about the carriage to the last when the music came to an end and it drove away. There had been no possible opportunity of passing close to it even had the presence of the young officer and the boy not presented an insurmountable obstacle.

Marco and The Rat went on their way and passed by the Hof-Theater and read the bills. *Tristan and Isolde* was to be presented at night, and a great singer would sing Isolde.

"He will go to hear that," both boys said at once. "He will be sure to go."

It was decided between them that Marco should go on his quest alone when night came. One boy who hung around the entrance of the opera would be observed less than two.

"People notice crutches more than they notice legs," The Rat said. "I'd better keep out of the way unless you need me. My time hasn't come yet. Even if it doesn't come at all, I've been on duty. I've gone with you, and I've been ready. That's what an aide-de-camp does."

He stayed at home and read such English papers as he could lay hands on, and he drew plans and refought battles on paper.

Marco went to the opera. Even if he had not known his way to the square near the place where the Hof-Theater stood, he could easily have found it by following the groups of people in the streets who all seemed walking in one direction. There were students in their odd caps walking three or four abreast, there were young couples and older ones, and here and there whole families. There were soldiers of all ages, officers and privates. And when talk was to be heard in passing, it was always talk about music.

For some time Marco waited in the square and watched the carriages roll up and pass under the huge pillared portico to deposit their contents at the entrance and at once drive away in orderly sequence. He must make sure that the grand carriage with the green and silver liveries rolled up with the rest. If it came, he would buy a cheap ticket and go inside.

It was rather late when it arrived. People in Munich are not late for the opera if it can be helped, and the coachman drove up hurriedly. The green and silver footman leaped to the ground and opened the carriage door almost before it stopped. The chancellor got out, looking less genial than usual because he was afraid that he might lose some of the overture. A rosy-cheeked girl in a white frock was with him, and she was evidently trying to soothe him.

"I do not think we are really late, Father," she said. "Don't feel cross, please. It will spoil the music for you."

This was not a time in which a man's attention could be attracted quietly. Marco ran to get the ticket that would give him a place among the rows of young

soldiers, artists, students, and musicians who were willing to stand throughout the performance of even the
longest opera. He knew that unless they were in one of
the few boxes that belonged only to the court, the chancellor and his rosy-cheeked daughter would be in the
best seats in the front curve of the balcony, which were
the most desirable of the house. He soon saw them.
They had secured the central places directly below the
large royal box where two quiet princesses and their attendants were already seated.

When he found he was not too late to hear the
overture, the chancellor's face become more genial than
ever. He settled himself down to an evening of enjoy-
ment and evidently forgot everything else in the world.
Marco did not lose sight of him. When the audience
went out between acts to promenade in the corridors,
he might go also, and there might be a chance to pass
near to him in the crowd. He watched him closely.
Sometimes his fine old face saddened at the beautiful
woe of the music, sometimes it looked enraptured, and
it was always evident that every note reached his soul.

The pretty daughter who sat beside him was attentive
but not so enthralled. After the first act two glittering
young officers appeared and made elegant and low bows,
drawing their heels together as they kissed her hand.
They looked sorry when they were obliged to return to
their seats again.

After the second act the chancellor sat for a few
minutes as if he were in a dream. The people in the seats
near him began to rise from their seats and file out into
the corridors. The young officers were to be seen rising

also. The rosy daughter leaned forward and touched her father's arm gently.

"She wants him to take her out," Marco thought. "He will take her because he is good-natured."

He saw him recall himself from his dream with a smile, and then he rose and after helping to arrange a silvery blue scarf round the girl's shoulders, gave her his arm just as Marco skipped out of his fourth row standing place.

It was a rather warm night, and the corridors were full. By the time Marco had reached the balcony floor, the pair had issued from the little door and were temporarily lost in the moving numbers.

Marco quietly made his way among the crowd, trying to look as if he belonged to somebody. Once or twice his strong body and his dense black eyes and lashes made people glance at him, but he was not the only boy who had been brought to the opera, so he felt safe enough to stop at the foot of the stairs and watch those who went up and those who passed by. It was a miscellaneous crowd made up of good unfashionable music lovers mixed here and there with grand people of the court.

Suddenly he heard a low laugh, and a moment later a hand lightly touched him.

"You *did* get out, then?" a soft voice said.

When he turned, he felt his muscles stiffen. He ceased to slouch and did not smile as he looked at the speaker. What he felt was a wave of fierce anger. It swept over him before he had time to control it.

A lovely lady who seemed swathed in several shades of soft violet drapery was smiling at him with lovely eyes.

It was the woman who had trapped him into Number 10 Brandon Terrace.

HELP!

21

"Did it take you very long to find it?" asked the lady with the smile. "Of course I knew you would find it in the end. But we had to give ourselves time. How long did it take?"

Marco removed himself from beneath the touch of her hand. It was quietly done, but there was disdain in his young face that made her wince though she pretended to shrug her shoulders amusedly.

"You refuse to answer?" she laughed.

"I refuse."

At that very moment he saw at the curve of the corridor the chancellor and his daughter approaching slowly. The two young officers were talking gaily to the girl. They were on their way back to their box. Was he going to lose them? Was he?

The delicate hand was laid on his shoulder again, but this time he felt that it grasped him firmly.

"Naughty boy," the soft voice said. "I am going to take you home with me. If you struggle, I shall tell these people that you are my bad boy who is here without permission. What will you answer? My escort is coming down the staircase and will help me. Do you see?" And in fact there appeared in the crowd at the head of the staircase the figure of the man he remembered.

He did see. A dampness broke out on the palms of his hands. If she did this bold thing, what could he say to those she told her lie to? How could he bring proof or explain who he was? And what story dare he tell? His protestations and struggles would merely amuse the lookers-on, who would see in them only the impotent rage of an insubordinate youngster.

There swept over him a wave of remembrance that brought back, as if he were living through it again, the moment when he had stood in the darkness of the wine cellar with his back against the door and heard the man walk away and leave him alone. But now he was in another land and far away from his father. He could do nothing to help himself unless something showed him a way.

He made no sound, and the woman who held him saw only a flame leap under his dense black lashes.

But something within him called out "Help!"

The chancellor was drawing nearer. Perhaps! Should he?

"You are too proud to kick and shout," the voice went on. "And people would only laugh. Do you see?"

The stairs were crowded and the man who was at the head of them could only move slowly. But he had seen the boy.

Marco turned so that he could face his captor squarely as if he were going to say something in answer to her. But he was not.

Even as he made the movement of turning, he knew what he should do. And he could do two things at once—save himself and give his Sign—because the Sign once given, the chancellor would understand.

"He will be here in a moment. He has recognized you," the woman said.

As he glanced up the stairs, the delicate grip of her hand unconsciously slackened.

Marco whirled away from her. The bell rang that was to warn the audience that they must return to their seats, and he saw the chancellor hasten his pace.

A moment later, the old aristocrat found himself amazedly looking down at the pale face of a breathless lad who spoke to him in German and in such a manner that he could not but pause and listen.

"Sir," he was saying, "the woman in violet at the foot of the stairs is a spy. She trapped me once, and she threatens to do it again. Sir, may I beg you to protect me?"

He said it low and fast. No one else could hear his words.

"What! What!" the chancellor exclaimed.

And then, drawing a step nearer and quite as low and rapidly but with perfect distinctness, Marco uttered four words, "The Lamp is lighted."

The help cry had been answered instantly. Marco saw it at once in the old man's eyes, notwithstanding that he turned to look at the woman at the foot of the staircase as if she only concerned him.

"What! What!" the chancellor said again and made a movement toward her, pulling his large moustache with a fierce hand.

Then Marco recognized that a curious thing happened. The lady saw the movement and the gray moustache, and that instant her smile died away, and she turned quite white—so white, that under the brilliant electric light she was almost green and scarcely looked lovely at all. She made a sign to the man on the staircase and slipped through the crowd like an eel. She was a slim flexible creature and never was a disappearance more wonderful in its rapidity. Between stout matrons and their thin or stout escorts and families she made her way and lost herself—but always making toward the exit. In two minutes there was no sight of her. She was gone and so, evidently, was her male companion.

It was plain to Marco that to follow the profession of a spy was not by any means a safe thing. The chancellor had recognized her. She had also recognized the chancellor, who turned looking ferociously angry and spoke to one of the young officers.

"She and the man with her are two of the most dangerous spies in Europe. She is a Rumanian, and he is a Russian. What they wanted of this innocent lad I don't

pretend to know. What did she threaten?" he asked
Marco.

Marco was feeling rather cold and sick and had lost
his healthy color for the moment.

"She said she meant to take me home with her and
would pretend I was her son who had come here without
permission," he answered. "She believes I know something I do not." He made a hesitating but grateful bow.
"The third act, sir. I must not keep you. Thank you.
Thank you!"

The chancellor moved toward the entrance door of
the balcony seats, but he did it with his hand on Marco's
shoulder.

"See that he gets home safely," he said to the younger
of the two officers. "Send a messenger with him. He's too
young to be attacked by creatures of that kind."

Polite young officers naturally obey the commands
of chancellors and such dignitaries. This one found
without trouble a young private who marched with
Marco through the deserted streets to his lodgings. He
was a stolid young Bavarian peasant and seemed to have
no curiosity or even any interest in the reason for the
command given him. He scarcely gave a glance to the
schoolboy he was to escort.

The Rat had fallen asleep over his papers and lay
with his head on his folded arms on the table. But he was
awakened by Marco's coming into the room and sat up
blinking his eyes in the effort to get them open.

"Did you see him? Did you get near enough?" he drowsed.

"Yes," Marco answered. "I got near enough."

The Rat sat upright suddenly. "It's not been easy," he exclaimed. "I'm sure something happened. Something went wrong."

"Something nearly went wrong—*very* nearly," answered Marco. But as he spoke he took the sketch of the Chancellor out of the slit in his sleeve and tore it and burned it with a match. "But I did get near enough. And that's *two*."

They talked long before they went to sleep that night. The Rat grew pale as he listened to the story of the woman in violet.

"I ought to have gone with you," he said. "I see now. An aide-de-camp must always be in attendance. It would have been harder for her to manage two than one. I must always be near to watch, even if I am not close by you. If you had not come back—if you had not come back!" He struck his clenched hands together fiercely. "What should I have done?"

When Marco turned toward him from the table near which he was standing, he looked like his father.

"You would have gone on with the game just as far as you could," he said. "You could not leave it. You remember the places, and the faces, and the Sign. There is some money; and when it was all gone, you could have begged, as we used to pretend we should. We have not had to do it yet, and it was best to save it for country places and villages. But you could have done it if you were obliged to. The game would have to go on."

The Rat caught at his thin chest as if he had been struck breathless. "Without you?" he gasped. "Alone?"

"Yes," said Marco. "And we must think of it and plan in case anything like that should happen."

He stopped himself quite suddenly and sat down, looking straight before him, as if at some faraway thing he saw.

"I said nothing aloud. But within me," Marco touched himself on the breast, "I called out, 'Help! Help!' with all my strength. And help came. The thought that flashed into my mind almost the next second came like lightning. All at once I knew if I ran to the chancellor and said the woman was a spy, it would startle him into listening to me; and that then I could give him the Sign; and that when I gave him the Sign, he would know I was speaking the truth and would protect me."

"It was a splendid thought!" The Rat said. "And it was quick."

Suddenly they heard a clumping step upon the staircase and when it reached the landing, it stopped at their door. Then there was a solid knock.

When Marco opened the door, the young soldier who had escorted him from the Hof-Theater was standing outside. He looked as uninterested and stolid as before, as he handed him a small flat package.

"You must have dropped it near your seat at the opera," he said. "I was to give it into your own hands. It is your purse."

After he had clumped down the staircase again, Marco and The Rat drew a quick breath at the same time.

"I had no seat, and I had no purse," Marco said. "Let us open it."

There was a flat limp leather note holder inside. In it was a paper, at the head of which were photographs of the lady and her companion. Beneath were a few lines that stated that they were the well-known spies Eugenia Karovna and Paul Varel and that the bearer must be protected against them. It was signed by the Chief of the Police. On a separate sheet was written the command: "Carry this with you as protection."

"That is help," The Rat said. "It would protect us even in another country. The chancellor sent it. But you made the call for help, and it's here!"

There was no streetlamp to shine into their windows when they went at last to bed. When the blind was drawn up, they were nearer the sky than they had been in the Marylebone Road. The last thing each of them saw as he went to sleep was the stars.

A Night Vigil

22

On a hill in the midst of a great Austrian plain, around which high Alps wait watching through the ages, stands a venerable fortress, almost more beautiful than anything one has ever seen. If it were not for the great plain flowering broadly about it with its widespread beauties of meadowland and wood, it might—though it is to be doubted—seem something less a marvel of medieval picturesqueness. But out of the plain rises the low hill, and surrounding it at a stately distance stands guard the giant majesty of the Alps with shoulders in the clouds, whose unchanging silence seems to know the secret of the everlasting. And on the hill which this august circle holds in its embrace, as though it enclosed a treasure, stands the old, old, towered fortress built as a citadel for the prince archbishops, who were kings in their domain in long past centuries.

As you approach the town, and as you leave it, and as you walk through its streets, the broad, calm, empty-looking ones, or the narrow thoroughfares whose houses seem so near to each other, whether you climb or descend or cross bridges or gaze at churches or step out on your balcony at night to look at the mountains, always it seems that from some point you can see it gazing down at you, the citadel of Hohen-Salzburg.

It was to Salzburg they went next, because at Salzburg was to be found the man who looked like a hairdresser and who worked in a barber's shop. Strange as it might seem, to him also must be carried the Sign.

"There may be people who come to him to be shaved—soldiers or men who know things," The Rat worked it out, "and he can speak to them when he is standing close to them. It will be easy to get near him. You can go and have your hair cut."

The journey from Munich was not a long one, and during the latter part of it they had the wooden seated third-class carriage to themselves. Even the drowsy old peasant who nodded and slept in one corner got out with his bundles at last. To Marco the mountains were long known wonders that could never grow old. They had always and always been so old! They were so silent, and yet it seemed as if they said some amazing thing—something that would take your breath from you if you could hear it. That was what the mountains said to Marco, which was why he did not want to talk much, but sat and gazed out of the carriage window.

The Rat had been very silent all the morning. He had been silent when they got up, and he had scarcely spoken when they made their way to the station at Munich and sat waiting for their train. It seemed to Marco that he was thinking so hard that he was like a person who was far away from the place he stood in. His brows were drawn together, and his eyes did not seem to see the people who passed by. Usually he saw everything and made shrewd remarks on almost all he saw. But today he was somehow otherwise absorbed. He sat in the train with his forehead against the window and stared out. He moved and gasped when he found himself staring at the Alps, but afterwards he was strangely still.

It was not until after the sleepy old peasant had gathered his bundles and got out at a station that he spoke, and he did it without turning his head.

"What if you want something that will harm somebody else?" he said. "What if you hate someone and wish you could kill him?"

Marco answered, "My father once said 'Let pass through thy mind, my son, only the image thou wouldst desire to see become a truth. Meditate only upon the wish of thy heart—seeing first that it is such as can wrong no man and is not ignoble. Let him who stretcheth forth his hand to draw the lightning to his brother recall that through his own soul and body will pass the bolt.' "

Then The Rat turned around. He had a shrewdly reasoning mind. "Wonder if there's anything in that?" he pondered. "It'd make a chap careful if he believed it! Revenging yourself on a man would be like holding him against a live wire to kill him and getting all the volts through yourself."

He hugged his knees for a few minutes. He was remembering his rags, and the fog-darkened room in the slums, and the loud, hideous laughter. A sudden anxiety revealed itself in his face. "Does your father believe it?" he asked. "Does he?"

"He knows it is true," Marco said.

"I'll own up," The Rat decided after further reflection. "I'll own up I'm glad that there isn't anyone left that I've a grudge against. There isn't anyone . . . now."

Then he fell again into silence and did not speak until their journey was at an end. As they arrived early in the day, they had plenty of time to wander about the marvelous little old city. But through the wide streets and through the narrow ones, under the archways into the market gardens, across the bridge and into the square where the Glockenspiel played its old tinkling tune, everywhere the Citadel looked down.

They found the hairdresser's shop in one of the narrow streets. There were no grand shops there, and this particular shop was a modest one. They walked past it once, and then went back. It was a shop so humble that there was nothing remarkable in two common boys going into it to have their hair cut. An old man came forward to receive them. He was evidently glad of their modest patronage. He undertook to attend to The Rat himself, but having arranged him in a chair, he turned about and called to someone in the back room.

"Heinrich," he said.

In the slit in Marco's sleeve was the sketch of the man with smooth curled hair, who looked like a hairdresser. They had found a corner in which to take their final look at it before they turned back to come in. Heinrich, who came forth from the small back room, had smooth curled hair. He looked extremely like a hairdresser. He had features like those in the sketch—his nose and mouth and chin and figure were like what Marco had drawn and committed to memory. But—

He gave Marco a chair and tied the white covering around his neck. Marco leaned back and closed his eyes a moment.

"That is *not* the man!" he was saying to himself. "He is *not* the man."

How he knew he was not, he could not have explained, but he felt sure. It was a strong conviction. But for the sudden feeling, nothing would have been easier than to give the Sign. And if he could not give it now, where was the one to whom it must be spoken, and what would be the result if that one could not be found? And if there were two who were so much alike, how could he be sure?

Each owner of each of the pictured faces was a link in a powerful secret chain; and if a link were missed, the chain would be broken. Each time Heinrich came within the line of his vision, he recorded every feature afresh and compared it with the remembered sketch. Each time the resemblance became more close, but each time some persistent inner conviction repeated, "No, the Sign is not for him!"

It was disturbing also to find that The Rat was all at once as restless as he had previously been silent and preoccupied. He moved in his chair to the great discomfort of the old hairdresser. He kept turning his head to talk. He asked Marco to translate divers questions he wished him to ask the two men—questions about the Citadel, about the Monchsberg, the Residenz, the Glockenspiel, the mountains. He added one query to another and could not sit still.

"The young gentleman will get an ear snipped," said the old man to Marco. "And it will not be my fault."

What shall I do? Marco was thinking. *He is not the man.*

He did not give the Sign. He must go away and think it out, though where his thoughts would lead him he did not know. This was a more difficult problem than he had ever dreamed of facing. There was no one to ask advice of. Only himself and The Rat, who was nervously wriggling and twisting in his chair.

"You must sit still," he said to him. "The hairdresser is afraid you will make him cut you by accident."

"But I want to know who lives at the Residenz?" said The Rat. "These men can tell us things if you ask them."

"It is done now," said the old hairdresser with a relieved air. "Perhaps the cutting of his hair makes the young gentleman nervous. It is sometimes so."

The Rat stood close to Marco's chair and asked questions until Heinrich also had done his work. Marco could not understand his companion's change of mood. He realized that if he had wished to give the Sign, he had been allowed no opportunity. He could not have given it. The restless questioning had so directed the older man's attention to his son and Marco that nothing could have been said to Heinrich without his observing it.

"I could not have spoken if he had been the man," Marco said to himself.

Their very exit from the shop seemed a little hurried. When they were fairly in the street, The Rat made a clutch at Marco's arm.

"You didn't give it?" he whispered breathlessly. "I kept talking and talking to prevent you."

Marco tried not to feel breathless, and he tried to speak in a low and level voice with no hint of exclamation in it. "Why did you say that?" he asked.

The Rat drew closer to him. "That was not the man!" he whispered. "It doesn't matter how much he looks like him, he isn't the right one." He was pale and swinging along swiftly as if he were in a hurry. "Let's get into a quiet place. I've been saying to myself that we should know the right things to do—for the game and for your father—and so that I could be the right sort of aide-de-camp. I've been working at it, and when he came out, I knew he was not the man in spite of his looks. And I couldn't be sure you knew, and I thought, if I kept on talking and interrupting you with silly questions, you could be prevented from speaking."

"There's a place not far away where we can get a look at the mountains. Let's go there and sit down," said Marco. "I knew he was not the right one too."

They got away from the streets and the people and reached the quiet place where they could see the mountains. There they sat down by the wayside. The Rat took off his cap and wiped his forehead, but it was not only the quick walking which had made it damp.

"The strangeness of it gave me a kind of fright," he said. "When he came out and he was near enough for me to see him, a sudden strong feeling came over me. It seemed as if I knew he wasn't the man. Then I said to myself, 'but he looks like him,' and I began to get nervous. And then I was sure again, and then I wanted to try to stop you from giving him the Sign. And then it all seemed foolishness."

Marco was very quiet. He was looking at the farthest and highest peaks and wondering about many things.

"It was the expression of his face that was different," he said. "And his eyes. They are rather smaller than the right man's are. The light in the shop was poor, and it was not until the last time he bent over me that I found out what I had not seen before. His eyes are gray, the other ones are brown."

"Did you see that?" The Rat exclaimed. "Then we're sure! We're safe."

"We're not safe till we've found the right man," Marco said. "Where is he? Who is he?"

He said the words quietly, as if he were lost in thought, but also rather as if he expected an answer. And he still looked at the far-off peaks. The Rat, after watching him a moment or so, began to look at them also. They were like a magnet to him too. There was something calming about them, and when your eyes had rested upon them a few moments, they did not want to move away.

"There must be a ledge up there somewhere," he said at last.

"Let's go up and look for it and sit there and think about finding the right man."

There seemed nothing fantastic in this to Marco. To go into some quiet place and sit and think about the thing he wanted to remember or to find out was an old way of his. To be quiet was always the best thing, his father had taught him.

"There is a little train which goes up the Gaisberg," he said. "When you are at the top, a world of mountains spreads around you. Lazarus went once and told me. And we can lie out on the grass all night. Let us go, Aide-de-camp."

So they went, each one thinking the same thought, and each mind holding its own vision.

They went up the Gaisberg in the little train, which pushed and dragged and panted slowly upward with them. It took them with it stubbornly and gradually higher and higher until it had left Salzburg and the Citadel below and had reached the world of mountains that rose and spread and lifted great heads behind each other and beside each other and beyond each other until there seemed no other land on earth but that on the mountainsides. One felt the absurdity of living upon flat ground, where life must be an insignificant thing.

There were only a few sightseers in the small carriages, and they were going to look at the view from the summit.

When the little train stopped at the top, they got out with the rest. They wandered about with them over the short grass on the treeless summit and looked out from this viewpoint and the other. The Rat grew more and more silent, and his silence was not merely a matter of speechlessness but of expression. They left the sightseers at last and wandered away by themselves. They found a ledge where they could sit or lie and where even the world of mountains seemed below them. They had brought some simple food with them, and they laid it behind a jutting bit of rock. When the sightseers boarded the laboring little train again and were dragged back down the mountain, their night of vigil would begin.

That was what it was to be. A night of stillness on the heights, where they could wait and watch and hold themselves ready for any thought which spoke to them.

The people returned to the train, and it set out upon its way down the steepness. They heard it laboring on its way, as though it was forced to make as much effort to hold itself back as it had made to drag itself upward.

Then they were alone, and it was a loneness such as an eagle might feel when it held itself poised high in the curve of blue. They sat and watched. They saw the sun go down and, shade by shade, deepen and make radiant and then draw away with it the last touches of color— rose, gold, purple, and gray.

One mountaintop after another held its blush a few moments and lost it. It took long to gather them all, but at length they were gone and the marvel of night fell.

The breath of the forests below was sweet about them, and soundlessness enclosed them that was of unearthly peace. The stars began to show themselves, and presently the two who waited found their faces turned upward to the sky, and they both were speaking in whispers.

"The stars look large here," The Rat said.

"Yes," answered Marco. "It seems like the top of the world."

"It is so still."

They had eaten their meal of black bread and cheese after the setting of the sun, and now they lay down on their backs and looked up until the first few stars had multiplied themselves into myriads. They began a little low talk, but the soundlessness was stronger than themselves.

The Rat said restlessly, "What if we don't find him? Don't find the right one, I mean?"

"Lie still—still—and look up at the stars," whispered Marco. "They give you a sure feeling."

There was something in the curious serenity of him that calmed even his aide-de-camp.

They were only two boys, and they had begun their journey on the earliest train and had been walking about all day and thinking of great and anxious things.

"It is so still," The Rat whispered again at last.

"It is so still," whispered Marco.

And the mountains rising behind each other and beside each other and beyond each other in the night, and also the myriads of stars that had so multiplied themselves, looking down knew that they were asleep.

"Someone is smoking," Marco found himself saying in a dream. He awakened and found that the smoke was

not part of a dream at all. It came from the pipe of a
young man who had an alpenstock and who looked as if
he had climbed to see the sun rise. He wore the clothes
of a climber and a green hat with a tuft at the back. He
looked down at the two boys, surprised.

"Good day," he said. "Did you sleep here so that
you could see the sun get up?"

"Yes," answered Marco.

"Were you cold?"

"We slept too soundly to know. And we brought our
thick coats."

"I slept halfway down the mountains," said the
man. "I am a guide in these days, but I have not been
one long enough to miss a sunrise. My father and
brother think I am mad about such things. They would
rather stay in their beds. Oh, he is awake, is he?" turning toward The Rat, who had risen on one elbow and
was staring at him. "What is the matter? You look as if
you were afraid of me."

Marco did not wait for The Rat to recover his breath
and speak. "I know why he looks at you so," Marco answered for him. "He is startled. Yesterday we went to a
hairdresser's shop down below there, and we saw a man
who was almost exactly like you, only," he looked up,
"his eyes were gray, and yours are brown."

"He was my twin brother," said the guide, puffing
at his pipe cheerfully. "My father thought he could make
hairdressers of us both, and I tried it for four years. But
I always wanted to be climbing the mountains, and there
were not holidays enough. So I cut my hair, and washed

the perfume out of it, and broke away. I don't look like a hairdresser now, do I?"

He did not. Not at all. But Marco knew him. He was the man. There was no one on the mountaintop but themselves, and the sun was just showing a rim of gold above the farthest and highest giant's shoulders. One need not be afraid to do anything, since there was no one to see or hear. Marco slipped the sketch out of the slit in his sleeve. He looked at it, and he looked at the guide, and then he showed it to him.

"That is not your brother. It is you!" he said.

The man's face changed a little more than any other face had changed when its owner had been spoken to. On a mountaintop as the sun rises, one is not afraid.

"The Lamp is lighted," said Marco. "The Lamp is lighted."

"God be thanked!" burst forth the man. And he took off his hat and bared his head. Then the rim behind the mountain's shoulder leaped forth into a golden torrent of splendor.

And The Rat stood up, resting his weight on his crutches in utter silence, and stared and stared.

"That is *three!*" said Marco.

The Silver Horn

23

During the next week, which they spent in journeying towards Vienna, they gave the Sign to three different persons at places that were on the way. In a village across the frontier in Bavaria they found a giant of an old man sitting on a bench under a tree before his mountain "Gasthaus" or inn; and when the four words were uttered, he stood up and bared his head as the guide had done.

When Marco gave the Sign in some quiet place to a man who was alone, he noticed that they all did this and said their "God be thanked" devoutly, as if it were part of some religious ceremony.

In a small town a few miles away, he had to search some hours before he found a stalwart young shoemaker with bright red hair and a horseshoe shaped scar on his forehead. He was not in his workshop when the boys first passed it, because as they found out later, he had been climbing a mountain the day before and had been detained in the descent because his companion had hurt himself.

When Marco went in and asked him to measure him for a pair of shoes, he was quite friendly and told them all about it.

"There are some good fellows who should not climb," he said. "When they find themselves standing on a bit of rock jutting out over emptiness, their heads begin to whirl round, and then if they don't turn head over heels a few thousand feet, it is because some comrade is near enough to drag them back. There can be no ceremony then, and they sometimes get hurt, as my friend did yesterday."

"Did you never get hurt yourself?" The Rat asked.

"When I was eight years old I did that," said the young shoemaker, touching the scar on his forehead. "But it was not much. My father was a guide and took me with him. He wanted me to begin early. There is nothing like it—climbing. I shall be at it again. This won't do for me. I tried shoemaking because I was in love with a girl who wanted me to stay at home. She married another man. I am glad of it. Once a guide, always a guide." He knelt down to measure Marco's foot, and Marco bent a little forward.

"The Lamp is lighted," he said.

There was no one in the shop, but the door was open and people were passing in the narrow street; so the shoemaker did not lift his red head. He went on measuring.

"God be thanked!" he said, in a low voice. "Do you want these shoes really, or did you only want me to take your measure?"

"I cannot wait until they are made," Marco answered. "I must go on."

"Yes, you must go on," answered the shoemaker. "But I'll tell you what I'll do—I'll make them and keep them. Some great day might come when I shall show them to people and swagger about them." He glanced around cautiously and then ended, still bending over his measuring. "They will be called the shoes of the Bearer of the Sign. And I shall say, 'He was only a lad. This was the size of his foot.' " Then he stood up with a great smile. "There'll be climbing enough to be done now," he said, "and I look to see you again somewhere."

When the boys went away, they talked it over.

"The hairdresser didn't want to be a hairdresser, and the shoemaker didn't want to make shoes," said The Rat. "They both wanted to be mountain climbers. There are mountains in Samavia and mountains on the way to it. You showed them to me on the map."

"Yes; and secret messengers who can climb any-where, and cross dangerous places, and reconnoiter from points no one else can reach, can find out things and give signals other men cannot," said Marco.

"That's what I thought," The Rat answered. "That was what he meant when he said, 'There will be climbing enough to be done now.' "

Strange were the places they went to and curiously unlike each other were the people to whom they carried their message. The most singular of all was an old woman who lived in so remote a place that the road wound around and around the mountain for miles and miles. It was not a bad road, and it was an amazing one to travel, dragged in a small cart by a mule when one could be dragged, and clambering slowly with rests between when one could not.

"How can anyone live higher than this?" said The Rat as they sat on the thick moss by the wayside after the mule and cart had left them. "Look at the bare crags looming up above there. Let us look at her again. Her picture looked as if she were a hundred years old."

Marco took out his hidden sketch. It seemed surely one of the strangest things in the world that a creature as old as this one seemed could reach such a place, or having reached it, could ever descend to the world again to give aid to any person or thing.

Her old face was crossed and recrossed with a thousand wrinkles. Her profile was splendid yet, and she had been a beauty in her day. Her eyes were like an eagle's— and not an old eagle's. And she had a long neck that held her old head high.

"How could she get here?" exclaimed The Rat.

"Those who sent us know, though we don't," said Marco. "Will you sit and rest while I go on further?"

"No," The Rat answered stubbornly. "I didn't train myself to stay behind. But we shall come to bare rock climbing soon, and then I shall be obliged to stop," and he said the last bitterly. He knew that if Marco had come alone, he would have ridden in no cart but would have trudged upward and onward sturdily to the end of his journey.

But they did not reach the crags, as they had thought must be inevitable. Suddenly halfway to the sky, as it seemed, they came to a bend in the road and found a mysterious, ancient, huddled village which, being snowed down, might have caught among the rocks and rested there through all time.

There it stood. There it huddled itself. And the monsters in the blue above it looked down upon it as if it were an incredible thing—this ancient, steep-roofed, hanging-balconied, crumbling cluster of human nests, which seemed a thousand miles from the world. Marco and The Rat stood and stared at it. Then they sat down and stared at it.

"How did it get here?" The Rat cried.

Marco shook his head. He certainly could see no explanation of its being there.

An old peasant driving a cow came down a steep path. He looked with a dull curiosity at The Rat and his crutches; but when Marco advanced and spoke to him in German, he did not seem to understand, but shook his head saying something in a dialect Marco did not know.

"If they all speak like that, we shall have to make signs when we want to ask anything," The Rat said. "What will she speak?"

"She will know the German for the Sign or we would not have been sent here," answered Marco. "Come on."

They made their way to the village, which huddled itself together evidently with the object of keeping itself warm when through the winter months the snows strove to bury it and the winds roared down from the huge mountain crags and tried to tear it from among its rocks. The doors and windows were few and small, and glimpses of the inside of the houses showed earthen floors and dark rooms. It was plain that it was counted a more comfortable thing to live without light than to let in the cold.

It was easy enough to reconnoiter. The few people they saw were evidently not surprised that strangers should be curious and want to look at them and their houses.

The boys wandered about as if they were casual explorers, who having reached the place by chance were interested in all they saw. They went into the little Gasthaus and got some black bread and sausage and some milk. The mountaineer owner was a brawny fellow who understood some German. He told them that few strangers knew of the village but that bold hunters and climbers came for sport. In the forests on the mountainsides were bears and in the high places, chamois. Now and again some great gentlemen came with parties of the daring kind—very great gentlemen indeed, he said, shaking his head with pride. There was one who had castles in other mountains, but he liked best to come here. Marco began to wonder if several strange things might not be true if great gentlemen sometimes climbed to the mysterious place. But he had not been sent to give the Sign to a great gentleman. He had been sent to give it to an old woman with eyes like a young eagle.

He had a sketch in his sleeve of her face, of her steep-roofed, black-beamed, balconied house. If they walked about a little, they would be sure to come upon it in this tiny place. Then he could go in and ask her for a drink of water.

They roamed about for an hour after they left the Gasthaus. They went into the little church and looked at the graveyard and wondered if it was not buried out of all sight in the winter. After they had done this, they sauntered out and walked through the huddled clusters of houses, examining each one as they drew near it and passed.

"I see it!" The Rat exclaimed at last. "It is that very old-looking one standing a little way from the rest. It is not as tumbled down as most of them. And there are some red flowers on the balcony."

"Yes. That's it," said Marco.

They walked up to the low black door, and as he stopped on the threshold, Marco took off his cap. He did this because sitting in the doorway on a low wooden chair was the old, old woman with the eagle eyes—sitting knitting.

There was no one else in the room and no one anywhere within sight. When the old woman looked up at him holding her head high on her long neck, Marco knew he need not ask for water or for anything else.

"The Lamp is lighted," he said in his low but strong and clear young voice.

She dropped her knitting upon her knees and gazed at him a moment in silence. She knew German it was clear, for it was in German she answered him.

"God be thanked!" she said. "Come in, young Bearer of the Sign, and bring your friend in with you. I live alone and not a soul is within hearing."

She was a wonderful old woman. Neither Marco nor The Rat would live long enough to forget the hours they spent in her strange dark house. She kept them and made them spend the night with her.

"It is quite safe," she said. "I live alone since my man fell into the crevasse and was killed. His rope broke while he was trying to save his comrade. I have two rooms to spare, and sometimes climbers are glad to sleep in them. Mine is a good warm house, and I am well known in the village. You are very young," she added shaking her head. "You are very young. You must have good blood in your veins to be trusted with this."

"I have my father's blood," answered Marco.

"You are like someone I once saw," the old woman said, and her eagle eyes set themselves hard upon him. "Tell me your name."

There was no reason why he should not tell it to her.

"It is Marco Loristan," he said.

"What? It is that!" she cried out, not loud but low.

To Marco's amazement she got up from her chair and stood before him, showing what a tall old woman she really was. There was a startled, even an agitated, look in her face. And suddenly she actually made a sort of curtsey to him—bending her knee as peasants do when they pass a shrine.

"It is that!" she said again. "And yet they dare let you go on a journey like this. That speaks for your courage and for theirs."

But Marco did not know what she meant. Her strange obeisance made him feel awkward. He stood up because his training had told him that when a woman stands a man also rises.

"The name speaks for the courage," he said, "because it is my father's."

She watched him almost anxiously. "You do not even know," she breathed. It was an exclamation and not a question.

"I know what I have been told to do," he answered. "I do not ask anything else."

"Who is that?" she asked, pointing to The Rat.

"He is the friend my father sent with me," said Marco smiling. "He called him my aide-de-camp. It was a sort of joke because we had played soldiers together."

It seemed as if she were obliged to collect her thoughts. She stood with her hand at her mouth, looking down at the earth floor.

"God guard you," she said at last. "You are very . . . very young!"

"But all his years," The Rat broke in, "he has been in training for just this thing. He did not know it was training, but it was. A soldier who had been trained for thirteen years would know his work."

He was so eager that he forgot she could not understand English. Marco translated what he said into German and added, "What he says is true."

She nodded her head, still with questioning and anxious eyes. "Yes. Yes," she muttered. "But you are very young." Then she asked in a hesitating way, "Will you not sit down until I do?"

"No," answered Marco. "I would not sit while my mother or grandmother stood."

"Then I must sit—and forget," she said.

She passed her hand over her face as though she were sweeping away the sudden puzzled trouble in her expression. Then she sat down, as if she had obliged herself to become again the old peasant she had been when they entered.

"All the way up the mountain you wondered why an old woman should be given the Sign," she said. "You asked each other how she could be of use."

Neither Marco nor The Rat said anything.

"When I was young and fresh," she went on. "I went to a castle over the frontier to be foster mother to a child who was born a great noble—one who was near the throne. He loved me, and I loved him. He was a strong child, and he grew up a great hunter and climber. When he was not ten years old, my man taught him to climb. He always loved these mountains better than his own. He comes to see me as if he were only a young mountaineer. He sleeps in the room there," with a gesture over her shoulder into the darkness. "He has great power, and if he chooses to do a thing, he will do it— just as he will attack the biggest bear or climb the most dangerous peak. He is one who can bring things about. It is very safe to talk in this room."

Then all was quite clear. Marco and The Rat understood.

No more was said about the Sign. It had been given and that was enough. The old woman told them that they must sleep in one of her bedrooms. The next morning one of her neighbors was going down to the valley with a cart, and he would help them on their way. The Rat knew that she was thinking of his crutches, and he became restless.

"Tell her," he said to Marco, "how I have trained myself until I can do what anyone else can. And tell her I am growing stronger every day. I'll show her what I can do. Your father wouldn't have let me come as your aide if I hadn't proved to him that I wasn't a cripple. Tell her. She thinks I'm no use."

Marco explained and the old woman listened attentively. When The Rat got up and swung himself about up and down the steep path near her house, she seemed relieved. His extraordinary dexterity and firm swiftness evidently amazed her and gave her a confidence she had not felt at first.

"If he has taught himself to be like that just for love of your father, he will go to the end," she said. "It is more than one could believe, that a pair of crutches could do such things."

The Rat was pacified and could afterwards give himself up to watching her as closely as he wished to. He was soon working out certain things in his mind. What he watched was her way of watching Marco. It was as if

she were fascinated and could not keep her eyes from
him. She told them stories about the mountains and the
strangers who came to climb with guides or to hunt. She
told them about the storms, which sometimes seemed
about to put an end to the little world among the crags.
She described the winter when the snow buried them and
the strong ones were forced to dig out the weak and some
lived for days under the masses of soft whiteness, glad to
keep their cows or goats in their rooms that they might
share the warmth of their bodies. The villagers were
forced to be good neighbors to each other, for the man
who was not ready to dig out a hidden chimney or buried
door today might be left to freeze and starve in his snow
tomb next week. Through the worst part of the winter,
no creature from the world below could make way to
them to find out whether they were all dead or alive.

While she talked, she watched Marco as if she were
always asking herself some question about him. The
Rat was sure that she liked him and greatly admired his
strong body and good looks. It was not necessary for
him to carry himself slouchingly in her presence, and he
looked glowing and noble. There was a sort of reverence
in her manner when she spoke to him. She reminded
him of Lazarus more than once. When she gave them
their evening meal, she insisted on waiting on him with
a certain respectful ceremony. She would not sit at table
with him, and The Rat began to realize that she felt that
he himself should be standing to serve Marco.

"She thinks I ought to stand behind your chair as
Lazarus stands behind your father's," he said to Marco.
"Perhaps an aide ought to do it. Shall I? I believe it
would please her."

"A Bearer of the Sign is not a royal person," answered Marco. "My father would not like it, and I should not. We are only two boys."

It was very wonderful when after their supper was over, they all three sat together before the fire.

The red glow of the bed of wood coal and the orange yellow of the flame from the big logs filled the room with warm light that made a mellow background for the figure of the old woman as she sat in her low chair and told them more and more enthralling stories.

Her eagle eyes glowed, and her long neck held her head splendidly high as she described great feats of courage and endurance in aiding those in awesome peril, and when she glowed most in the telling, they always knew that the hero of the adventure had been her foster child who was the baby born a great noble and near the throne. To her he was the most splendid and adorable of human beings. Almost an emperor, but so warm and tender of heart that he never forgot the long past days when she had held him on her knee and told him tales of bear hunting and of the mountaintops in midwinter.

"Yes, yes," she said. "*Good Mother,* he calls me. And I bake him a cake on the hearth as I did when he was ten years old and my man was teaching him to climb. And when he chooses that a thing shall be done—done it is! He is a great lord."

The flames had died down and only the big bed of red coal made the room glow, and they were thinking of going to bed when the old woman started very suddenly, turning her head as if to listen.

Marco and The Rat heard nothing, but they saw that she did, and they sat so still that each held his breath. There was utter stillness for a few moments. Utter stillness.

Then they did hear something—a clear silver sound, piercing the pure mountain air.

The old woman sprang upright with the fire of delight in her eyes. "It is his silver horn!" she cried out, striking her hands together. "It is his own call to me when he is coming. He has been hunting somewhere and wants to sleep in his good bed here. Help me to put on more brushwood so that he will see the flame of them through the open door as he comes."

"Shall we be in the way?" said Marco. "We can go at once."

She was going towards the door to open it, and she stopped a moment and turned. "No, no!" she said. "He must see your face. He will want to see it. I want him to see . . . how young you are."

She threw the door wide open, and they heard the silver horn send out its cheerful call again. The brushwood The Rat had thrown on the coals crackled and sparkled and roared into fine flames which cast their light into the road and threw out in fine relief the old figure that stood on the threshold and looked so tall.

In but a few minutes her great lord came to her. In his green hunting suit with its green hat and eagle's feather he was as splendid as she had said he was. He was big and royal looking and laughing, and he bent and kissed her as if he had been her own son.

"Yes, Good Mother," they heard him say. "I want my warm bed and one of your good suppers. I sent the others to the Gasthaus."

He came into the glowing room and his head almost touched the blackened rafters. Then he saw the two boys.

"Who are these, Good Mother?" he asked.

She lifted his hand and kissed it. "They are the Bearers of the Sign," she said rather softly. "The Lamp is lighted."

Then his whole look changed. His laughing face became quite grave and for a moment looked even anxious. Marco knew it was because he was startled to find them only boys. He made a step forward to look at them more closely.

"The Lamp is lighted. And you two bear the Sign!" he exclaimed.

Marco stood in the fire glow that he might see him well. He saluted with respect. "My name is Marco Loristan, Highness," he said. "And my father sent me."

The change that came upon his face was even greater than at first. For a second Marco even felt that there was a flash of alarm in it. But almost at once that passed.

"Loristan is a great man and a great patriot," he said. "If he sent you, it is because he knows you are the one safe messenger. He has worked too long for Samavia not to know what he does."

Marco saluted again. He knew what it was right to say next.

"If we have Your Highness's permission to retire," he said, "we will leave you and go to bed. We go down the mountain at sunrise."

"Where next?" asked the hunter, looking at him with curious intentness.

"To Vienna, Highness," Marco answered.

His questioner held out his hand, still with the intent interest in his eyes. "Good night, fine lad," he said. "Samavia has need to vaunt itself on its Sign bearer. God go with you."

He stood and watched as Marco went toward the room in which he and his aide-de-camp were to sleep. The Rat followed him closely. At the little back door the old woman stood, having opened it for them. As Marco passed and bade her good night, he saw that she again made the strange obeisance, bending the knee as he went by.

How Shall
We Find Him?

24

In Vienna they came upon a pageant. The broad pavements of the huge chief thoroughfare were crowded with a cheering populace watching the martial pomp and splendor as it passed by with marching feet, prancing horses, and glitter of scabbard and chain, which all seemed somehow part of music in triumphant bursts.

The Rat was enormously thrilled by the magnificence of the imperial place. Its immense spaces, the squares and gardens reigned over by statues of emperors, made him feel that all things on earth were possible. The palaces and stately piles of architecture seemed to sweep out of his world all atmosphere but that of splendid cities down whose broad avenues emperors rode with golden trumpets blaring forth. It seemed as if it must always be like this—that lances and cavalry and emperors would never cease to ride by. "I should like to stay here a long time," he said almost as if he were in a dream. "I should like to see it all."

He leaned on his crutches in the crowd and watched the glitter of the passing pageant. Now and then he glanced at Marco, who watched also with a steady eye which The Rat saw nothing would escape. How absorbed he always was in the game. How impossible it was for him to forget it or to remember it only as a boy would. Often it seemed that he was not a boy at all. And the game, The Rat knew in these days, was a game no more, but a thing of deep and deadly earnest—a thing which touched kings and thrones and concerned the ruling and swaying of great countries. And they—two lads pushed about by the crowd as they stood and stared at the soldiers—carried with them that which was even now lighting the Lamp.

The blood in The Rat's veins ran quickly and made him feel hot as he remembered certain thoughts that had forced themselves into his mind during the past weeks. As his brain had the trick of working things out, it had during the last fortnight at least, been following a wonderful, if fantastic fancy. A mere trifle had set it at work, but its labor once begun, things which might have once seemed to be trifles appeared so no longer.

When Marco was asleep, The Rat lay awake thrilled and sometimes almost breathless through midnight hours, looking backward and recalling every detail of their lives since they had known each other. Sometimes it seemed to him that almost everything he remembered—the game from first to last above all—had pointed to but one thing. And then again he would all at once feel that he was a fool and had better keep his head steady. Marco, he knew, had no wild fancies. He had learned too much and his mind was too well balanced. He did not try to work out things. He only thought of what he was under orders to do.

"But," said The Rat more than once in these midnight hours, "if it ever comes to a draw whether he is to be saved or I am, he is the one that must come to no harm."

This thought passed through his mind as the tramping feet went by. As a sudden splendid burst of approaching music broke upon his ear, a look twisted his face. He realized the contrast between this day and that first morning behind the churchyard, when he had sat on his platform among the Squad and looked up and saw Marco in the arch at the end of the passage. And because he had been good looking and had held himself so well, he had thrown a stone at him. Yes, blind gutter-bred fool that he'd been, his first greeting to Marco had been a stone, just because he was what he was. As they stood here in the crowd in this far-off foreign city, it did not seem as if it could be true that it was he who had done it.

The Rat managed to work himself closer to Marco's side. "Isn't it splendid?" he said. "I wish I was an emperor myself. I'd have these fellows out like this every day." He said it only because he wanted to say something, to speak as a reason for getting closer to him. He wanted to be near enough to touch him and feel that they were really together and that the whole thing was not a sort of magnificent dream from which he might awaken to find himself lying on his heap of rags in his corner of the room in Bone Court.

The crowd swayed forward in its eagerness to see the principal feature of the pageant—the emperor in his carriage. The Rat swayed forward with the rest to look as it passed.

A handsome white-haired and mustached personage in splendid uniform decorated with jeweled orders and with a cascade of emerald green plumes nodding in his military hat gravely saluted the shouting people on either side. By him sat a man uniformed, decorated, and emerald plumed also, but many years younger.

Marco's arm touched The Rat's almost at the same moment that his own touched Marco. Under the nodding plumes each saw the rather tired and cynical pale face, a sketch of which was hidden in the slit in Marco's sleeve.

"Is the one who sits with the emperor an archduke?" Marco asked the man nearest to him in the crowd. The man answered amiably enough. No, he was not, but he was a certain prince, a descendant of the one who was the hero of the day. He was a great favorite of the emperor's and was also a great personage, whose palace contained pictures celebrated throughout Europe.

"He pretends it is only pictures he cares for," he went on, shrugging his shoulders and speaking to his wife, who had begun to listen, "but he is a clever one, who amuses himself with things he professes not to concern himself about—big things. It's his way to look bored and interested in nothing, but it's said he's a wizard for knowing dangerous secrets."

"Does he live at the Hofburg with the emperor?"
asked the woman, craning her neck to look after the
imperial carriage.

"No, but he's often there. The emperor is lonely
and bored too, no doubt, and this one has ways of
making him forget his troubles. It's been told me that
now and then the two dress themselves roughly, like
common men, and go out into the city to see what it's
like to rub shoulders with the rest of the world. I daresay
it's true. I should like to try it myself once in a while, if I
had to sit on a throne and wear a crown."

The two boys followed the celebration to its end.
They managed to get near enough to see the entrance to
the church where the service was held and to get a view
of the ceremonies at the banner-draped and laurel-
wreathed statue. They saw the man with the pale face several times, but he was always so enclosed that it was not
possible to get within yards of him. It happened once,
however, that he looked through a temporary break in
the crowding people and saw a dark strong-featured and
remarkably intent boy's face, whose vivid scrutiny of him
caught his eye. There was something in the fixedness of
its attention that caused him to look at it curiously for a
few seconds, and Marco met his gaze squarely.

Look at me! Look at me! the boy was saying to him mentally. *I have a message for you. A message!*

The tired eyes in the pale face rested on him with a
certain growing light of interest and curiosity, but the
crowding people moved and the temporary break closed
up so that the two could see each other no more. Marco
and The Rat were pushed backward by those taller and

stronger than themselves until they were on the outskirts of the crowd.

"Let us go to the Hofburg," said Marco. "They will come back there, and we shall see him again, even if we can't get near."

To the Hofburg they made their way through the less-crowded streets, and there they waited as near to the great palace as they could get. They were there when, the ceremonies at an end, the imperial carriages returned, but though they saw their man again, they were at some distance from him and he did not see them.

Then followed four singular days. They were singular days because they were full of tantalizing incidents. Nothing seemed easier than to hear talk of and see the emperor's favorite, but nothing was more impossible than to get near to him. He seemed rather a favorite with the populace, and the common people of the shop-keeping or laboring classes were given to talking freely of him—of where he was going and what he was doing. Tonight he would be sure to be at this great house or that, at this ball or that banquet. There was no difficulty in discovering that he would be sure to go to the opera, or the theatre, or to drive to Schonbrunn with his imperial master.

Marco and The Rat heard casual speech of him again and again, and from one part of the city to the other they followed and waited for him. But it was like chasing a will-o'-the-wisp. He was evidently too brilliant and important a person to be allowed to move about alone. There were always people with him who seemed absorbed in his languid, cynical talk. Marco thought that he never seemed to care much for his companions, though they on their part always seemed highly entertained by what he was saying. It was noticeable that they laughed a great deal, though he himself scarcely even smiled.

"He's one of those chaps with the trick of saying witty things as if he didn't see the fun in them himself," The Rat summed him up. "Chaps like that are always cleverer than the other kind."

"He's too high in favor and too rich not to be followed about," they heard a man in a shop say one day, "but he gets tired of it. Sometimes when he's too bored to stand it any longer, he lets it be thought that he's gone into the mountains somewhere, and all the time he's shut up alone with his pictures in his own palace."

That very night The Rat came in to their attic looking pale and disappointed. He had been out to buy some food after a long and arduous day in which they had covered much ground, had seen their man three times, and each time under circumstances which made him more inaccessible than ever. They had come back to their poor quarters both tired and ravenously hungry.

The Rat threw his purchase on to the table and himself into a chair. "He's gone to Budapest," he said. "*Now* how shall we find him?"

Marco was rather pale also, and for a moment he looked paler. The day had been a hard one, and in their haste to reach places at a long distance from each other they had forgotten their need of food.

They sat silent for a few moments because there seemed to be nothing to say. "We are too tired and hungry to be able to think well," Marco said at last. "Let us eat our supper and then go to sleep. Until we've had a rest, we must 'let go.' "

"Yes. There's no good in talking when you're tired," The Rat answered a trifle gloomily. "You don't reason straight."

Their meal was simple, but they ate well and without words.

Even when they had finished and undressed for the night, they said very little.

Sleep made it for them—deep, restful, healthy sleep. If they had been more resentful of their ill luck and lost labor, it would have come less easily and have been less natural. In their talks of strange things, they had learned that one great secret of strength and unflagging courage is to know how to let go—to cease thinking over an anxiety until the right moment comes. It was their habit to let go for hours sometimes and wander about looking at places and things—galleries, museums, palaces, giving themselves up with boyish pleasure and eagerness to all they saw. Marco was too intimate with the things worth seeing, and The Rat too curious and feverishly wide-awake to allow their missing much.

The Rat's image of the world had grown until it seemed to know no boundaries that could hold its wealth of wonders. He wanted to go on and on and see them all.

When Marco opened his eyes in the morning, he found The Rat lying looking at him. Then they both sat up in bed at the same time.

"I believe we are both thinking the same thing," Marco said.

They frequently discovered that they were thinking the same things.

"So do I," answered The Rat. "It shows how tired we were that we didn't think of it last night."

"Yes, we are thinking the same thing," said Marco. "We have both remembered what we heard about his shutting himself up alone with his pictures and making people believe he had gone away."

"He's in his palace now," The Rat announced.

"Do you feel sure of that too?" asked Marco. "Did you wake up and feel sure of it the first thing?"

"Yes," answered The Rat. "As sure as if I'd heard him say it himself."

"So did I," said Marco.

The day was a brilliant one, and though their attic had only one window, the sun shone in through it as they ate their breakfast. Then they leaned on the window's ledge and talked about the prince's garden. They talked about it because it was a place open to the public, and they had walked round it more than once. The palace, which was not a large one, stood in the midst of it. The prince was good-natured enough to allow quiet and well-behaved people to saunter through. It was not a fashionable promenade but a pleasant retreat for people who sometimes took their work or books and sat on the seats placed here and there among the shrubs and flowers.

"When we were there the first time, I noticed two things," Marco said. "There is a stone balcony that juts out from the side of the palace that looks on the Fountain Garden. That day there were chairs on it as if the prince and his visitors sometimes sat there. Near it there was a very large evergreen shrub, and I saw that there was a hollow place inside it. If someone wanted to stay in the gardens all night to watch the windows when they were lighted and see if anyone came out alone upon the balcony, he could hide himself in the hollow place and stay there until the morning."

"Is there room for two inside the shrub?" The Rat asked.

"No. I must go alone," said Marco.

A Voice
in the Night

25

Late that afternoon there wandered about the gardens two quiet, inconspicuous, rather poorly dressed boys. They looked at the palace, the shrubs, and the flower beds as strangers usually did, and they sat on the seats and talked as people were accustomed to seeing boys talk together. It was a sunny day and exceptionally warm, and there were more saunterers and sitters than usual, which was perhaps the reason why the porter at the entrance gates gave such slight notice to the pair that he did not observe that, though two boys came in, only one went out. He did not remember when he saw The Rat swing by on his crutches at closing time, that he had entered in company with a dark-haired lad who walked without any aid.

It happened that, when The Rat passed out, the porter at the entrance was much interested in the aspect of the sky, which was curiously threatening. There had been heavy clouds hanging about all day and now and then blotting out the sunshine entirely, but the sun had refused to retire altogether. Just now, however, the clouds had piled themselves in thunderous, purplish mountains, and the sun had been forced to set behind them.

"It's been a sort of battle since morning," the porter said. "There will be some crashes and cataracts tonight."

That was what The Rat had thought when they had sat in the Fountain Garden on a seat which gave them a good view of the balcony and the big evergreen shrub with the hollow in its middle.

"If there should be a big storm, the evergreen will not save you much, though it may keep off the worst," The Rat said. "I wish there was room for two."

He would have wished there was room for two if he had seen Marco marching to the stake. As the gardens emptied, the boys rose and walked around once more, as if on their way out. By the time they had sauntered toward the big evergreen, nobody was in the Fountain Garden, and the last loiterers were moving toward the arched stone entrance to the streets.

When they drew near one side of the evergreen, the two were together. When The Rat swung out on the other side of it, he was alone. No one noticed that any-thing had happened; no one looked back. So The Rat swung down the walks and around the flowerbeds and passed into the street. And the porter looked at the sky and made his remark about the crashes and cataracts.

As the darkness came on, the hollow in the shrub seemed a very safe place. It was not in the least likely that anyone would enter the closed gardens; and if by rare chance some servant passed through, he would not be in search of people who wished to watch all night in the middle of an evergreen instead of going to bed and to sleep. The hollow was well enclosed with greenery, and there was room to sit down when one tired of standing.

Marco stood for a long time because by doing so, he could see plainly the windows opening on the balcony if he gently pushed aside some flexible young boughs. He had managed to discover in his first visit to the gardens that the windows overlooking the Fountain Garden were those which belonged to the prince's own suite of rooms. Those which opened on to the balcony lighted his favorite apartment, which contained his best loved books and pictures and in which he spent most of his secluded leisure hours.

Marco watched these windows anxiously. If the prince had not gone to Budapest, if he were really only in retreat and hiding from his merry world among his treasures, he would be living in his favorite rooms and lights would show themselves. And if there were lights, he might pass before a window because, since he was enclosed in his garden, he need not fear being seen. The twilight deepened into darkness and because of the heavy clouds, it was very dense. Faint gleams showed themselves in the lower part of the palace, but none was lighted in the windows Marco watched. He waited so long that it became evident that none was to be lighted at all. At last he loosed his hold on the young boughs and after standing a few moments in thought, sat down upon the earth in the midst of his embowered tent. The prince was not in his retreat. He was probably not in Vienna, and the rumor of his journey to Budapest had no doubt been true. So much time lost through making a mistake, but it was best to have made the venture. Not to have made it would have been to lose a chance.

The entrance was closed for the night, and there was no getting out of the gardens until they were opened for the next day. He must stay in his hiding place until the time when people began to come and bring their books and knitting and sit on the seats. Then he could stroll out without attracting attention. But he had the night before him to spend as best he could. That would not matter at all. He could tuck his cap under his head and go to sleep on the ground. He could command himself to waken once every half hour and look for the lights. He would not go to sleep until it was long past midnight—so long past that there would not be one chance in a hundred that anything could happen. But the clouds that made the night so dark were giving forth low rumbling growls. At intervals a threatening gleam of light shot across them, and a sudden swish of wind rushed through the trees in the garden.

This happened several times, and then Marco began to hear the patter of raindrops. They were heavy and big drops, but few at first, and then there was a new and more powerful rush of wind, a jagged dart of light in the sky and a tremendous crash. After that the clouds tore themselves open and poured forth their contents

in floods. After the protracted struggle of the day, it all
seemed to happen at once, as if a horde of huge lions
had at one moment been let loose—flame after flame of
lightning, roar and crash and sharp reports of thunder,
shrieks of wind, torrents of rain, as if some tidal wave
of the skies had gathered and rushed and burst upon
the earth. It was such a storm as people remember for a
lifetime and which in few lifetimes is seen at all.

Marco stood still in the midst of the rage and flooding, blinding roar of it. After the first few minutes he
knew he could do nothing to shield himself. Down the
garden paths he heard cataracts rushing. He held his cap
pressed against his eyes because he seemed to stand in
the midst of darting flames. The crashes, cannon reports and thunderings, and the jagged streams of light
came so close to one another that he seemed deafened
as well as blinded. He wondered if he would ever be able
to hear human voices again when it was over. That he
was drenched to the skin and that the water poured from
his clothes as if he were himself a cataract was so small
a detail that he was scarcely aware of it. He stood still,
bracing his body, and waited. If he had been a Samavian
soldier in the trenches and such a storm had broken
upon him and his comrades, they could only have
braced themselves and waited. This was what he found
himself thinking when the tumult and downpour were
at their worst. There were men who had waited in the
midst of a rain of bullets.

It was not long after this thought had come to him
that there occurred the first temporary lull in the storm.
Its fury perhaps reached its height and broke at that
moment. A yellow flame had torn its jagged way across

the heavens, and an earth-rending crash had thundered itself into rumblings that actually died away before breaking forth again. Marco took his cap from his eyes and drew a long breath. He drew two long breaths. It was as he began drawing a third and realizing the strange feeling of the almost stillness about him that he heard a new kind of sound at the side of the garden nearest his hiding place. It sounded like the creak of a door opening somewhere in the wall behind the laurel hedge. Someone was coming into the garden by a private entrance.

He pushed aside the young boughs again and tried to see, but the darkness was too dense. Yet he could hear if the thunder did not break again. There was the sound of feet on the wet gravel, the footsteps of more than one person coming toward where he stood. They were not afraid of being heard; merely at liberty to come in by what entrance they chose. Marco remained very still. A sudden hope gave him a shock of joy. If the man with the tired face chose to hide himself from his acquaintances, he might choose to go in and out by a private entrance. The footsteps drew near, crushing the wet gravel, passed by, and seemed to pause somewhere near the balcony. Then flame lit up the sky again, and the thunder burst forth once more.

But this was its last great peal. The storm was at an end. Only fainter and fainter rumblings and mutterings and paler and paler darts followed. Even they were soon over, and the cataracts in the paths had rushed themselves silent. But the darkness was still deep.

It was black in the hollow of the evergreen. Marco stood in it, streaming with rain, but feeling nothing because he was full of thought. He pushed aside his greenery and kept his eyes on the place in the blackness where the windows must be, though he could not see them. It seemed that he waited a long time, but he knew it only seemed so. He began to breathe quickly because he was waiting for something.

Suddenly he saw exactly where the windows were, because they were all lighted.

His feeling of relief was great, but it did not last very long. It was true that something had been gained in the certainty that his man had not left Vienna. But what next? It would not be so easy to follow him if he chose only to go out secretly at night. What next? To spend the rest of the night watching a lighted window was not enough. Tomorrow night it might not be lighted. But he kept his gaze fixed upon it.

"I must speak to you. I must speak to you!" he found himself saying in a low intense voice. "I am outside here waiting. Listen! I must speak to you!"

He said it many times and kept his eyes fixed upon the window that opened on to the balcony. Once he saw a man's figure cross the room, but he could not be sure who it was. The last distant rumblings of thunder had died away, and the clouds were breaking. It was not long before the dark mountainous billows broke apart, and a brilliant full moon showed herself sailing in the rift, suddenly flooding everything with light. Parts of the garden were silver white, and the tree shadows were like black velvet. A silvery lance pierced even into the hollow of Marco's evergreen and struck across his face.

Perhaps it was this sudden change which attracted the attention of those inside the balconied room. A man's figure appeared at the long windows. Marco saw now that it was the prince. He opened the windows and stepped out on to the balcony.

"It is all over," the prince said quietly. And he stood with his face lifted, looking at the great white sailing moon. He stood very still and seemed for the moment to forget the world and himself. It was a wonderful, triumphant queen of a moon.

But something brought him back to earth. A low, but strong and clear voice came up to him from the garden path below.

"The Lamp is lighted. The Lamp is lighted," it said, and the words sounded almost as if someone were uttering a prayer. They seemed to call to him, to arrest him, to draw him.

He stood still a few seconds in dead silence. Then he bent over the balustrade. The moonlight had not broken the darkness below.

"That is a boy's voice," he said in a low tone, "but I cannot see who is speaking."

"Yes, it is a boy's voice," it answered in a way which somehow moved him, because it was so ardent. "It is the son of Stefan Loristan. The Lamp is lighted."

"Wait. I am coming down to you," the prince said.

In a few minutes Marco heard a door open gently not far from where he stood. Then the man he had been following so many days appeared at his side.

"How long have you been here?" he asked.

"Before the gates closed. I hid myself in the hollow of the big shrub there, Highness," Marco answered.

"Then you were out in the storm?"

"Yes, Highness."

The prince put his hand on the boy's shoulder. "I cannot see you, but it is best to stand in the shadow. You are drenched to the skin."

"I have been able to give your Highness the Sign," Marco whispered. "A storm is nothing."

There was a silence. Marco knew that his companion was pausing to turn something over in his mind.

"So-o?" he said slowly, at length. "The Lamp is lighted, and *you* are sent to bear the Sign." Something in his voice made Marco feel that he was smiling. "What a race you are! What a race—you Samavian Loristans!"

He paused as if to think the thing over again. "I want to see your face," he said next. "Here is a tree with a shaft of moonlight striking through the branches. Let us step aside and stand under it."

Marco did as he was told. The shaft of moonlight fell upon his uplifted face and showed its young strength and darkness, quite splendid for the moment in a triumphant glow of joy in obstacles overcome. Raindrops hung on his hair, but he did not look draggled, only very wet and picturesque. He had reached his man. He had given the Sign.

The prince looked him over with interest. "Yes," he said in his cool, rather dragging voice. "You are the son of Stefan Loristan, and you must be taken care of. You must come with me. I have trained my household to remain in its own quarters until I require its service. I have attached to my own apartments a good safe little room where I sometimes keep people. You can dry your clothes and sleep there. When the gardens are opened again, the rest will be easy."

But though he stepped out from under the trees and began to move towards the palace in the shadow, Marco noticed that he moved hesitatingly, as if he had not quite decided what he should do. He stopped rather suddenly and turned again to Marco, who was following him.

"There is someone in the room I just now left," he said, "an old man whom it might interest to see you. It might also be a good thing for him to feel interest in you. I choose that he shall see you . . . as you are."

"I am at your command, Highness," Marco answered. He knew his companion was smiling again.

"You have been in training for more centuries than you know," he said, "and your father has prepared you to encounter the unexpected without surprise."

They passed under the balcony and paused at a low stone doorway hidden behind shrubs. The door was a beautiful one Marco saw when it was opened, and the corridor disclosed was beautiful also though it had an air of quiet and aloofness which was not so much secret as private. A perfect though narrow staircase mounted from it to the next floor. After ascending it, the prince led the way through a short corridor and stopped at the door at the end of it. "We are going in here," he said.

It was a wonderful room—the one that opened on to the balcony. Each piece of furniture in it, the hangings, the tapestries, and pictures on the wall were all such as might well have found themselves adorning a museum. Marco remembered the common report of his escort's favorite amusement of collecting wonders and furnishing his house with the things others exhibited only as marvels of art and handicraft. The place was rich and mellow with exquisitely chosen beauties.

In a massive chair upon the hearth sat a figure with bent head. It was a tall old man with white hair and moustache. His elbows rested upon the arm of his chair, and he leaned his forehead on his hand as if he were weary.

Marco's companion crossed the room and stood beside him, speaking in a lowered voice. Marco could not at first hear what he said. He himself stood quite still waiting.

The white-haired man lifted his head and listened. It seemed as though almost at once he was singularly interested. The lowered voice was slightly raised at last, and Marco heard the last two sentences: "The only son of Stefan Loristan. Look at him."

The old man in the chair turned slowly and looked steadily and with questioning curiosity touched with grave surprise. He had keen and clear blue eyes.

Then Marco, still erect and silent, waited again. The prince had merely said to him, "an old man whom it might interest to see you." He had plainly intended that, whatever happened, he must make no outward sign of seeing more than he had been told he would see—an old man. It was for him to show no astonishment or recognition. He had been brought here not to see but to be seen. The power of remaining still under scrutiny, which

The Rat had often envied him, stood him now in good stead because he had seen the white head and tall form not many days before in the royal carriage, escorted by banners, and helmets, and following troops whose tramping feet kept time to bursts of military music while the populace bared their heads and cheered.

"He is like his father," this personage said to the prince. "But if anyone but Loristan had sent him . . . His looks please me." Then suddenly to Marco, "You were waiting outside while the storm was going on?"

"Yes, sir," Marco answered.

Then the two exchanged some words still in the lowered voice.

"You read the news as you made your journey?" he was asked. "You know how Samavia stands?"

"She does not stand," said Marco. "The Iarovitch and the Maranovitch have fought as hyenas fight, until each has torn the other into fragments and neither has blood or strength left."

The two glanced at each other.

"A good simile," said the older person. "You are right. If a strong party rose—and a greater power chose not to interfere—the country might see better days." He looked at him a few moments longer and then waved his hand kindly.

"You are a fine Samavian," he said. "I am glad of that. You may go. Good night."

Marco bowed respectfully, and the man with the tired face led him out of the room.

It was just before he left him in the small quiet chamber in which he was to sleep that the prince gave him a final curious glance. "I remember now," he said. "In the room when you answered the question about Samavia, I was sure that I had seen you before. It was the day of the celebration. There was a break in the crowd, and I saw a boy looking at me. It was you."

"Yes," said Marco, "I have followed you each time you have gone out since then, but I could never get near enough to speak. Tonight seemed only one chance in a thousand."

"You are doing your work more like a man than a boy," was the next speech, and it was made reflectively. "No man could have behaved more perfectly than you did just now when discretion and composure were necessary." Then, after a moment's pause, "He was deeply interested and deeply pleased. Good night."

When the gardens had been thrown open the next morning and people were passing in and out again, Marco passed out also. He was obliged to tell himself two or three times that he had not wakened from an amazing dream. He quickened his pace after he had crossed the street, because he wanted to get home to the attic and talk to The Rat. There was a narrow side street that was necessary for him to pass through if he wished to make a shortcut. As he turned into it, he saw a curious figure leaning on crutches against a wall. It looked damp and forlorn, and he wondered if it could be a beggar. It was not. It was The Rat, who suddenly saw who was approaching and swung forward. His face was pale and haggard, and he looked worn and frightened. He dragged off his cap and spoke in a voice that was hoarse as a crow's.

"God be thanked!," he said. *God be thanked!* as people always said it when they received the Sign, alone. But there was a kind of anguish in his voice as well as relief.

"Aide-de-camp!" Marco cried out, for The Rat had begged him to call him so. "What have you been doing? How long have you been here?"

"Ever since I left you last night," said The Rat clutching tremblingly at his arm as if to make sure he was real. "If there was not room for two in the hollow, there was room for one in the street. Was it my place to go off duty and leave you alone? Was it?"

"You were out in the storm?"

"Weren't you?" said The Rat fiercely. "I huddled against the wall as well as I could. What did I care? Crutches don't prevent a fellow waiting. I wouldn't have left you if you'd given me orders. That would have been mutiny. When you did not come out as soon as the gates opened, I felt as if my head got on fire. How could I know what had happened? I've not the nerve and back-bone you have. I go half mad." For a second or so Marco did not answer. But when he put his hand on the damp sleeve, The Rat actually started, because it seemed as though he were looking into the eyes of Stefan Loristan.

"You look just like your father!" he exclaimed in spite of himself. "How tall you are."

"When you are near me," Marco said in Loristan's own voice, "when you are near me, I feel . . . I feel as if I were a royal prince attended by an army. You *are* my army." And he pulled off his cap with quick boyishness and added, "God be thanked."

The sun was warm in the attic window when they reached their lodging, and the two leaned on the rough sill as Marco told his story. It took some time to relate, and when he ended, he took an envelope from his pocket and showed it to The Rat. It contained a flat package of money.

"He gave it to me just before he opened the private door," Marco explained. "And he said to me, 'It will not be long now. After Samavia, go back to London as quickly as you can—*as quickly as you can!*' "

"I wonder what he meant?" The Rat said, slowly. A tremendous thought had shot through his mind. But it was not a thought he could speak of to Marco.

"I cannot tell. I thought that it was for some reason he did not expect me to know," Marco said. "We will do as he told us. As quickly as we can." They looked over the newspapers, as they did every day. All that could be gathered from any of them was that the opposing armies of Samavia seemed each to have reached the culmination of disaster and exhaustion. Which party had the power left to take any final step that could call itself a victory, it was impossible to say. Never had a country been in a more desperate case.

"It is the time," said The Rat, glowering over his map. "If the Secret Party rises suddenly now, it can take Melzarr almost without a blow. It can sweep through the country and disarm both armies.

"They're weakened. They're half starved. They're bleeding to death, They *want* to be disarmed. Only the

Iarovitch and the Maranovitch keep on with the struggle because each is fighting for the power to tax the people and make slaves of them. If the Secret Party does not rise, the people will, and they'll rush on the palaces and kill every Maranovitch and Iarovitch they find. And serve them right!"

"Let us spend the rest of the day in studying the road map again," said Marco. "Tonight we must be on the way to Samavia."

Across the Frontier

26

That one day a week later two tired and travel-worn boy beggars should drag themselves with slow and weary feet across the frontier line between Jiardasia and Samavia was not an incident to awaken suspicion or even to attract attention. War and hunger and anguish had left the country stunned and broken. Since the worst had happened, no one was curious as to what would befall them next. If Jiardasia herself had become a foe, instead of a friendly neighbor, and had sent galloping hordes of soldiery across the border, there would only have been more shrieks, and home burnings, and slaughter which no one dare resist. But so far Jiardasia had remained peaceful.

The two boys—one of them on crutches—had evidently traveled far on foot. Their poor clothes were dusty and travel stained, and they stopped and asked for water at the first hut across the line. The one who walked without crutches had some coarse bread in a bag slung over his shoulder, and they sat on the roadside and ate it as if they were hungry.

The old grandmother who lived alone in the hut sat and stared at them without any curiosity. She may have vaguely wondered why anyone crossed into Samavia in these days. But she did not care to know their reason. Her big son had lived in a village that belonged to the Maranovitch, and he had been called out to fight for his lords. He had not wanted to fight and had not known what the quarrel was about, but he was forced to obey. He had kissed his handsome wife and four sturdy children, crying aloud when he left them. His village and his good crops and his house must be left behind.

Then the Iarovitch swept through the pretty little cluster of homesteads that belonged to their enemy. They were mad with rage because they had met with great losses in a battle not far away, and as they swooped through, they burned and killed, and trampled down fields and vineyards. The old woman's son never saw either the burned walls of his house or the bodies of his wife and children, because he had been killed himself in the battle for which the Iarovitch were revenging themselves. Only the old grandmother who lived in the hut near the frontier line and stared vacantly at the passersby remained alive. She wearily gazed at people and wondered why she did not hear news from her son and her grandchildren. But that was all.

When the boys were over the frontier and well on their way along the roads, it was not difficult to keep out of sight if it seemed necessary. The country was mountainous, and there were deep and thick forests by the way—forests so far-reaching and with such thick undergrowth that full-grown men could easily have hidden themselves. It was because of this perhaps, that this part of the country had seen little fighting. There was too great opportunity for secure ambush for a foe. As the two travelers went on, they heard of burned villages and towns destroyed, but they were towns and villages nearer Melzarr and other fortress-defended cities, or they were in the country surrounding the castles and estates of powerful nobles and leaders. It was true, as Marco had said to the white-haired man, that the Maranovitch and Iarovitch had fought with the savageness of hyenas until at last the forces of each side lay torn and bleeding, their strength, their resources, their supplies exhausted.

Each day left the country weaker and more desperate. Europe looked on with small interest in either party but with growing desire that the disorder should end and cease to interfere with commerce. All this and much more Marco and The Rat knew, but as they made their cautious way through byways of the maimed and tortured little country, they learned other things. They learned that the stories of its beauty and fertility were not romances. The two boys traveled through forest and woodland when it was possible to leave the road. It was safe to thread a way among huge trees and tall ferns and young saplings. It was not always easy, but it was safe.

Sometimes they saw a charcoal burner's hut or a shelter where a shepherd was hiding with the few sheep left to him. Each man they met wore the same look of stony suffering in his face, but when the boys begged for bread and water as was their habit, no one refused to share the little he had. It soon became plain to them that they were thought to be two young fugitives whose homes had probably been destroyed and who were wandering about with no thought but that of finding safety until the worst was over. That one of them traveled on crutches added to their apparent helplessness, and that he could not speak the language of the country made him more an object of pity. The peasants did not know what language he spoke. Sometimes a foreigner came to find work in this small town or that. The poor lad might have come to the country with his father and mother and then have been caught in the whirlpool of war and tossed out on the world parentless. But no one asked questions. Even in their desolation they were silent and noble people who were too courteous for curiosity.

"In the old days they were simple and stately and kind. All doors were open to travelers. The master of the poorest hut uttered a blessing and a welcome when a stranger crossed his threshold. It was the custom of the country," Marco said. "I read about it in a book of my father's. Above most of the doors the welcome was carved in stone. It was this—'The Blessing of the Son of God, and Rest within these Walls.' "

"They are big and strong," said The Rat. "And they have good faces. They carry themselves as if they had been drilled—both men and women."

It was not through the blood-drenched part of the unhappy land their way led them, but they saw hunger and dread in the villages they passed. Crops which should have fed the people had been taken for the use of the army. Flocks and herds had been driven away, and faces were gaunt and gray. Those who had as yet lost only crops and herds knew that homes and lives might be torn from them at any moment. Old men and women and children were left to wait for any fate that the war might deal out to them.

When they were given food from some poor store, Marco would offer a little money in return. He dare not excite suspicion by offering much. He was obliged to let it be imagined that in his flight from his ruined home he had been able to snatch at and secrete some poor hoard which might save him from starvation. Often the women would not take what he offered.

The journey was a hard and hungry one. They must make it all on foot, and there was little food to be found, but each of them knew how to live on scant fare. They traveled mostly by night and slept among the ferns and undergrowth through the day. They drank from running brooks and bathed in them. Moss and ferns made soft and sweet-smelling beds, and trees roofed them. Sometimes they lay long and talked while they rested. A day came when they knew they were nearing their journey's end.

"It is nearly over now," Marco said after they had thrown themselves down in the forest in the early hours of one dewy morning. "He said 'After Samavia, go back to London as quickly as you can—*as quickly as you can.*' He said it twice. As if something were going to happen."

"Perhaps it will happen more suddenly than we think. The thing he meant," answered The Rat.

Suddenly he sat up on his elbow and leaned towards Marco. "We are in Samavia!" he said "We two are in Samavia! And we are near the end."

Marco rose on his elbow also. He was very thin as a result of hard travel and scant feeding. His thinness made his eyes look immense and black as pits, but they burned and were beautiful with their own fire.

"Yes," he said, breathing quickly. "And though we do not know what the end will be, we have obeyed orders. The prince was next to the last one. There is only one more. The old doctor."

"I have wanted to see him more than I have wanted to see any of the others," The Rat said.

"So have I," Marco answered. "His house is built on the side of this mountain. I wonder what he will say to us."

Both had the same reason for wanting to see him. In his youth he had served in the clinic over the frontier—the one that, till it was destroyed in a revolt, had treasured the five-hundred-year-old story of the beautiful royal lad brought to be hidden by the ancient shepherd. But the clinic had been burned, and the young man had in later years crossed the frontier and become the doctor of a few mountaineers. He had worked hard and faithfully and was respected by the people. Only the secret Forgers of the Sword knew that his most ardent followers were those whom he visited in dark caverns under the earth, where arms were piled high, and men with dark strong faces sat together in the dim light and laid plans and wrought schemes.

This Marco and The Rat did not know as they talked of their desire to see him.

"He may not choose to tell us anything," said Marco. "When we have given him the Sign, he may turn away and say nothing as some of the others did. He may have nothing to say that we should hear. Silence may be the order for him too."

It would not be a long or dangerous climb to the little house on the mountainside. They could sleep or rest all day and begin it at twilight. So after they had talked of the old doctor and had eaten their black bread, they settled themselves to sleep under cover of the thick tall ferns.

It was a long and deep sleep that nothing disturbed. So few human beings ever climbed the hill, except by the narrow rough path leading to the church, that the little wild creatures had not learned to be afraid of them. Once during the afternoon, a hare stopped by Marco's head and after looking at him a few seconds with his lustrous eyes began to nibble the ends of his hair. He only did it from curiosity and because he wondered if it might be a new kind of grass, but he did not like it and stopped nibbling almost at once, and then hopped away to attend to his own affairs.

A very large and handsome green stag beetle crawled from one end of The Rat's crutches to the other, but having done it, he went away also. Two or three times a bird, searching for his dinner under the ferns, was surprised to find the two sleeping figures, but as they lay so quietly, there seemed nothing to be frightened about. A beautiful little field mouse running past discovered that there were crumbs lying about and ate all she could find on the moss. After that she crept into Marco's pocket and found some excellent crumbs and had quite a feast. But she disturbed nobody, and the boys slept on.

It was a bird's evening song that awakened them both. The bird alighted on the branch of a tree near them, and her trill was rippling clear and sweet. The evening air had freshened and was fragrant with hillside scents. When Marco first rolled over and opened his eyes, he thought the most delicious thing on earth was to waken from sleep on a hillside at evening and hear a bird singing. It seemed to make exquisitely real to him the fact that he was in Samavia, that the Lamp was lighted and his work was nearly done. The Rat awakened when he did, and for a few minutes both lay on their backs without speaking. At last Marco said, "The stars are coming out. We can begin to climb, aide-de-camp."

Then they both got up and looked at each other.

"The *last one*!" The Rat said. "Tomorrow we shall be on our way back to London. Number 7 Philibert Place. After all the places we've been to—what will it look like?"

"It will be like wakening out of a dream," said Marco. "It's not beautiful—Philibert Place. But *he* will be there." And it was as if a light lighted itself in his face and shone through the very darkness of it.

And The Rat's face lighted in almost exactly the same way. He pulled off his cap and stood bare headed. "We've obeyed orders," he said. "We've not forgotten one. No one has noticed us; no one has thought of us. We've blown through the countries as if we had been grains of dust."

Marco's head was bared too, and his face was still shining. "God be thanked," he said. "Let us begin to climb."

They pushed their way through the ferns and wandered in and out through trees until they found the little path. The hill was thickly clothed with forest, and the little path was sometimes dark and steep; but they knew that if they followed it, they would at last come out to a place where there were scarcely any trees at all, and on a crag they would find the tiny house waiting for them. The doctor might not be there. They might have to wait for him, but he would be sure to come back from visiting wherever he wandered between times.

There were many stars in the sky when at last a turn of the path showed them the house above them. It was little and built of rough stone. It looked as if the doctor himself might have broken and carried or rolled bits of the hill to put it together. It had the small, round summit the Turks had brought into Europe in centuries past. The two boys stopped on the path to look at it.

"There is a candle burning in one of the little windows," said Marco.

"There is a well near the door, and someone is beginning to draw water," said The Rat next. "It is too dark to see who it is. Listen."

They listened and heard the bucket descend on the chains and splash in the water. Then it was drawn up, and it seemed someone drank long. Then they saw a dim figure move forward and stand still. Then they heard a voice begin to pray aloud, as if the owner, being accustomed to utter solitude, did not think of earthly hearers.

"Come," Marco said. And they went forward.

Because the stars were so many and the air so clear, the doctor heard their feet on the path and saw them almost as soon as he heard them. He ended his prayer and watched them coming. A lad on crutches, who moved as lightly and easily as a bird, and a lad who, even yards away, was noticeable for a bearing of his body that was neither haughty nor proud but set him somehow aloof from every other lad one had ever seen. A magnificent lad though. As he drew near, the starlight showed his face thin and his eyes hollow as if with fatigue or hunger.

"And who is this one?" the old doctor murmured to himself. "Who?"

Marco drew up before him and bowed respectfully. Then he lifted his black head, squared his shoulders and uttered his message for the last time.

"The Lamp is lighted, sir," he said. "The Lamp is lighted."

The old doctor stood quite still and gazed into his face. The next moment he bent his head so that he could look at him closely. It seemed almost as if he were frightened and wanted to make sure of something. At the moment it flashed through The Rat's mind that the old, old woman on the mountaintop had looked frightened in quite the same way.

"I am an old man," he said. "My eyes are not good. If I had a light . . ." He glanced towards the house.

It was The Rat who with one whirl swung through the door and seized the candle. He guessed what he wanted. He held it himself so that the flare fell on Marco's face.

The old doctor drew nearer. He gasped for breath. "You are the son of Stefan Loristan!" he cried. "It is *his son* who brings the Sign."

He fell upon his knees and hid his face in his hands. Both the boys heard him sobbing and praying—praying and sobbing at once.

They glanced at each other. The Rat was bursting with excitement, but he felt a little awkward also and wondered what Marco would do. An old fellow on his knees crying made a chap feel as if he didn't know what to say. Must you comfort him or must you let him go on?

Marco only stood quite still and looked at him with understanding and gravity.

"Yes, sir," he said. "I am the son of Stefan Loristan, and I have given the Sign to all. You are the last one. The Lamp is lighted. I could weep for gladness too."

The doctor's tears and prayers ended. He rose to his feet—a rugged-faced old man with long and thick white hair that fell on his shoulders—and smiled at Marco while his eyes were still wet.

"You have passed from one country to another with the message?" he said. "You were under orders to say those four words?"

"Yes, sir," answered Marco.

"That was all? You were to say no more?"

"I know no more. Silence has been the order since I took my oath of allegiance when I was a child. I was not old enough to fight, or serve, or reason about great things. All I could do was to be silent and to train myself to remember and be ready when I was called. When my father saw I was ready, he trusted me to go out and give the Sign. He told me the four words. Nothing else."

The old man watched him with a wondering face. "If Stefan Loristan does not know best," he said, "who does?"

"He always knows," answered Marco proudly. "Always." He waved his hand like a young king toward The Rat. He wanted each man they met to understand the value of The Rat. "He chose for me this companion," he added. "I have done nothing alone."

"He let me call myself his aide-de-camp," burst out The Rat. "I would be cut into inch long strips for him."

Marco translated.

Then the doctor looked at The Rat and slowly nodded his head. "Yes," he said. "He knew best. He always knows best. That I see."

"How did you know I was my father's son?" asked Marco. "You have seen him?"

"No," was the answer, "but I have seen a picture that is said to be his image. And you are the picture's self. It is indeed a strange thing that two of God's creatures should be so alike. There is a purpose in it." He led them into his bare small house and made them rest, and drink goat's milk, and eat food. As he moved about the hutlike place, there was a mysterious and exalted look on his face.

"You must be refreshed before we leave here," he said at last. "I am going to take you to a place hidden in the mountains where there are men whose hearts will leap at the sight of you. To see you will give them new power and courage and new resolve. Tonight they meet as they or their ancestors have met for centuries, but now they are nearing the end of their waiting. And I shall bring them the son of Stefan Loristan, who is the Bearer of the Sign!"

They ate the bread and cheese and drank the goat's milk he gave them, but Marco explained that they did not need rest as they had slept all day. They were prepared to follow him when he was ready.

The last faint hint of twilight had died into night, and the stars were at their thickest when they set out together. The white-haired old man took a thick knotted staff in his hand and led the way. He knew it well, though it was a rugged and steep one with no track to mark it. Sometimes they seemed to be walking around the mountain, sometimes they were climbing, sometimes they dragged themselves over rocks or fallen trees or struggled through almost impassable thickets. The Rat was called upon to use all his prowess, and sometimes Marco and the doctor helped him across obstacles with the aid of his crutch.

"Haven't I shown tonight whether I'm a cripple or not?" he said once to Marco. "You can tell *him* about this, can't you? And that the crutches helped instead of being in the way?"

They had been out nearly two hours when they came to a place where the undergrowth was thick and a huge tree had fallen crashing down among it in some storm.

Not far from the tree was an outcropping rock. Only the top of it was to be seen above the heavy tangle.

They had pushed their way through the jungle of bushes and young saplings led by their companion. They did not know where they would be led next and were supposed to push forward further when the doctor stopped by the outcropping rock. He stood silent a few minutes—quite motionless—as if he were listening to the forest and the night. But there was utter stillness. There was not even a breeze to stir a leaf, or a half-wakened bird to sleepily chirp.

He struck the rock with his staff—twice, and then twice again.

Marco and The Rat stood with bated breath.

They did not wait long. Presently each of them found himself leaning forward, staring with almost unbelieving eyes, not at the doctor or his staff, but at the rock itself!

It was moving. Yes, it moved. The doctor stepped aside, and it slowly turned, as if worked by a lever. As it turned, it gradually revealed a chasm of darkness dimly lighted, and the doctor spoke to Marco. "There are hiding places like this all through Samavia," he said. "Patience and misery have waited long in them. They are the caverns of the Forgers of the Sword. Come."

The Forgers
of the Sword

27

Many times since their journey had begun the boys had found their hearts beating with the thrill and excitement of things. The story of which their lives had been a part was a pulse-quickening experience. But as they carefully made their way down the steep steps leading seemingly into the bowels of the earth, both Marco and The Rat felt as though the old doctor must hear the thudding in their young sides.

"*The Forgers of the Sword.* Remember every word they say," The Rat whispered, "so that you can tell it to me afterwards. Don't forget anything. I wish I knew Samavian."

At the foot of the steps stood the man who was evidently the sentinel who worked the lever that turned the rock. He was a big burly peasant with a good watchful face, and the doctor greeted him as he took from him the lantern he held out.

They went through a narrow and dark passage, and down some more steps, and turned a corner into another corridor cut out of rock and earth. It was a wider corridor, but still dark so that Marco and The Rat had walked some yards before their eyes became sufficiently accustomed to the dim light to see that the walls themselves seemed made of arms stacked closely together.

"The Forgers of the Sword," The Rat was unconsciously mumbling to himself. "The Forgers of the Sword."

It must have taken years to cut out the rounding passage they threaded their way through, and longer years to forge the solid, bristling walls. But The Rat remembered the story the stranger had told his drunken father, of the few mountain herdsmen who in their savage grief and wrath over the loss of their prince had banded themselves together with a solemn oath that had been handed down from generation to generation. The Samavians were a long-memoried people, and the fact that their passion must be smothered had made it burn all the more fiercely. Five hundred years ago they had first sworn their oath; and kings had come and gone, had died or been murdered, and dynasties had changed, but the Forgers of the Sword had not changed or forgotten their oath or wavered in their belief that some time—some time, even after the long dark years—the soul of their Lost Prince would be among them once more. For the last hundred years their number and power and their hiding places had so increased that Samavia was at last honeycombed with them. And they only waited, breathless . . . for the Lighting of the Lamp.

The old doctor knew what he was bringing them. Marco and The Rat in spite of their fond imaginings were not quite old enough to know how fierce and full of flaming eagerness the breathless waiting of savage full-grown men could be. But there was a tense thrill in knowing that they were being led in as the Bearers of the Sign. The Rat went hot and cold; he gnawed his fingers as he went. He could almost have shrieked aloud in the intensity of his excitement when the old doctor stopped before a big black door.

Marco made no sound. Excitement or danger always made him look tall and quite pale. He looked both now.

The doctor touched the door, and it opened.

They were looking into an immense cavern. Its walls and roof were lined with arms—guns, swords, bayonets, javelins, daggers, pistols, and every weapon a desperate man might use. The place was full of men, who turned towards the door when it opened. They all greeted the doctor, but Marco realized almost at the same instant that they were startled seeing that he was not alone.

They were a strange and picturesque crowd as they stood under their canopy of weapons in the lurid torchlight. Marco saw at once that they were men of all classes, though all were roughly dressed. They were huge mountaineers and plainsmen young and old. Some of the biggest were men with white hair but with bodies of giants and with determination in their strong jaws. There were many of these, Marco saw, and in each man's eyes, whether he were young or old, glowed a steady unconquered flame. They had been beaten so often, they had been oppressed and robbed, but in the eyes of each one was this unconquered flame that throughout all the long tragedy of years had been handed down from father to son. It was this which had gone on through centuries, keeping its oath and forging its swords in the caverns of the earth, and that today was waiting.

The old doctor laid his hand on Marco's shoulder and gently pushed him through the crowd that parted to make way for them. He did not stop until the two stood in the very midst of the circle, which fell back gazing wonderingly. Marco looked up at the old man because for several seconds he did not speak. It was plain that he did not speak because he also was excited, and could not. He opened his lips, and his voice seemed to fail him. Then he tried again and spoke so that all could hear—even the men at the back of the gazing circle.

"My friends," he said, "this is the son of Stefan Loristan, and he comes to bear the Sign. My son," he said to Marco, "speak."

Then Marco understood what he wished and also what he felt. He felt it himself, that magnificent uplifting gladness as he spoke, holding his black head high and lifting his right hand.

"The Lamp is lighted, brothers!" he cried. "The Lamp is lighted!"

Then The Rat, who stood apart watching, thought that the strange world within the cavern had gone mad! Wild smothered cries broke forth, men caught each other in embraces, they fell upon their knees, they clutched one another sobbing, they wrung each other's hands, and they leaped into the air. It was as if they could not bear the joy of hearing that the end of their waiting had come at last. They rushed upon Marco and fell at his feet. The Rat saw big peasants kissing his shoes, his hands, every scrap of his clothing they could seize. The wild circle swayed and closed upon him until The Rat was afraid. He did not know that overpowered by this frenzy of emotion, his own excitement was making him shake from head to foot like a leaf, and that tears were streaming down his cheeks. The swaying crowd hid Marco from him, and he began to fight his way towards him because his excitement increased with fear. The frenzied crowd of men seemed for the moment to have almost ceased to be sane. Marco was only a boy. They did not know how fiercely they were pressing upon him and keeping away the very air.

"Don't kill him! Don't kill him!" yelled The Rat, struggling forward. "Stand back, you fools! I'm his aide-de-camp! Let me pass!"

And though no one understood his English, one or two suddenly remembered they had seen him enter with the doctor and so gave way. But just then the old doctor lifted his hand above the crowd and spoke in a voice of stern command.

"Stand back, my friends!" he cried. "Madness is not the homage you must bring to the son of Stefan Loristan. Obey! Obey!" His voice had a power in it that penetrated even the wildest herdsmen. The frenzied mass swayed back and left space about Marco, whose face The Rat could at last see. It was very white with emotion, and in his eyes there was a look that was like awe.

The Rat pushed forward until he stood beside him. He did not know that he almost sobbed as he spoke.

"I'm your aide-de-camp," he said. "I'm going to stand here. Your father sent me! I'm under orders! I thought they'd crush you to death."

He glared at the circle about them as if instead of friends distraught with excitement, they had been enemies. The old doctor seeing him, touched Marco's arm.

"Tell him he need not fear," he said. "It was only for the first few moments. The passion of their souls drove them wild. They are your servants."

"Those at the back might have pushed the front ones on until they trampled you under foot in spite of themselves," The Rat persisted.

"No," said Marco. "They would have stopped if I had spoken."

"Why didn't you speak then?" snapped The Rat.

"All they felt was for Samavia and for my father," Marco said, "and for the Sign. I felt as they did."

The Rat was somewhat softened. It was true after all. How could he have tried to quell the outbursts of their honor for Loristan, of the country he was saving for them, of the Sign that called them to freedom? He could not.

Then followed a strange and picturesque scene. The doctor went about among the encircling crowd and spoke to one man after another—sometimes to a group. A larger circle was formed. As the pale old man moved about, The Rat felt as if some ceremony were going to be performed. Watching it from first to last, he was thrilled to the core.

At the end of the cavern a block of stone had been cut out to look like a platform. It was covered with white, and against the wall above it hung a large picture veiled by a curtain. From the roof there swung before it an ancient lamp of metal suspended by chains. There the doctor asked Marco to stand with his aide-de-camp on the lower level in attendance. A knot of the biggest herdsmen went out and returned. Each carried a huge sword that had perhaps been of the earliest made in the dark days gone by. The bearers formed themselves into a line on either side of Marco. They raised their swords and formed a pointed arch above his head and a passage twelve-men long.

When the points first clashed together, The Rat struck himself hard upon his breast. His exultation was too keen to endure. He gazed at Marco standing still in that curiously splendid way that both he and his father *could* stand still and wondered how he could do it. He looked as if he were prepared for any strange thing that could happen to him, because he was *under orders.* The Rat knew that Marco was doing whatever he did merely for his father's sake. It was as if he felt that he was representing his father, though he was a mere boy, and that because of this, boy as he was, he must bear himself nobly and remain outwardly undisturbed.

At the end of the arch of swords, the old doctor stood and gave a sign to one man after another. When the sign was given to a man, he walked under the arch to the platform, and there knelt, and lifting Marco's hand to his lips, kissed it with passionate fervor. Then he returned to the place he had left. One after another passed up the aisle of swords, one after another knelt, and one after the other kissed the young brown hand, rose and went away. Sometimes The Rat heard a few words which sounded almost like a murmured prayer; sometimes he heard a sob as a shaggy head bent; again and again he saw eyes wet with tears. Once or twice Marco spoke a few Samavian words, and the face of the man spoken to flamed with joy. The Rat had time to see as Marco had seen that many of the faces were not those of peasants. Some of them were clear cut and subtle and of the type of scholars or nobles. It took a long time for them all to kneel and kiss the lad's hand, but no man omitted the ceremony. When at last it was at an end, a strange silence filled the cavern. They stood and gazed at each other with burning eyes.

The doctor moved to Marco's side and stood near the platform. He leaned forward and took in his hand a cord that hung from the veiled picture. He drew it and the curtain fell apart. There seemed to stand gazing at them from between its folds a tall kingly youth with deep eyes in which the stars of God were shining and with a smile wonderful to behold. Around the heavy locks of his black hair, the long dead painter had set a faint glow of light.

"Son of Stefan Loristan," the old doctor said, in a shaken voice, "it is the Lost Prince! It is Ivor!"

Then every man in the room fell on his knees. Even the men who had upheld the archway of swords dropped their weapons with a crash and knelt also. He was their hero—this boy. Dead for five hundred years, he was their hero still.

"Ivor! Ivor!" the voices broke into a heavy murmur. "Ivor! Ivor!" as if they chanted a chorus.

Marco started forward, staring at the picture, his breath caught in his throat, his lips apart.

"But . . . but . . ." he stammered, "but if my father were as young as he is—he would be *like* him!"

"When you are as old as he is, *you* will be like him. *You!*" said the doctor. And he let the curtain fall.

The Rat stood staring with wide eyes from Marco to the picture and from the picture to Marco. And he breathed faster and faster and gnawed his finger ends. But he did not utter a word. He could not have done it, if he tried.

Then Marco stepped down from the platform as if he were in a dream, and the old man followed him. The men with swords sprang to their feet and made their archway again with a new clash of steel. The old man and the boy passed under it together. Now every man's eyes were fixed on Marco. At the heavy door by which he had entered, he stopped and turned to meet their glances. He looked very young and thin and pale, but suddenly his father's smile was lighted in his face. He said a few words in Samavian clearly and gravely, saluted, and walked out.

"What did you say to them?" gasped The Rat, stumbling after him as the door closed behind them and shut in the murmur of impassioned sound.

"There was only one thing to say," was the answer. "They are men. I am only a boy. I thanked them for my father, and told them he would never—never forget."

Extra! Extra! Extra!

28

It was raining in London. Pouring. It had been raining for two weeks more or less, generally more. When the train from Dover drew in at Charing Cross, the weather seemed suddenly to have considered that it had so far been too lenient and must express itself much more vigorously. So it had gathered together its resources and poured them forth in a deluge that surprised even Londoners.

The rain so beat against and streamed down the windows of the third-class carriage in which Marco and The Rat sat that they could not see through them.

They had made their homeward journey much more rapidly than they had made the one on which they had been outward bound. It had of course taken them some time to tramp back to the frontier, but there had been no reason for stopping anywhere after they had once reached the railroads. They had been tired sometimes, but they had slept heavily on the wooden seats of the railway carriages. Their one desire was to get home. Number 7 Philibert Place rose before them in its noisy dinginess as the one desirable spot on earth. To Marco it held his father.

And it was Loristan alone that The Rat saw when he thought of it. Loristan as he would look when he saw him come into the room with Marco, and stand up and salute, and say, "I have brought him back, sir. He has carried out every single order you gave him. Every single one. So have I."

And so he had. He had been sent as a companion and attendant, and he had been faithful in every thought. If Marco had allowed him, he would have waited upon him like a servant and have been proud of the service. But Marco would never let him forget that they were only two boys and that one was of no more importance than the other.

He had secretly even felt this attitude to be a sort of grievance. It would have been more like a game if one of them had been the mere servant of the other, and if that other had blustered a little and issued commands. If the faithful vassal could have been wounded or cast into a dungeon for his young commander's sake, the adventure would have been more complete. But though their journey had been full of wonders and rich with beauties, though the memory of it hung in The Rat's mind like a background of tapestry embroidered in all the hues of the earth with all the splendors of it, there had been no dungeons and no wounds. After the adventure in Munich their unimportant boyishness had not even been observed by such perils as might have threatened them. As The Rat had said, they had "blown like grains of dust" through Europe and had been as nothing. And this was what Loristan had planned. This was what his grave thought had wrought out. If they had been men, they would not have been so safe.

From the time they had left the old doctor on the hillside to begin their journey back to the frontier, they both had been given to long silences as they tramped side by side or lay on the moss in the forests. Now that their work was done, a sort of reaction had set in. There were no more plans to be made and no more uncertainties to contemplate. They were on their way back to Number 7 Philibert Place—Marco to his father, The Rat to the man he adored. Each of them was thinking of many things.

Marco was full of longing to see his father's face and hear his voice again. He wanted to feel the pressure of his hand on his shoulder—to be sure that he was real and not a dream. This last was because during this homeward journey everything that had happened often seemed to be a dream. It had all been so wonderful! Now that they were left behind, they all seemed like things he had dreamed. But he had not dreamed them. He was going back to tell his father about them. And how _good_ it would be to feel his hand on his shoulder!

The Rat gnawed his finger ends a great deal. His thoughts were more wild and feverish than Marco's. They leaped forward in spite of him. It was no use to pull himself up and tell himself that he was a fool. Now that all was over, he had time to be as great a fool as he was inclined to be. But how he longed to reach London and stand face to face with Loristan. The Sign was given. The Lamp was lighted. What would happen next? His crutches were under his arms before the train drew up.

"We're there! We're there!" he cried restlessly to Marco. They had no luggage to delay them. They took their bags and followed the crowd along the platform. The rain was rattling like bullets against the high-glassed roof. People turned to look at Marco, seeing the glow of exultant eagerness in his face. They thought he must be some boy coming home for the holidays and going to make a visit at a place he delighted in. The rain was dancing on the pavements when they reached the entrance.

"A cab won't cost much," Marco said, "and it will take us quickly."

They called one and got into it. Each of them had flushed cheeks, and Marco's eyes looked as if he were gazing at something a long way off—gazing at it and wondering.

"We've come back," said The Rat, in an unsteady voice. "We've been. And we've come back." Then suddenly he turned to look at Marco. "Does it ever seem to you as if, perhaps, it . . . it wasn't true?"

"Yes," Marco answered, "but it was true. And it's done." Then he added after a second or so of silence, just what The Rat had said to himself, "What next?" He said it very low.

The way to Philibert Place was not long. When they turned into the roaring, untidy road where the busses and carts struggled past each other with their loads, and the tired-faced people hurried in crowds along the pavement, they looked at them all feeling that they had left their dream far behind indeed. But they were at home.

It was a good thing to see Lazarus open the door and stand waiting before they had time to get out of the cab. Cabs stopped so seldom before houses in Philibert Place that the inhabitants were always prompt to open their doors. When Lazarus had seen this one stop at the broken iron gate, he had known whom it brought. He had kept an eye on the windows faithfully for many a day, even when he knew that it was too soon—even if all was well—for any travelers to return.

He bore himself with an air more than usually military and his salute when Marco crossed the threshold was formal stateliness itself. But his greeting burst from his heart.

"God be thanked!" he said in his deep growl of joy. "God be thanked!"

When Marco put forth his hand, he bent his grizzled head and kissed it devoutly.

"God be thanked!" he said again.

"My father?" Marco began, "my father is out?" If he had been in the house, he knew he would not have stayed in the back sitting room.

"Sir," said Lazarus, "will you come with me into his room? You, too, sir," to The Rat. He had never said "sir" to him before.

He opened the door of the familiar room, and the boys entered. The room was empty.

Marco did not speak; neither did The Rat. They both stood still in the middle of the shabby carpet and looked up at the old soldier. Both had suddenly the same feeling that the earth had dropped from beneath their feet. Lazarus saw it and spoke fast and with tremor. He was almost as agitated as they were.

"He left me at your service—at your command," he began.

"Left you?" said Marco.

"He left us, all three, under orders . . . to *wait*," said Lazarus. "The master has gone."

The Rat felt something hot rush into his eyes. He brushed it away that he might look at Marco's face. The shock had changed it very much. Its glowing eager joy had died out; it had turned paler and his brows were drawn together. For a few seconds he did not speak at all, and when he did speak, The Rat knew that his voice was steady only because he willed that it should be so.

"If he has gone," he said, "it is because he had a strong reason. It was because he also was under orders."

"He said that you would know that," Lazarus answered. "He was called in such haste that he had not a moment in which to do more than write a few words. He left them for you on his desk there."

Marco walked over to the desk and opened the envelope that was lying there. There were only a few lines on the sheet of paper inside and they had evidently been written in the greatest haste. They were these: "The Life of my life—for Samavia."

"He was called . . . to Samavia," Marco said, and the thought sent his blood rushing through his veins. "He has gone to Samavia."

Lazarus drew his hand roughly across his eyes, and his voice shook and sounded hoarse.

"There has been great disaffection in the camps of the Maranovitch," he said. "The remnant of the army has gone mad. Sir, silence is still the order, but who knows? Who knows? God alone."

He had not finished speaking before he turned his head as if listening to sounds in the road. They were the kind of sounds that had broken up The Squad and sent it rushing down the passage into the street to seize on a newspaper. There was to be heard a commotion of newsboys shouting riotously some startling piece of news that had called out an "Extra."

The Rat heard it first and dashed to the front door. As he opened it, a newsboy running by shouted at the topmost power of his lungs the news he had to sell. "Assassination of King Michael Maranovitch by his own soldiers! Assassination of the Maranovitch! Extra! Extra! Extra!"

When The Rat returned with a newspaper, Lazarus interposed himself between him and Marco with great and respectful ceremony. "Sir," he said to Marco, "I am at your command, but the master left me with an order that I was to repeat to you. He requested you *not* to read the newspapers until he himself could see you again."

Both boys fell back.

"Not read the papers!" they exclaimed together.

Lazarus had never before been quite so reverential and ceremonious.

"Your pardon, sir," he said. "I may read them at your orders and report such things as it is well that you should know. There have been dark tales told, and there may be darker ones. He asked that you would not read for yourself. If you meet again—when you meet again," he corrected himself hastily, "when you meet again, he says you will understand. I am your servant. I will read and answer all such questions as I can."

The Rat handed him the paper, and they returned to the back room together.

"You shall tell us what he would wish us to hear," Marco said.

The news was soon told. The story was not a long one, as exact details had not yet reached London. It was briefly that the head of the Maranovitch party had been put to death by infuriated soldiers of his own army. It was an army drawn chiefly from a peasantry that did not love its leaders or wish to fight, and suffering and brutal treatment had at last roused it to furious revolt.

"What next?" said Marco.

"If I were a Samavian," began The Rat, and then he stopped.

Lazarus stood biting his lips, but staring stonily at the carpet. Not The Rat alone but Marco also noted a grim change in him. It was grim because it suggested that he was holding himself under an iron control. It was as if while tortured by anxiety he had sworn not to allow himself to look anxious, and the resolve set his jaw hard and carved new lines in his rugged face. Each boy thought this in secret, but did not wish to put it into words. If he was anxious, he could only be so for one reason, and each realized what the reason must be. Loristan had gone to Samavia—to the torn and bleeding country filled with riot and danger. If he had gone, it could only have been because its danger called him, and he went to face it at its worst. Lazarus had been left behind to watch over them. Silence was still the order, and what he knew he could not tell them, and perhaps he knew little more than that a great life might be lost.

Because his master was absent, the old soldier seemed to feel that he must comfort himself with a greater ceremonial reverence than he had ever shown before. He held himself within call and at Marco's orders, as it had been his custom to hold himself with regard to Loristan. The ceremonious service even extended itself to The Rat, who appeared to have taken a new place in his mind. He also seemed now to be a person to be waited upon and replied to with dignity and formal respect.

When the evening meal was served, Lazarus drew out Loristan's chair at the head of the table and stood behind it with a majestic air.

"Sir," he said to Marco, "the master requested that you take his seat at the table until . . . while he is not with you."

Marco took the seat in silence.

At two o'clock in the morning, when the roaring road was still, the light from the streetlamp shining into the small bedroom fell on two pale boy faces. The Rat sat up on his sofa bed in the old way with his hands clasped round his knees. Marco lay flat on his hard pillow. Neither of them had been to sleep, and yet they had not talked a great deal. Each had secretly guessed a good deal of what the other did not say.

"There is one thing we must remember," Marco had said early in the night. "We must not be afraid."

"No," answered The Rat, almost fiercely, "we must not be afraid."

"We are tired. We came back expecting to be able to tell it all to him. We have always been looking forward to that. We never thought once that he might be gone. But he *was* gone. Did you feel as if," he turned towards the sofa, "as if something had struck you on the chest?"

"Yes," The Rat answered heavily. "Yes."

"We weren't ready," said Marco. "He had never gone before, but we ought to have known he might someday be . . . called. He went because he was called. He told us to wait. We don't know what we are waiting for, but we know that we must not be afraid."

The Rat lifted his head and looked at the bed sideways. "Did you think," he said slowly, "did you *ever* think that perhaps he knew where the descendant of the Lost Prince was?"

Marco answered even more slowly. "If anyone knew, surely he might. He has known so much," he said.

"Listen to this," broke forth The Rat. "I believe he has gone to tell the people. If he does, if he could show them, all the country would run mad with joy. It would not be only the Secret Party. All Samavia would rise and follow any flag he chose to raise. They've prayed for the Lost Prince for five hundred years, and if they believed they'd got him once more, they'd fight like madmen for him. But there would not be anyone to fight. They'd all want the same thing. If they could see the man with Ivor's blood in his veins, they'd feel he had come back to them. They'd believe it!"

He beat his fists together in his frenzy of excitement. "It's the time! It's the time!" he cried. "No man could let such a chance go by! He must tell them. He must. That *must* be what he's gone for. He knows. He's always known!" And he threw himself back on his sofa and flung his arms over his face, lying there panting.

"If it is the time," said Marco in a low, strained voice, "if it is, and he knows, he will tell them." And he threw his arms up over his own face and lay quite still.

Neither of them said another word, and the street-lamp shone in on them as if it were waiting for something to happen. But nothing happened. In time they were asleep.

'Twixt Night
and Morning

29

After this, they waited. They did not know what they waited for, nor could they guess even vaguely how the waiting would end. All that Lazarus could tell them he told. He would have been willing to stand respectfully for hours relating to Marco the story of how the period of their absence had passed for his Master and himself. He told how Loristan had spoken each day of his son, how he had often been pale with anxiousness, how in the evenings he had walked to and fro in his room deep in thought as he looked down unseeingly at the carpet.

"He permitted me to talk of you, sir," Lazarus said. "I saw that he wished to hear your name often. I reminded him of the times when you had been so young that most children of your age would have been in the hands of nurses, and yet you were strong and silent and sturdy and traveled with us as if you were not a child at all—never crying when you were tired and were not properly fed. As if you understood . . . as if you understood," he added proudly. "If through the power of God a creature can be a man at six years old, you were that one. Many a dark day I have looked into your solemn, watching eyes and have been half afraid because that a child should answer one's gaze so gravely seemed almost an unearthly thing."

"The chief thing I remember of those days," said Marco, "is that he was with me and that whenever I was hungry or tired, I knew he must be too."

The feeling that they were just *waiting* was so intense that it filled the days with strangeness. When the postman's knock was heard at the door, each of them endeavored not to start. A letter might some day come that would tell them—they did not know what. But no letters came. When they went out into the streets, they found themselves hurrying on their way back in spite of themselves. Something might have happened. Lazarus read the papers faithfully and in the evening told Marco and The Rat all the news it was "well that they should hear." But the disorders of Samavia had ceased to occupy much space. They had become an old story, and after the excitement of the assassination of Michael Maranovitch had died out, there seemed to be a lull in events. Michael's son had not dared to try to take his father's place, and there were rumors that he also had been killed. The head of the Iarovitch had declared himself king but had not been crowned because of disorders in his own party. The country seemed existing in a night-mare of suffering, famine, and suspense.

"Samavia is waiting too," The Rat broke forth one night as they talked together, "but it won't wait long. It can't. If I were a Samavian and in Samavia—"

"My father is a Samavian, and he is in Samavia," Marco's grave young voice interposed.

The Rat flushed red as he realized what he had said. "What a fool I am," he groaned. "I . . . I beg your pardon . . . sir." He stood up when he said the last words and added the "sir" as if he suddenly realized that there was a distance between them that was something akin to the distance between youth and maturity, but yet was not the same.

"You are a good Samavian, but . . . you forget," was Marco's answer.

Lazarus's intense grimness increased with each day that passed. The ceremonious respectfulness of his manner toward Marco increased also. It seemed as if the more anxious he felt, the more formal and stately his bearing became. It was as though he braced his own courage by doing the smallest things life in the back sitting room required. The Rat found himself feeling almost as if he were an attendant in a court, and that dignity and ceremony were necessary on his own part. He began to experience a sense of being somehow a person of rank for whom doors were opened grandly and who had vassals at his command. The watchful obedience of fifty vassals embodied itself in the manner of Lazarus.

"I am glad," The Rat said once reflectively, "that my father was once . . . different. It makes it easier to learn things perhaps. If he had not talked to me about people who . . . well, who had never seen places like Bone Court, this might have been harder for me to understand."

When at last they managed to call the Squad together and went to spend a morning at the Barracks behind the churchyard, that body of armed men stared at their commander in great and amazed uncertainty. They felt that something had happened to him. They did not know what had happened, but it was some experience that had made him mysteriously different. He did not look like Marco, but in some extraordinary way he seemed more akin to him. They only knew that some necessity in Loristan's affairs had taken the two away from London and the game. Now they had come back, and they seemed older.

At first, The Squad felt awkward and shuffled its feet uncomfortably. After the first greetings it did not know exactly what to say. It was Marco who saved the situation.

"Drill us first," he said to The Rat, "then we can talk about the game."

" 'Tention!" shouted The Rat, magnificently. And then they forgot everything else and sprang into line. After the drill was ended, and they sat in a circle on the broken flags, the game became more resplendent than it had ever been.

"I've had time to read and work out new things," The Rat said. "Reading is like traveling."

Marco himself sat and listened, enthralled by the adroitness of the imagination he displayed. Without revealing a single dangerous fact, he built up of their journeyings and experiences a totally new structure of adventures that would have fired the whole being of any group of lads. It was safe to describe places and people, and he so described them that the Squad squirmed in its delight at feeling itself marching in a procession attending the emperor in Vienna; standing in line before palaces; climbing with knapsacks strapped tight, up precipitous mountain roads; defending mountain fortresses; and storming Samavian castles.

The Squad glowed and exulted. The Rat glowed and exulted himself. Marco watched his sharp-featured, burning-eyed face with wonder and admiration. This strange power of making things alive was, he knew, what his father would call genius.

"Let's take the oath of 'legiance again," shouted Cad, when the game was over for the morning.

"The papers never said nothin' more about the Lost Prince, but we are all for him yet! Let's take it!" So they stood in line again, Marco at the head, and renewed their oath.

"The sword in my hand—for Samavia!

"The heart in my breast—for Samavia!

"The swiftness of my sight, the thought of my brain, the life of my life—for Samavia.

"Here grow twelve men—for Samavia.

"God be thanked!"

It was more solemn than it had been the first time. The Squad felt it tremendously. Both Cad and Ben were conscious that thrills ran down their spines into their boots. When Marco and The Rat left them, they first stood at salute and then broke out into a ringing cheer.

On their way home, The Rat asked Marco a question.

"Did you see Mrs. Beedle standing at the top of the basement steps and looking after us when we went out this morning?"

Mrs. Beedle was the landlady of the lodgings at Number 7 Philibert Place. She was a mysterious and dusty female who lived in the "cellar kitchen" part of the house and was seldom seen by her lodgers.

"Yes," answered Marco, "I have seen her two or three times lately, and I do not think I ever saw her before. Lazarus says she used to watch my father round corners. Why is she suddenly so curious about us?"

"I'd like to know," said The Rat. "I've been trying to work it out. Ever since we came back, she's been peeping around the door of the kitchen stairs, or over balustrades, or through the cellar kitchen windows. I believe she wants to speak to you and knows Lazarus won't let her if he catches her at it. When Lazarus is about, she always darts back."

"What does she want to say?" said Marco.

"I'd like to know," said The Rat again.

When they reached Number 7 Philibert Place, they found out, because when the door opened they saw at the top of cellar kitchen stairs at the end of the passage, the mysterious Mrs. Beedle in her dusty black dress and with a dusty black cap on, evidently having that minute mounted from her subterranean hiding place. She had come up the steps so quickly that Lazarus had not yet seen her.

"Young Master Loristan!" she called out authoritatively. Lazarus wheeled about fiercely.

"Silence!" he commanded. "How dare you address the young master?"

She snapped her fingers at him and marched forward folding her arms tightly. "You mind your own business," she said. "It's young Master Loristan I'm speaking to, not his servant. It's time he was talked to about this."

"Silence, woman!" shouted Lazarus.

"Let her speak," said Marco. "I want to hear. What is it you wish to say, madam? My father is not here."

"That's just what I want to find out about," put in the woman. "When is he coming back?"

"I do not know," answered Marco.

"That's it," said Mrs. Beedle. "You're old enough to understand that two big lads and a big fellow like that can't have food and lodgin's for nothing. You may say you don't live high—and you don't—but lodgin's are lodgin's, and rent is rent. If your father's coming back and you can tell me when, I mayn't be obliged to let the rooms over your heads, but I know too much about foreigners to let bills run when they are out of sight. Your father's out of sight. He," jerking her head towards Lazarus, "paid me for last week. How do I know he will pay me for this week?"

"The money is ready," roared Lazarus.

The Rat longed to burst forth. He knew what people in Bone Court said to a woman like that; he knew the exact words and phrases. But they were not words and phrases an aide-de-camp might deliver himself of in the presence of his superior officer. They were not words and phrases an attendant uses at court. He dare not allow himself to burst forth. He stood with flaming eyes and a flaming face and bit his lips till they bled. He wanted to strike with his crutches. The son of Stefan Loristan! The Bearer of the Sign! There sprang up before his furious eyes the picture of the luridly lighted cavern and the frenzied crowd of men kneeling at this same boy's feet. If he dared speak his mind now, he felt he could have endured it better. But being an aide-de-camp he could not.

"Do you want the money now?" asked Marco. "It is only the beginning of the week, and we do not owe it to you until the week is over. Is it that you want to have it now?"

Lazarus had become deadly pale. He looked huge in his fury, and he looked dangerous.

"Young master," he said slowly, in a voice as deadly as his pallor, and he actually spoke low, "this woman—"

Mrs. Beedle drew back towards the cellar steps.

"There's police outside," she shrilled. "Young Master Loristan, order him to stand back."

"No one will hurt you," said Marco. "If you have the money here, Lazarus, please give it to me."

Lazarus literally ground his teeth. But he drew himself up and saluted with ceremony. He put his hand into his breast pocket and produced an old leather wallet. There were but a few coins in it. He pointed to a gold one.

"I obey you, sir—since I must—" he said, breathing hard. "That one will pay her for the week."

Marco took out the sovereign and held it out to the woman.

"You hear what he says," he said. "At the end of this week if there is not enough to pay for the next, we will go."

Lazarus looked so like a hyena, only held back from springing by chains of steel, that the dusty Mrs. Beedle was afraid to take the money.

"If you say that you will not lose it, I'll wait until the week's ended," she said. "You're nothing but a lad, but you're like your father. You've got a way that a body can trust. If he was here and said he hadn't the money but he'd have it in time, I'd wait for a month. He'd pay it if he said he would. But he's gone, and two boys and a fellow like that one don't seem much to depend on. But I'll trust *you*."

"Be good enough to take it," said Marco. And he put the coin in her hand and turned into the back sitting room as if he did not see her.

The Rat and Lazarus followed him.

"Is there so little money left?" said Marco. "We have always had very little. When we had less than usual, we lived in poorer places and were hungry if it was necessary. We know how to go hungry. One does not die of it."

The big eyes under Lazarus's beetling brows filled with tears.

"No, sir," he said, "one does not die of hunger. But the insult—the insult! That is not endurable."

"She would not have spoken if my father had been here," Marco said. "And it is true that boys like us have no money. Is there enough to pay for another week?"

"Yes, sir," answered Lazarus, swallowing hard as if he had a lump in his throat, "perhaps enough for two, if we eat but little. If the master would accept money from those who would give it, he would always have had enough. But how could such a one as he? How could he? When he went away, he thought . . . he thought that—" but there he stopped himself suddenly.

"Never mind," said Marco. "Never mind. We will go away the day we can pay no more."

"I can go out and sell newspapers," said The Rat's sharp voice. "I've done it before. Crutches help you to sell them. The platform would sell 'em faster still. I'll go out on the platform."

"I can sell newspapers too," said Marco.

Lazarus uttered an exclamation like a groan. "Sir," he cried, "no, no! Am I not here to go out and look for work? I can carry loads. I can run errands."

"We will all three begin to see what we can do," Marco said.

Then, exactly as had happened on the day of their return from their journey, there arose in the road outside the sound of newsboys shouting. This time the outcry seemed even more excited than before. The boys were running and yelling, and there seemed more of them than usual. And above all other words was heard "Samavia! Samavia!"

But today The Rat did not rush to the door at the first cry. He stood still—for several seconds they all three stood still—listening. Afterwards each one remembered and told the others that he had stood still because some strange, strong feeling held him *waiting* as if to hear some great thing.

It was Lazarus who went out of the room first, and The Rat and Marco followed him.

One of the upstairs lodgers had run down in haste and opened the door to buy newspapers and ask questions. The newsboys were wild with excitement and danced about as they shouted. The piece of news they were yelling had evidently a popular quality.

The lodger bought two papers and was handing out coppers to a lad who was talking loud and fast. "Here's a go!" he was saying. "A Secret Party's risen up and taken Samavia! 'Twixt night and mornin' they done it! That there Lost Prince descendant 'as turned up, an' they've *crowned* him—'twixt night and mornin' they done it! Clapt 'is crown on 'is 'ead, so's they'd lose no time." And off he bolted, shouting, " 'Cendant of Lost Prince! 'Cendant of Lost Prince made King of Samavia!"

It was then that Lazarus, forgetting even ceremony, bolted also. He bolted back to the sitting room, rushed in, and the door closed behind him.

Marco and The Rat found it shut when having secured a newspaper they went down the passage. At the closed door, Marco stopped. He did not turn the handle. From the inside of the room there came the sound of big convulsive sobs and passionate Samavian words of prayer and gratitude.

"Let us wait," Marco said, trembling a little. "He will not want anyone to see him. Let us wait."

His black pits of eyes looked immense, and he stood at his tallest, but he was trembling slightly from head to foot. The Rat had begun to shake as if from chills. His face was scarcely human in its fierce unboyish emotion.

"Marco, Marco," his whisper was a cry. "That was what he went for. *Because he knew!*"

"Yes," answered Marco, "that was what he went for." And his voice was unsteady as his body was.

Presently the sobs inside the room choked themselves back suddenly. Lazarus had remembered. They had guessed he had been leaning against the wall during his outburst. Now it was evident that he stood upright, probably shocked at the forgetfulness of his frenzy.

So Marco turned the handle of the door and went into the room. He shut the door behind him, and they all three stood together.

When the Samavian gives way to his emotions, he is emotional indeed. Lazarus looked as if a storm had swept over him. He had choked back his sobs, but tears still swept down his cheeks.

"Sir," he said hoarsely, "your pardon. It was as if a convulsion seized me. I forgot everything—even my duty.

Pardon, pardon!" And there on the worn carpet of the dingy back sitting room in the Marylebone Road, he actually went on one knee and kissed the boy's hand.

"You mustn't ask pardon," said Marco. "You have waited so long, good friend. You have given your life as my father has. You have known all the suffering a boy has not lived long enough to understand. Your big heart— your faithful heart—" his voice broke and he stood and looked at him with an appeal which seemed to ask him to remember his boyhood and understand the rest.

"Don't kneel," he said next. "You mustn't kneel." And Lazarus, kissing his hand again, rose to his feet.

"Now, we shall hear," said Marco. "Now the waiting will soon be over."

"Yes, sir. Now, we shall receive commands," Lazarus answered.

The Rat held out the newspapers. "May we read them yet?" he asked.

"Until further orders, sir," said Lazarus hurriedly and apologetically, "until further orders, it is still better that I should read them first."

THE GAME
IS AT AN END

30

So long as the history of Europe is written and read, the unparalleled story of the rising of the Secret Party in Samavia will stand out as one of its most startling and romantic records. When it is related, it always begins with the story of the tall and kingly Samavian youth who walked out of the palace in the early morning sunshine singing the herdsmen's song of beauty of old days.

Then comes the outbreak of the ruined and re-volting populace; then the legend of the morning on the mountainside, and the old shepherd coming out of his cave and finding the apparently dead body of the handsome young hunter. Then the secret nursing in the cavern; then the jolting cart piled with sheep-skins crossing the frontier and ending its journey at the barred entrance of the church and leaving its mysterious burden behind. And then the bitter hate and struggle of dynasties, and the handful of shepherds and herdsmen meeting in their cavern and binding themselves and their unborn sons and sons' sons by an oath never to be broken.

Then comes the passing of generations and the slaughter of peoples and the changing of kings—and always that oath remembered, and the Forgers of the Sword at their secret work hidden in forests and caves. Then the strange story of the uncrowned kings who, wandering in other lands, lived and died in silence and seclusion, often laboring with their hands for their daily bread but never forgetting that they must be kings, and ready, even though Samavia never called. Perhaps the whole story would fill too many volumes to admit of it ever being told fully.

But history makes the growing of the Secret Party clear, when it is forced to deal with the Bearing of the Sign by two mere boys, who being blown as unremarkable as any two grains of dust across Europe, lit the Lamp whose flame so flared up to the high heavens that as if from the earth itself there sprang forth Samavians by the thousands ready to feed it. Iarovitch and Maranovitch were swept aside forever, and only Samavians remained to cry aloud in ardent praise and worship of the God who had brought back to them their Lost Prince.

The battle cry of his name had ended every battle. Swords fell from hands because swords were not needed. The Iarovitch fled in terror and dismay; the Maranovitch were nowhere to be found. Between night and morning, as the newsboy had said, the standard of Ivor was raised and waved from palace and citadel alike. From mountain, forest, and plain, from city, village, and town, its followers flocked to swear allegiance. Broken and wounded legions staggered along the roads to join and kneel to it. Women and children followed, weeping with joy and chanting songs of praise.

The nations of power held out their scepters to the lately prostrate and ignored country. Trainloads of food and supplies of all things needed began to cross the frontier; the aid of nations was bestowed. Samavia at peace to till its land, to raise its flocks, to mine its ores would be able to pay all back. Samavia in past centuries had been rich enough to make great loans and had stored such harvests as warring countries had been glad to call upon.

The story of the crowning of the king had been the wildest of all—the multitude of ecstatic people, famished, in rags, and many of them weak with wounds, kneeling at his feet, praying that he would go attended by them to their bombarded and broken cathedral, and at its high altar let the crown be placed upon his head so that even those who perhaps must die of their past sufferings would at least have paid their poor homage to the King Ivor who would rule their children and bring back to Samavia her honor and her peace.

Ivor! Ivor! they chanted like a prayer. *Ivor! Ivor!* in their houses, by the roadside, in the streets.

"The story of the coronation in the shattered cathedral, whose roof had been torn to fragments by bombs," said an important London paper, "reads like a legend of the Middle Ages. But upon the whole, there is in Samavia's national character something of the medieval still."

Lazarus, having bought and read in his top floor room every newspaper recording the details that had reached London, returned to report almost verbatim, standing erect before Marco, the eyes under his shaggy brows sometimes flaming with exultation, sometimes filled with a rush of tears. He could not be made to sit down. His whole big body seemed to have become rigid with magnificence. Meeting Mrs. Beedle in the passage, he strode by her with an air so thunderous that she turned and scuttled back to her cellar kitchen, almost falling down the stone steps in her nervous terror. In such a mood he was not a person to face without something like awe.

In the middle of the night, The Rat suddenly spoke to Marco as if he knew that he was awake and would hear him.

"He has given all his life to Samavia," he said. "When he traveled from country to country and lived in holes and corners, it was because by doing it he could escape spies and see the people who must be made to understand. No one else could have made them listen. An emperor would have begun to listen when he had seen his face and heard his voice. And he could be silent and wait for the right time to speak. He could keep still when other men could not. He could keep his face still— and his hands—and his eyes. Now all Samavia knows what he has done, and that he has been the greatest patriot in the world. We both saw what Samavians were like that night in the cavern. They will go mad with joy when they see his face!"

"They *have* seen it now," said Marco in a low voice from his bed.

Then there was a long silence, though it was not quite silence because The Rat's breathing was so quick and hard. "He must have been at that coronation!" he said at last. "The king. What will the king do to . . . repay him?"

Marco did not answer. His breathing could be heard also. His mind was picturing that same coronation—the shattered, roofless cathedral, the ruins of the ancient and magnificent high altar, the multitude of kneeling, famine-scourged people, the battle-worn, wounded, and bandaged soldiery. And the king. And his father! Where had his father stood when the king was crowned? Surely he had stood at the king's right hand, and the people had adored and acclaimed them equally!

"King Ivor," he murmured as if he were in a dream. "King Ivor!"

The Rat started up on his elbow. "You will see him," he cried out. "He's not a dream any longer. The game is not a game now—and it is ended. It is won! It was real. He was real."

"Yes," answered Marco, "but it is almost more a dream now than when it was one."

"The greatest patriot in the world is like a king himself," raved The Rat. "If there is no bigger honor to give him, he will be made a prince—and commander-in-chief—and prime minister! Can't you hear those Samavians shouting and singing? You'll see it all! Do you remember the mountain climber who was going to save the shoes he made for the Bearer of the Sign?

He said a great day might come when one could show them to the people. It's come! He'll show them. I know how they'll take it." His voice suddenly dropped, as if it dropped into a pit. "You'll see it all. But I shall not."

Then Marco awoke from his dream and lifted his head. "Why not?" It sounded like a demand.

"Because I know better than to expect it," The Rat groaned. "You've taken me a long way, but you can't take me to the palace of a king. I'm not such a fool as to think that, even if your father—"

He broke off because Marco did more than lift his head. He sat upright. "You bore the Sign as much as I did," he said. "We bore it together."

"Who would have listened to *me*?" cried The Rat. "*You* were the son of Stefan Loristan."

"You were the friend of his son," answered Marco. "You went at the command of Stefan Loristan. You were the *army* of the son of Stefan Loristan. That I have told you. Where I go, you will go. We will say no more of this—not one word."

And he lay down again in the silence of a prince of the blood. And The Rat knew that he meant what he said, and that Stefan Loristan also would mean it. And because he was a boy, he began to wonder what Mrs. Beedle would do when she heard what had happened—what had been happening all the time a tall, shabby foreigner had lived in her dingy back sitting room and been closely watched lest he should go away without paying his rent, as shabby foreigners sometimes did.

The Rat saw himself managing to poise himself very erect on his crutches while he told her that the shabby

foreigner was—well, was at least the friend of a king
and had given him his crown, that he would be made a
prince, and a commander in chief, and a prime minister because there was no higher rank or honor to
give him. And his son—whom she had insulted—was
Samavia's hero because he had borne the Sign. And also
that if she were in Samavia, and Marco chose to do it, he
could batter her wretched lodging house to the ground
and put her in a prison "and serve her jolly well right!"

The next day passed and the next, and then there
came a letter. It was from Loristan, and Marco turned
pale when Lazarus handed it to him. Lazarus and The
Rat went out of the room at once and left him to read
it alone. It was evidently not a long letter, because it was
not many minutes before Marco called them again into
the room.

"In a few days, messengers—friends of my father's—
will come to take us to Samavia. You and I and Lazarus
are to go," he said to The Rat.

"God be thanked," said Lazarus. "God be thanked!"

Before the messengers came, it was the end of the
week. Lazarus had packed their few belongings, and on
Saturday Mrs. Beedle was to be seen hovering at the top
of the cellar steps when Marco and The Rat left the back
sitting room to go out.

"You needn't glare at me!" she said to Lazarus, who
stood glowering at the door that he had opened for
them. "Young Master Loristan, I want to know if you've
heard when your father is coming back?"

"He will not come back," said Marco.

"He won't, won't he? Well, how about next week's rent?" said Mrs. Beedle. "Your man's been packing up, I notice. He's not got much to carry away, but it won't pass through that front door until I've got what's due me. People that can pack easy think they can get away easy, and they'll bear watching. The week's up today."

Lazarus wheeled and faced her with a furious gesture. "Get back to your cellar, woman," he commanded. "Get back underground and stay there. Look at what is stopping before your miserable gate."

A carriage was stopping—a very perfect carriage of dark brown. The coachman and footman wore dark brown and gold liveries, and the footman had leaped down and opened the door with respectful alacrity. "They are friends of the master's come to pay their respects to his son," said Lazarus. "Are their eyes to be offended by the sight of you?"

"Your money is safe," said Marco. "You had better leave us."

Mrs. Beedle gave a sharp glance at the two gentlemen who had entered the broken gate. They were of an order that did not belong to Philibert Place. They looked as if the carriage and the dark brown and gold liveries were everyday affairs to them.

"At all events, they're two grown men and not two boys without a penny," she said. "If they're your father's friends, they'll tell me whether my rent's safe or not."

The two visitors were upon the threshold. They were both men of a certain self-contained type of dignity, and when Lazarus opened wide the door, they stepped into the shabby entrance hall as if they did not see it.

They looked past its dinginess, and past Lazarus and The Rat and Mrs. Beedle—*through* them, as it were—at Marco.

He advanced towards them at once. "You come from my father," he said and gave his hand first to the elder man, then to the younger.

"Yes, we come from your father. I am Baron Rastka, and this is the Count Vorversk," said the elder man bowing.

"If they're barons and counts and friends of your father's, they are well-to-do enough to be responsible for you," said Mrs. Beedle, rather fiercely, because she was somewhat overawed and resented the fact. "It's a matter of next week's rent, gentlemen. I want to know where it's coming from."

The elder man looked at her with a swift cold glance. He did not speak to her but to Lazarus. "What is she doing here?" he demanded.

Marco answered him. "She is afraid we cannot pay our rent," he said. "It is of great importance to her that she should be sure."

"Take her away," said the gentleman to Lazarus. He did not even glance at her. He drew something from his coat pocket and handed it to the old soldier. "Take her away," he repeated.

And because it seemed as if she were not any longer a person at all, Mrs. Beedle actually shuffled down the passage to the cellar kitchen steps. Lazarus did not leave her until he too had descended into the cellar kitchen, where he stood and towered above her like an infuriated giant.

"Tomorrow he will be on his way to Samavia, miserable woman," he said. "Before he goes, it would be well for you to implore his pardon."

But Mrs. Beedle's point of view was not his. She had recovered some of her breath.

"I don't know where Samavia is," she raged, as she struggled to set her dusty, black cap straight. "I'll warrant it's one of these little foreign countries you can scarcely see on the map—and not a decent English town in it. He can go as soon as he likes, so long as he pays his rent before he does it. Samavia, indeed! You talk as if it was Buckingham Palace!"

THE SON OF
STEFAN LORISTAN

31

When a party composed of two boys attended by
a big soldierly manservant and accompanied by two
distinguished-looking, elderly men of a marked foreign type appeared on the platform of Charing Cross
Station, they attracted a good deal of attention. In
fact the good looks and strong, well-carried body of
the handsome lad with the thick black hair would have
caused eyes to turn towards him even if he had not
seemed to be regarded as so special a charge by those
who were with him. But in a country where people are
accustomed to seeing a certain manner and certain
forms observed in the case of persons—however young—
who are set apart by the fortune of rank and distinction,
and where the populace also rather enjoys the sight of

such demeanor, it was inevitable that more than one
quick-sighted looker-on should comment on the fact
that this was not an ordinary group of individuals.

"See that fine, big lad over there," said a workman
who stuck his head out of a third-class carriage window.
"He's some sort of a young swell, I'll lay a shillin'! Take a
look at him," to his mate inside.

The mate took a look. The pair were of the decent,
educated type and were shrewd at observation.

"Yes, he's some sort of young swell," he summed
him up. "But he's not English by a long chalk. He must
be a young Turk or Russian sent over to be educated.
His suit looks like it. All but the ferret-faced chap on
crutches. Wonder what he is."

A good-natured-looking guard was passing, and the
first man hailed him.

"Have we got any swells traveling with us this
morning?" he asked, jerking his head towards the
group. "That looks like it. Anyone leaving Windsor or
Sandringham to cross from Dover today?"

The man looked at the group curiously for a
moment and then shook his head. "They do look like
something or other," he answered, "but no one knows
anything about them. Everybody's safe at home in
Buckingham Palace and Marlborough House this week.
No one either going or coming."

No observer, it is true, could have mistaken Lazarus
for an ordinary attendant escorting an ordinary charge.
If silence had not still been strictly the order, he could
not have restrained himself. As it was, he bore himself

like a grenadier and stood by Marco as if across his dead body alone could anyone approach the lad.

"Until we reach Melzarr," he had said with passion to the two gentlemen, "until I can stand before my master and behold him embrace his son—*behold* him—I implore that I may not lose sight of him night or day. On my knees I implore that I may travel, armed, at his side. I am but his servant and have no right to occupy a place in the same carriage, but put me anywhere. I will be deaf, dumb, blind to all but himself. Only permit me to be near enough to give my life if it is needed. Let me say to my master, 'I never left him.' "

"We will find a place for you," the elder man said, "and if you are so anxious, you may sleep across his threshold when we spend the night at a hotel."

"I will not sleep," said Lazarus. "I will watch. Suppose there should be demons of Maranovitch loose and infuriated in Europe? Who knows?"

"The Maranovitch and Iarovitch who have not already sworn allegiance to King Ivor are dead on battlefields. The remainder are now Fedorovitch and praising God for their king," was the answer Baron Rastka made him.

But Lazarus kept his guard unbroken. When he occupied the next compartment to the one in which Marco traveled, he stood in the corridor throughout the journey. When they descended at any point to change trains, he followed close at the boy's heels, his fierce eyes on every side at once and his hand on the weapon hidden in his broad leather belt. When they stopped to rest in some city, he planted himself in a chair by the bedroom door of his charge, and if he slept he was not aware that nature had betrayed him into doing so.

If the journey made by the young Bearers of the Sign had been a strange one, this was strange by its very contrast. Throughout that pilgrimage, two uncared-for waifs in worn clothes had traveled from one place to another, sometimes in third- or fourth-class continental railroad carriages, sometimes in jolting diligences, sometimes in peasants' carts, sometimes on foot by side roads and mountain paths and forest ways. Now, two well-dressed boys in the charge of two men of the class whose orders are obeyed, journeyed in compartments reserved for them, their traveling accessories supplying every comfort that luxury could provide.

The Rat had not known that there were people who traveled in such a manner; that wants could be so perfectly foreseen; that railroad officials, porters at stations, the staff of restaurants could be by magic transformed into active and eager servants. To lean against the upholstered back of a railway carriage and in luxurious ease look through the window at passing beauties, and then to find books at your elbow and excellent meals appearing at regular hours—these unknown perfections made it necessary for him at times to pull himself together and give all his energies to believing that he was quite awake. Awake he was and with much on his mind to work out. So much indeed that on the first day of the journey he had decided to give up the struggle and wait until it became clear to him such things as he was to be allowed to understand of the mystery of Stefan Loristan.

What he realized most clearly was the fact that the
son of Stefan Loristan was being escorted in private state
to the country his father had given his life's work to—a
fact never for a moment forgotten. The Baron Rastka
and Count Vorversk were of the dignity and courteous
reserve that marks men of distinction. Marco was not
a mere boy to them; he was the son of Stefan Loristan,
and they were Samavians. They watched over him,
not as Lazarus did, but with a gravity and forethought
that somehow seemed to encircle him with a rampart.
Without any air of subservience, they constituted themselves his attendants. His comfort, his pleasure, and
even his entertainment were their private care. The Rat
felt sure they intended that, if possible, he should enjoy
his journey and that he should not be fatigued by it.

They conversed with him as The Rat had not
known that men ever conversed with boys until he had
met Loristan. It was plain that they knew what he would
be most interested in and that they were aware he was
as familiar with the history of Samavia as they were
themselves. When he showed a disposition to hear of
events that had occurred, they were as prompt to follow
his lead as they would have been to follow the lead of a
man. That, The Rat argued with himself, was because
Marco had lived so intimately with his father that his
life had been more like a man's than a boy's and had
trained him in mature thinking. He was very quiet
during the journey, and The Rat knew he was thinking
all the time.

The night before they reached Melzarr, they slept at
a town some hours distant from the capital. They arrived
at midnight and went to a quiet hotel.

"Tomorrow," said Marco as The Rat left him for the night, "tomorrow, we shall see him. God be thanked!"

"God be thanked!" said The Rat also. And each saluted the other before they parted.

In the morning Lazarus came into the bedroom with an air so solemn that it seemed as if the garments he carried in his hands were part of some religious ceremony.

"I am at your command, sir," he said. "And I bring you your uniform."

He carried a richly decorated Samavian uniform, and the first thing Marco had seen when he entered was that Lazarus himself was in uniform also. His was the uniform of an officer of the king's bodyguard.

"The master," he said, "asks that you wear this on your entrance to Melzarr. I have a uniform also for your aide-de-camp."

When Rastka and Vorversk appeared, they were in uniforms also. It was a uniform that had a touch of the Orient in its picturesque splendor. A short mantle bordered in fur hung by a jeweled chain from the shoulders, and there was much magnificent embroidery of color and gold.

"Sir, we must drive quickly to the station," Baron Rastka said to Marco. "These people are excitable and patriotic, and His Majesty wishes us to remain incognito and avoid all chance of public demonstration until we reach the capital." They passed rather hurriedly through the hotel to the carriage that awaited them. The Rat saw that something unusual was happening in the place. Servants were scurrying around corners, and guests were coming out of their rooms and even hanging over the balustrades.

As Marco got into his carriage, he caught sight of a boy about his own age who was peeping from behind a bush. Suddenly he darted away, and they all saw him tearing down the street towards the station as fast as his legs would carry him.

But the horses were faster than he was. The party reached the station and was escorted quickly to its place in a special carriage that awaited it. As the train made its way out of the station, Marco saw the boy who had run before them rush onto the platform, waving his arms and shouting something with wild delight. The people who were standing about turned to look at him, and the next instant they had all torn off their caps and thrown them up in the air and were shouting also. But it was not possible to hear what they said.

"We were only just in time," said Vorversk, and Baron Rastka nodded.

The train went swiftly and stopped only once before they reached Melzarr. This was at a small station, and on the platform stood peasants with big baskets of garlanded flowers and evergreens. They put them on the train, and soon both Marco and The Rat saw that something un-usual was taking place. At one time a man standing on the narrow outside platform of the carriage was plainly seen to be securing garlands and handing up flags to men who worked on the roof.

"They are doing something with Samavian flags and a lot of flowers and green things!" cried The Rat in excitement.

"Sir, they are decorating the outside of the carriage," Vorversk said. "The villagers on the line obtained permission from His Majesty. The son of Stefan Loristan could not be allowed to pass their homes without their doing homage."

"I understand," said Marco, his heart thumping hard against his uniform. "It is for my father's sake."

At last, embowered, garlanded, and hung with waving banners, the train drew in at the chief station at Melzarr.

"Sir," said Rastka, as they were entering, "will you stand up that the people may see you? Those on the outskirts of the crowd will have the merest glimpse, but they will never forget." Marco stood up. The others grouped themselves behind him. There arose a roar of voices that ended almost in a shriek of joy that was like the shriek of a tempest. Then there burst forth the blare of brass instruments playing the National Hymn of Samavia, and mad voices joined in singing it.

If Marco had not been a strong boy and long trained in self-control, what he saw and heard might have been almost too much to be borne. When the train had come to a full stop, and the door was thrown open, even Rastka's dignified voice was unsteady as he said, "Sir, lead the way. It is for us to follow."

And Marco erect in the doorway stood for a moment, looking out upon the roaring, acclaiming, weeping, singing, and swaying multitude . . . and saluted just as he had saluted the Squad, looking just as much a boy, just as much a man, just as much a thrilling young human being.

Then at the sight of him standing so, it seemed as if the crowd went mad—as the Forgers of the Sword had seemed to go mad on the night in the cavern. The tumult rose and rose, the crowd rocked and leapt, and in its frenzy of emotion threatened to crush itself to death. But for the lines of soldiers, there would have seemed no chance for anyone to pass through it alive.

"I am the son of Stefan Loristan," Marco said to himself in order to hold himself steady. "I am on my way to my father."

Afterward he was moving through the line of guarding soldiers to the entrance where two great state carriages stood, and there outside waited a larger and more frenzied crowd than that left behind. He saluted there again and again and again on all sides. It was what they had seen the emperor do in Vienna. He was not an emperor, but he was the son of Stefan Loristan, who had brought back the king.

"You must salute too," he said to The Rat when they got into the state carriage. "Perhaps my father has told them. It seems as if they knew you."

The Rat had been placed beside him on the carriage seat. He was inwardly shuddering with a rapture of exultation that was almost anguish. The people were looking at him—shouting at him—surely it seemed like it when he looked at the faces nearest in the crowd. Perhaps Loristan—

"Listen!" said Marco suddenly, as the carriage rolled on its way. "They are shouting to us in Samavian, _The Bearers of the Sign!_ That is what they are saying now. _The Bearers of the Sign._"

They were being taken to the palace. That Baron Rastka and Count Vorversk had explained in the train. His Majesty wished to receive them.

The city had once been noble and majestic. It was somewhat Oriental, as its uniforms and national costumes were. There were domed and pillared structures of white stone and marble. There were great arches and city gates and churches. But many of them were half in ruins through war and neglect and decay. They passed the half-unroofed cathedral standing in the sunshine in its great square, still in all its disaster one of the most beautiful structures in Europe. In the exultant crowd were still haggard faces, men with bandaged limbs and heads or hobbling on sticks and crutches. The richly colored native costumes were most of them worn to rags. But their wearers had the faces of creatures plucked from despair to be lifted to heaven.

"Ivor! Ivor!" they cried. "Ivor! Ivor!" and they sobbed with rapture.

The palace was as wonderful in its way as the white cathedral. The immensely wide steps of marble were guarded by soldiers. The huge square in which it stood was filled with people whom the soldiers held in check.

"I am his son," Marco said to himself, as he descended from the state carriage and began to walk up the steps that seemed so enormously wide that they appeared almost like a street. Up he mounted, step by step, The Rat following him. And as he turned from side to side to salute those who made deep obeisance as he passed, he began to realize that he had seen their faces before.

"These who are guarding the steps," he said quickly under his breath to The Rat, "are the Forgers of the Sword!"

There were rich uniforms everywhere when he entered the palace and people who bowed almost to the ground as he passed. He was very young to be confronted with such an adoring adulation and royal ceremony; but he hoped it would not last too long and that after he had knelt to the king and kissed his hand, he would see his father and hear his voice. Just to hear his voice again and feel his hand on his shoulder!

Through the vaulted corridors to the wide opened doors of a magnificent room he was led at last. The end of it seemed a long way off as he entered. There were many richly dressed people who stood in line as he passed up toward the canopied platform. He felt that he had grown pale with the strain of excitement, and he had begun to feel that he must be walking in a dream as on each side people bowed low and curtsied to the ground.

He realized vaguely that the king himself was standing, awaiting his approach. But as he advanced, each step bearing him nearer to the throne, the light and color about him, the strangeness and magnificence, the wildly joyous acclamation of the populace outside the palace made him feel rather dazzled, and he did not clearly see any one single face or thing.

"His Majesty awaits you," said a voice behind him that seemed to be Baron Rastka's. "Are you faint, sir? You look pale."

He drew himself together and lifted his eyes. For one full moment after he had so lifted them, he stood

quite still and straight, looking into the deep beauty of
the royal face. Then he knelt and kissed the hands held
out to him—kissed them both with a passion of boy love.

The king had the eyes he had longed to see—the
king's hands were those he had longed to feel again
upon his shoulder—the king was his father! The "Stefan
Loristan" who had been the last of those who had waited
for five hundred years and who had labored for Samavia
and had lived and died kings, though none of them till
now had worn a crown!

His *father* was the king!

It was not that night, nor the next, nor for many
nights that the telling of the story was completed. The
people knew that their king and his son were rarely
separated from each other, and that the prince's suite of
apartments were connected by a private passage with his
father's. The two were bound together by an affection of
singular strength and meaning, and their love for their
people added to their feeling for each other.

In the history of what their past had been, there was
a romance that swelled the emotional Samavian heart
near to bursting. By mountain fires, in huts, under the
stars, in fields and in forests, all that was known of their
story was told and retold a thousand times, with sobs of
joy and prayer breaking in upon the tale.

But none knew it as it was told in a certain quiet but
stately room in the palace, where the man once known
only as "Stefan Loristan"—but whom history would call
the first King Ivor of Samavia—told his share of it to the
boy whom Samavians had a strange honor for, because

he seemed so surely their Lost Prince restored in body
and soul—almost the kingly lad in the ancient portrait.

It was a wonderful and intense story, that of the
long wanderings and the close hiding of the dangerous
secret. Among all those who had known that a man who
was an impassioned patriot was laboring for Samavia
and using all the power of a great mind and the delicate
ingenuity of a great genius to gain friends and favor for
his unhappy country. There had been just one who had
known that Stefan Loristan had a claim to the Samavian
throne. Yet he had made no claim; he had sought—not a
crown—but the final freedom of the nation for which his
love had been his life.

"Not the crown," he said to the two young Bearers
of the Sign as they sat at his feet like schoolboys, "not
a throne. *The life of my life—for Samavia.* That was what I
worked for—what we have all worked for. If there had
risen a wiser man in Samavia's time of need, it would
not have been for me to remind them of their Lost
Prince. I could have stood aside. But no man arose. The
crucial moment came. And the one man in Samavia who
knew the secret revealed it. Then . . . Samavia called,
and I answered."

He tousled the thick, black hair of his son's head.

"There was a thing we never spoke of together,"
he said. "I believed always that your mother died of her
bitter fears for me and the unending strain of them.
She was very young and loving and knew that there was
no day when we parted that we were sure of seeing each
other alive again. When she died, she begged me to

promise that your boyhood and youth should not be burdened by the knowledge that she had found so terrible to bear. I would have kept the secret from you even if she had not so implored me. I had never meant that you should know the truth until you were a man. If I had died, a certain document would have been sent to you that would have left my task in your hands and made my plans clear. You would have known then that you also were a Prince Ivor, who must take up his country's burden and be ready when Samavia called. I tried to help you to train yourself for any task, and you never failed me."

"Your Majesty," said The Rat, "I began to work it out and think it must be true that night when we were with the old woman on the top of the mountain. It was the way she looked at . . . at His Highness."

"Say *Marco*," said Prince Ivor. "It's easier. He was my army, Father."

Stefan Loristan's grave eyes melted. "Yes. Say *Marco*. You were his army—and more—when we both needed one. It was you who invented the game."

"Thank you . . . Your Majesty," said The Rat, reddening scarlet. "You do me great honor! But he would never let me wait on him when we were traveling. He said we were nothing but two boys. I suppose that's why it's hard to remember at first. But my mind went on working until sometimes I was afraid I might let something out at the wrong time. When we went down into the cavern, and I saw the Forgers of the Sword go mad over him—I *knew* it must be true. But I didn't dare to speak. I knew you meant us to wait; so I waited."

"You are a faithful friend," said the king.

A great moon was sailing in the sky that night—just such a moon as had sailed among the torn rifts of storm clouds when the prince at Vienna had come out upon the balcony and the boyish voice had startled him from the darkness of the garden below.

The clearer light of this night's splendor drew them out on a balcony also—a broad balcony of white marble that looked like snow. The pure radiance fell upon all they saw spread before them—the lovely but half-ruined city, the great palace square with its broken statues and arches, the splendid ghost of the unroofed cathedral whose High Altar was bare to the sky.

They stood and looked at it. There was a stillness in which all the world might have ceased breathing.

"What next?" said Prince Ivor at last, speaking quietly and low. "What next, Father?"

"Great things will come, one by one," said the king, "if we hold ourselves ready."

Prince Ivor turned his face from the lovely, white, broken city and put his brown hand on his father's arm.